Comes the Darkness

Comes the Darkness

The Land of Marqueria, Volume 2

Shana Ren

Published by Shana Ren, 2024.

COMES THE DARKNESS

First edition. April 2, 2024.

ISBN: 979-8989921041

Written by Shana Ren.

This story is for you, P. I wouldn't have finished this book if you hadn't asked to read my daily pages every night at bedtime. Thank you, sweetheart. Thanks to my family for always encouraging me and helping me work through tough times. Thanks to my husband for the morning coffee, the heated blankets, hot baths, and being my cheerleader. I love you all.

"We don't hide in the safe places. We never have. That isn't us." Kenna

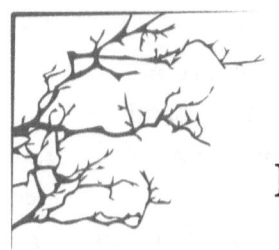

Prologue

Jamie and Kenna appeared at the base of a giant mountain covered in trees and boulders. It reminded Kenna of Mount Rainier, but much more significant and with an assortment of colored trees mixed in with the Evergreens. Trees one wouldn't find in the Mortal world. Glancing up at the trail, Kenna groaned and tucked a strand of cinnamon-red hair behind her ear, then groaned, "That's quite a hike, isn't it, husband?" Jamie grinned at his wife and said, "I have all the confidence in the world that you can take on that mountain. Did the Dragon sisters tell you how long this hike should take?" Kenna shook her head and said, "No, they didn't. We're really on our own out here, aren't we? Do you realize this trip is our first time alone since before the girls were born?" Kenna was staring at Jamie, her face a little worried and sad. Jamie said quietly, "They will be ok, sweetheart. They promised to stay within the Castle grounds and not to go off alone." Kenna smiled, green eyes shining with unshed tears, then whispered, "I know you're right; I just worry. They're my life," She sighed, took a deep breath, exhaled, straightened her back, and said, "I'm okay. I can do this. I need to feel the sadness every once in a while." Kenna closed her eyes, took a deep breath, then let it out slowly. She opened her eyes and smiled at her husband, Jamie. Then, she determinedly said, "Now, let's get hiking, husband."

Jamie and Kenna walked to the beginning of the trail, where Kenna noticed a small wooden sign partially hidden within a tall red berry bush. Kenna turned to Jamie and asked, "Can you make out what this says?" Jamie leaned in, pushing aside the limbs of the bush, and read, "Mount Parnassus. This is Dragon Mountain, it's where the Sacred Grove of the Dragons is located. Somewhere on this vast mountain is the Grove where the wild Dragons live." Grinning, Kenna gleefully exclaimed, "Wild Dragons! We are far from Montana right now in more ways than just geographically. Throughout my childhood in Montana, I dreamed of dragons; I was obsessed with them. You don't understand how excited I am to meet our dragons." "Even though I grew up in Marqueria, I've never been to this part of it. There was no reason for me to seek out the Dragons, as I am Bear," Jamie said, his golden eyes thoughtful, then he shrugged, continuing, "Historically, Bears and Dragons had no relationship. Dragons were for the Elves only."

Kenna reached for Jamie's hand and said, "That has changed. Look at our daughters. They are half Bear and have each bonded to a Dragon. We are on a quest to find our Dragons, and you're a full Bear. Marqueria is evolving." Jamie smiled softly at his wife, raised her hand to kiss her palm, and said, "I believe it is mostly due to you, wife. You are the beginning of the Matriarchal line of the Elves, with a direct line to the Goddess. Marqueria is entering an age of enlightenment because of you."

He gave her a gentle kiss on the forehead, then playfully swatted her butt and said, "Now, get walking. We have a long way to go." Kenna laughed, took out her AirPods, and handed one to Jamie, saying, "A little hiking music is needed." Jamie put his in and mumbled, "As long as it's not Nickelback." "I heard you. There are a few on this playlist, so be nice," Kenna laughingly said, then they began walking up the trail that disappeared into the trees. The trail looked like it wrapped around the massive mountain as it ascended. 'A long way indeed,' she thought.

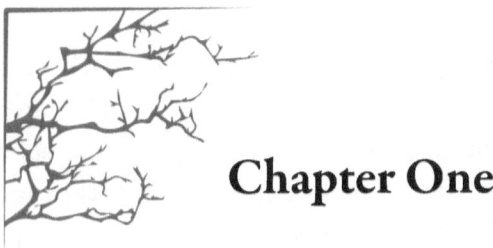

Chapter One

Noelle entered the Library in search of her Papa. She found him standing before the massive fireplace, staring into the flames. "Papa, it's been several days, and they're still not back. I haven't been able to reach them through our mind connection; neither has Ember. I'm very worried," Noelle said to her Papa as she joined him in front of the fire. Bram patted her shoulder and said, "Calm, granddaughter. I'm sure they're fine. Your mother is the most powerful magic wielder in Marqueria, and your father is the most powerful Bear, with the exception of Otso. They can take care of themselves, sweetheart." Bram, his mind on other things, patted her shoulder as he continued to stare into the flames. Noelle sighed heavily and quickly left the room in search of her sister, Ember.

She found Ember, her fifteen-year-old sister, in the sitting room of their suite, playing a game on her laptop. Alaric, one of the Wolf Princes and Ember's fated mate, sat across from her. Looking around, Noelle spotted Blaze, the other Wolf Prince, sitting on the other couch with a sketchbook on his lap, sketching something that held all his attention. Noelle watched Blaze quietly for a few moments, thinking how weird it was that just a month ago, she had been living in Montana being a relatively typical teenager, and now she was in Marqueria, Princess to the Bears and Elves, and fated to fight a great war from the back of a Dragon. Plus, she was 'fated' to be Blaze's mate. 'The fates are not choosing whom I love and marry,' Noelle thought grumpily. When Blaze realized Noelle was standing close by, he quickly closed the cover of his sketchbook and stood up. "What did the Elf King, your grandfather, say?" Blaze asked quietly. The look on Noelle's face told Blaze all he needed to know. He gave a quiet sigh, knowing this meant the sisters were going to have a plan, and it would probably land them all in trouble. He nodded and asked her, "What do you want to do? What is your plan?" This caught the attention of Ember and Alaric, who closed their laptops and stood up, too.

"Our dragons, Sage and Jade, said they should have returned by now. We know our parents would never miss Christmas or Yule with us, and that's next week plus the Dragon sisters have been unable to contact our parents. We need to take the Dragon sisters and ride them to where our parents were going and start our search from there," Noelle said. Scrunching up her face, Ember asked, "Can't we do that transfer thing like mom? We're strong enough, aren't we?" Considering it, Noelle bit her lip and said, "Let me contact Jade and see what she thinks." Noelle closed her eyes and was still for a few minutes while communicating with her bonded Dragon, Jade. The green and gold tattoo, which was her bonding mark with her Dragon, on her left wrist gave off a faint glow while she was doing this, then her green and gold eyes popped open, and she grinned. "The Dragon sisters believe we are strong enough to transfer several people to the exact spot Mom and Dad were going. They said they would fly to that location and meet us there. They're leaving now." Ember, green and gold eyes shining with excitement, turned to Blaze and Alaric and said, "Pack your bags, boys! We're taking a trip."

"Not alone, you're not," growled a low voice from the back of the sitting room by the staircase door. They all turned towards the back of the sitting room. There stood the Bear Brothers, Tai, and Kai. They were part of the Bear clan and appointed to protect the two Princesses by their grandfather, Otso, who was King of the Bears. They were already dressed for travel, each with a bag slung over a shoulder. Ember tilted her head slightly and asked in a surprised voice, "You're not going to try and stop us?" They both shook their heads, their faces fierce-looking. Tai said, "We know better than to try. You'd only sneak away. This way, we can go and try to keep you out of trouble, as well as be added protection." Turning to Blaze and Alaric, "Okay, Wolf Boys, grab your short swords and bows, but don't let anyone see you doing it. Also, travel clothes and supplies. We will meet at the Dragon stables in twenty minutes." Blaze and Alaric quickly left for their suite of rooms to gather their travel gear. "Go change into travel clothing, Princesses. Please bring your bows and your short swords too. And hurry, I also have a bad feeling," growled Tai.

The Dragon stables were a sight to behold. They were as large and round as the main castle and built with the same lovely white stones. Their walls contained the same twinkling jewels embedded into each stone. The structure was vast, with multiple spacious rooms designed to accommodate Dragons of various sizes and breeds.

The interior was lit by the same soft, glowing light that lit the hallway to their tower of suites, plus softly flickering torches helped illuminate the interior. The air was thick with a mix of earthy scents and a hint of smoke from the torches and the Dragons. The floor was covered with a thick layer of soft black sand, providing a comfortable resting place for the Dragons' massive claws and bodies.

Noelle, Ember, Tai, and Kai stood just inside one of the giant doors, waiting for the Wolf brothers, Blaze and Alaric, to join them. The four were dressed for travel in the super soft, form-fitting, yet stretchy tunics and leggings of Marqueria. They had all opted to wear muted shades of brown paired with tall brown suede boots. The material was rip-proof and fireproof and kept them warm, even with being so thin. Each was carrying a soft, flexible backpack made from material similar to their clothing. These bags weren't like normal backpacks but were woven with a spell, which allowed them to carry anything. No matter how large or heavy the item was, it would fit and never weigh more than seven pounds.

They also each carried matching pairs of short swords at their waists and had bows and a quiver of arrows slung over their backs. They were prepared for anything on this journey, not knowing what they would encounter. Noelle and Ember's parents, Jamie and Kenna, had gone missing several days ago while on a quest to find their Dragons. The girls were unable to contact their parents via the mind links they shared with them. Plus, Jade and Sage, the girls' bonded Dragons, weren't able to contact their parents either. 'Something is definitely wrong, even if the other rulers of Marqueria don't agree,' thought Noelle as she waited for Blaze and Alaric to join them in the Dragon Stables. "Do you think they got caught?" whispered Noelle, worry in her deep green and gold eyes. "No, otherwise the entire castle would be in an uproar, and everyone would be here by now," whispered Ember to her sister as she peeked through the door, looking for the wolf brothers, her green and gold eyes squinting from the bright light. From behind the group, there was a chuckle, and Blaze asked, "Did you honestly think we would get caught? We are Wolf. We are silence personified." "Plus, we came in the back way to avoid the guards. That way, they'll think the Bear brothers were escorting you both to see your Dragons," said Alaric, grinning at Ember. Ember grinned back and said, "Brilliant! Now, let's go!" With some surprise, Kai looked at the teen brothers and said, "Smart. I'm impressed, boys." Then, the six of them moved into a circle, clasping hands. Suddenly, Ember cried softly, "I forgot my AirPods and phone! I need my music." Noelle gave her sister a grin and said, "I grabbed them. Don't worry, you'll get your Taylor Swift and Linkin Park fix." Ember whispered, "Thanks, sis." Then, the girls began to glow silvery, and their curly cinnamon-red hair softly floated around their heads. Suddenly, they all disappeared.

The next instant, they appeared at the base of a giant mountain with a snow-covered peak and slopes covered in many different species of trees, shrubbery, and huge boulders. "Hey! This reminds me of Mount Rainier in Washington, only much, much larger. Don't you think so, Noelle?" Ember asked her sister. Noelle nodded as she looked around, then said, "Where are our Dragons? They were supposed to meet us here." Tai and Kai, the bear brothers who were their protectors, walked the perimeter with their noses lifted as if scenting the air. "I don't smell your Dragons, so don't start worrying. They just haven't made it here yet," said Tai, the blonde Bear brother. After checking out the perimeter, Tai and Kai came over and joined the teenagers. Tai asked, "Do either one of you feel the Darkness? When the Darkness took Hilda over, I caught a faint scent similar to the one in the Grove above your red house in Montana in the Mortal realm. It's over at the beginning of the trail, by the sign." The girls walked over to the trail, where the sign had the words 'Mount Parnassus' carved into it. Ember and Noelle held hands and closed their eyes. Their bodies began to glow faintly, and their hair started to float gently about their head, cinnamon-red strands catching the sun and turning to floating fire. "Yes, we feel the Darkness. It has been here. It's faint, a couple of days old," they said in unison, one voice. Slowly, their hair returned to fall down their backs and around their shoulders, and the glow faded. Opening worry-filled eyes, they stared at each other, saying nothing and still holding hands. "Did your bracelet get warm?" Ember asked as she let go of her Noelle's hands and rolled the Black Tourmaline and Amethyst gems between her fingers, feeling their warmth. Noelle nodded and said, "Yes, it did. The Darkness has definitely been through here." Their bracelets were a match for the one their mom always wore. They are meant to indicate evil's presence and protect against it. They are not as good as casting a circle, but they are a good early warning.

Blaze stepped closer to Noelle, placing his hands gently on her shoulders and squeezing them softly. He said quietly, "Tell us what you felt and saw, please. We need to know what we're walking into." Noelle took a deep, steadying breath and said, "We saw It here at the beginning of the trail. It still remains in Hilda, but it is a different Hilda. She was younger and looked to be the same age as Papa, around thirty-eight human years, but she had long silver hair and ice-blue eyes. We also know It was following our parents, but keeping back from them so they wouldn't sense It was there," Ember said, "Our Dragons haven't made it here, either. We saw them leaving the Castle grounds and flying, but they are still on their way." Alaric moved to Ember's side and put his arm around her shoulder, pulling her close to his side. She let go of her sister's hands and turned into his body, putting her arms around his waist as he pulled her into a comforting embrace, his six-foot frame towering over her diminutive body and his scent soothing her anger and worry. Alaric whispered, "SShhh, it's going to be okay. Take deep, calming breaths. We will find your parents and their Dragons." As he soothingly rubbed his hand up and down her back. She laid her head down on his chest and took a deep breath, feeling immediately calmer. From a near distance, there was the sound of a throat being cleared, and then Kai said, "OK, pup. Enough cuddling with the Princess. You may be her fated mate, but she's still under our protection while her parents are away." Ember stepped back from Alaric and, turning to Kai and Tai, heatedly said, "It's called comforting. Maybe if you understood that, you'd have found your mates by now." The Bear brothers froze and stared at Ember, expressions unreadable. Then, with a raw, pained expression, Tai said in a low, gruff voice, "You know nothing of our pasts, Princess. From now on, avoid assuming that you do." Kai laid a hand on his brother's shoulder and said, "Tai. It's ok. She meant nothing by it. She's just upset." Tai took a deep breath and blew it out slowly, nodded his head, and then continued walking to the beginning of the trail.

A little way up the trail, Noelle, with Blaze at her side, called out, " Please remember, emotions are running high right now, so let's just be patient with each other. But, seriously, we need to go now." Ember was looking at the Bear brothers, and the expression on her face showed her remorse. She caught up to Tai, grabbing his sleeve and pulling him to a stop. He didn't look at her, just waited. "Tai, I'm sorry. I never meant to hurt your feelings. I get defensive and lash out. I apologize," Ember said softly. Tai gave a quiet sigh and said, "I, too, apologize, Princess. We don't like to talk about our past, but I will this one time so you can understand us and why we act as we do." Tai took a deep breath and let it out slowly before saying, "Before the war that Hilda started almost 40 years ago, Kai and I both had mates. We were happy and just living our lives like normal inhabitants of Marqueria. But then the war came for the first time ever in our history. One day, while Kai and I were fighting Hilda's army near your grandparents' castle, our mates decided to go to the river to sunbathe and swim. When we got home later that night, our mates were not there. We went in search of them and soon found them by the river, where they had been killed by the retreating army. They had both been pregnant with our first young. When your mother was stolen away, and Otso sent your father through the Tree soon after, we volunteered to travel through to keep an eye on him. We had nothing left here, and the thought that our Prince, your father, was unprotected didn't sit well with us. And this is the last time I will discuss this with anyone." Tai nodded his head at Ember and walked up the trail to join the others, who had stopped and been listening to Tai while he was speaking to Ember.

Tai moved to the front of the group and began hiking up the trail. Nobody said anything. Ember and Noelle stared at each other, obviously using their mind link. Ember nodded, put in one of her AirPods, handed the other to Alaric, and then began following Noelle and Blaze up the trail, Alaric behind her and Kai at the rear guard.

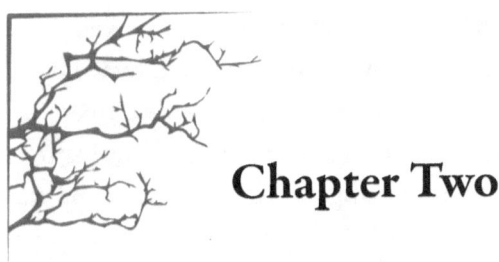

Chapter Two

Kenna woke up slowly, her head pounding painfully and her eyes squinting at the firelight coming from the fireplace at the back of the cave. Sitting up carefully on the side of the cot she had been lying on and trying not to jar the wound in her side, she placed her feet gently upon the soft rug lying on the cave's smooth black rock floor. Playing with the Black Tourmaline and Amethyst bracelet on her right wrist, she glanced sluggishly around.

Examining the cave, she found a smooth black stone floor with several plush rugs scattered over it. The walls, although covered in a few colorful tapestries, were the same smooth black stone as the floor. There were two cots side by side, one she was sitting on. In front of the fire were two large cushy chairs and a table. The cave was round with a small fireplace towards the back, where Jamie was squatting down in front of, feeding wood into the fire. He was shirtless and had a blood-stained white cloth wrapped around his head and another one around his chest. "Jamie," whispered Kenna, her voice coarse and raspy. He immediately stood and came to her side, kneeling down in front of her. "Where are we, Jamie? What happened to us?" she asked softly. Jamie reached up with both hands and gently smoothed her hair back from her face, softly caressing her cheeks with his thumbs. He then leaned in and gave her a gentle kiss. "We are in a protected cave. We were brought here by a Dryad and her sisters, who found us wounded near their trees. We are safe for the moment," Jamie said, golden eyes staring into Kenna's deep green ones, seeking confirmation that she was truly okay. Kenna started to shake her head but stopped immediately due to a jolt of pain. "I don't remember much of what happened. I recall we were setting up camp, and then we ate dinner. The last thing I remember is going to sleep in the tent," Kenna said, grimacing at the pain in her head.

She placed a hand on the wound to her left side, under her rib cage. "How did I get this? What caused it?" She asked Jamie. She then gingerly touched the back of her head at the base, feeling the large lump and dried blood in her cinnamon-red hair. "I was hit in the back of the head, wasn't I?" she murmured, looking questioningly at Jamie. He heaved a deep sigh and cautiously sat next to her on the cot, trying not to jostle her. He softly said, "Yes, you were hit with a club. We were attacked in our sleep by the followers of Hilda and the Darkness. We were so exhausted that we forgot to cast a circle of protection around our tent. It was such a stupid, amateur mistake. There was a time when I knew better than to make such a grave error. Living in the Mortal Realm has made me less cautious and soft. This will never happen again, my wife. I promise I will be more careful with you." Jamie sighed and ran his hand over the black hair on his head, grimacing when he touched his temple. Then he continued, "I was stabbed in the chest with a short sword and hit in the temple with a club. That's the last thing I remember. When the Dryads found us, we were surrounded by the followers of Hilda, but they were all dead." Kenna gasped softly and asked, "But how? Who killed them?" Jamie turned towards her and took her hands in his, softly rubbing his thumbs over the backs of her hands, and said, "The Dryads said you were the source of the energy burst that killed them all." Kenna stared blankly at Jamie, slowly shaking her head and then stopping due to the pain.

"I don't understand. How could I possibly be responsible for those deaths? I don't remember anything after going to bed," she whispered in a confused voice, rolling the gems on her Black Tourmaline and Amethyst bracelet between her fingers, a small frown between her eyes. "Sweetheart, I woke up while they were trying to heal our wounds and applying our dressings. The position of the bodies with respect to you and me leads me to believe that you were, indeed, the source of the energy burst. You protected me and yourself from the followers of the Darkness, and you have no reason to feel guilty. The Goddess worked through you to ensure we would survive and return to our daughters," Jamie softly explained, gently pulling her into his arms. Kenna breathed in deeply of her husband's scent, allowing it to calm her. "Okay. It's okay. I accept this, and I will be okay with it. Jamie, I'm okay, really. We are at war with Evil, and I will not allow us to lose. Other than a killer headache and the burning wound in my side, I'm okay," she said, trying to convince herself, as well as her husband.

Kenna gave a small gasp, clutching Jamie's arm. "Jamie, I can't link with our daughters. Why can't I link with our daughters?" Kenna asked in a soft, slightly panicked voice. "Sshhh, it's okay. This cave is a barrier and is protective.

We can't connect with our daughters while we are in this cave. Nothing and no one will know we are here, which will allow us to heal and be at our full strength when we leave," Jamie explained softly. "You said the Dryads tried to heal us. Why couldn't they heal us completely?" Kenna asked. "Their magic is for the earth fauna and doesn't work as well on Elves and Weres," Jamie said.

Kenna grimaced as she stood up, gripping Jamie's arm as he helped her maintain her balance. "I can heal us, Jamie. I have the magic to do it," she said with soft urgency. "No, I want you to rest and conserve your energy, wife," he replied in a soft, growly voice. Kenna turned towards her husband and placed her right hand over his chest wound, then her left hand over the wound on his temple, pushing aside the long dark hair. She closed her eyes and began to glow softly, with her hair gently floating up off her shoulders and back. They stayed like this for a few moments until Kenna stopped glowing, and her hair returned to rest down her back. Opening her eyes, she looked up into rather angry golden eyes. "I said I wanted you to rest," Jamie growled softly. "And I said I wanted to heal us. You don't get to tell me what to do, husband. You didn't do it when we were in Montana, and you're not going to start now that we're in Marqueria," Kenna growled right back at him, her green eyes shooting glowing sparks.

"Are you healed?" Jamie asked her, his eyes going to the wound to her side. Kenna removed the dressing wrap and looked at the skin. There was no wound, not even a scar. "Yes, I am. Now, let's get dressed and go find our Dragons and mind link with our daughters," she replied, already walking to the pile of clothes that were hers. Jamie gave a low growl and started to gather his clothing together, along with the backpack and supplies. He then gave a loud sigh and said gruffly, "Thank you for healing me. I appreciate it, and I'm sorry I tried to control your actions. I'm just crazy worried about you and the girls. The role you and our girls play in this coming war is messing with my mind. I've been questioning our decision to move here and wonder if we should have stayed in Montana, enjoying our quiet life." He sat on the cot, elbows on his knees, head in his hands. Kenna sat next to him and began rubbing his back, saying softly, "That's not us anymore, Jamie. If it ever was. We are not ones to hide in the safe places. You are the Prince of the Were Bears, father to the Princesses of the Elves and Bears, husband to me. You are brave and strong, and you always fight for those who can't fight for themselves. Staying safe isn't how you or I are made. Neither are our girls, for that matter."

Jamie reached over and picked Kenna up, placing her in his lap and holding her close. "I couldn't survive without you, Kenna. I will protect you with my body, with my blood and soul, if need be. Our girls need you just as much as I do. Please, take care of yourself too," Jamie whispered into her sweet-scented hair, inhaling deeply and feeling calm settle over him. Kenna softly kissed his neck and, playing with his hair, whispered, "I promise I will take care of myself and not do anything too reckless. I love you, husband, and don't want to leave you alone in this life." They stayed cuddled together for a few more moments, then Kenna sighed and said, "We need to get going. Our quest is waiting, as are our daughters, and they must be so worried about not being able to contact us." They both stood up, completed dressing, then loaded their pack and headed to the solid rock door at the front of the cave. Standing by the door, Kenna looked closely at Jamie and then gave a gasp. "Your hair! Your hair grew! I just realized! How did this happen?" she asked. Jamie ran a hand through his shoulder-length dark hair and chuckled. "It grew after the Dryads tried to heal me. I guess your husband isn't bald anymore. If you mind, I'll shave every day for you," he said, grinning at her. Kenna stood on tip-toe and gave him a soft kiss, saying, "I love it. If you like it, I like it. It is rather scintillating having you look entirely different." She winked and pushed through the door.

When they passed through the door, they discovered the cave was deep within a forest filled with a variety of very ancient tall trees, berry bushes, and a few wildflowers pushing up through the snow. Waiting patiently a few yards from the cave opening stood seven Dryads. Kenna gazed in awe at the beautiful women who resembled the trees surrounding them. Three Dryads had skin that resembled brown bark, with hair the vibrant colors of autumn, which flowed down their backs and about their shoulders. Three Dryads had skin resembling grey bark and flowing hair of vibrant autumn. The last Dryad was faintly glowing, and something about her made it obvious she was the leader. Her skin was the white and black bark of a birch tree, and her long, flowing hair was the stunning gold, orange, and red of its autumn leaves. She reminded Kenna of the Tree back in the Grove for some reason.

COMES THE DARKNESS

The Birch Dryad gracefully moved forward until she was just a couple of feet from them. When she spoke, her voice was musical and soothing. "We are pleased to see you both healed and able to travel again. Our healing magic is not meant for any other than the plants in our forests, so I am relieved you had the ability to heal yourselves, Princess Kenna," the Dryad said, smiling at them softly. "You know who we are?" asked Kenna. There were nods and gentle laughs from all seven Dryads. "Yes, of course, we know who you are. You and your family have been passing through my Tree for many generations. Your daughters many, many times since they were younglings," spoke the Birch Dryad. Kenna gave a soft gasp and exclaimed, "You're the Tree in the Grove! I thought so, but I wasn't sure. Thank you so much for bringing us to a safe place to rest and heal. We are in your debt." The Birch Dryad shook her head, causing her leaf hair to move wildly about her head, and chuckled, saying, "No, that is not how it is, Princess. We are in your debt. You and your family are the saviors of Marqueria, and we will do anything and everything to help you in your battle against the Darkness. But you must be on your way quickly and unite with your Dragons as soon as possible. The Darkness grows more powerful each day, and we must all prepare for the war to come. Even now, your daughters and the four Weres are on a journey to find you. They have already made it halfway to the Sacred Grove of the Dragons, where they will meet their own Dragons, who are flying there as we speak. But you must get there first and join with your Dragons so that you are ready for the coming battle. We bid you farewell and safe journeys."

The Dryads all nodded to Jamie and Kenna and slowly melted into the forest, disappearing into the trees. Kenna and Jamie were left staring at each other as they absorbed the news that the Dryad had just delivered. "I'm going to ground them forever," growled Jamie softly. "Stand in line, husband," whispered Kenna, but after a few moments, she laughed, shaking her head. "I don't see anything funny about this, wife," said Jamie, all growly and annoyed. "Oh, Jamie, this is Noelle and Ember we are talking about. Since when have they ever done what was expected? They came through the Tree when they were practically babies, alone. They have been independent and fierce since the day they were born. I'm not surprised they have come looking for us, are you?" asked Kenna, grinning at Jamie. Jamie gave a bark of laughter and shook his head, saying, "No, you're right. I guess it's not a surprise at all. I was just really hoping those two would stay put for once until we got back. Well, at least they have Tai and Kai, plus the Wolf brothers, to protect them."

Kenna scoffed and said rather heatedly, "You seriously think they need protection? Our daughters are as powerful as I am when it comes to magic and spells of protection. Their skills at archery are excellent, not to mention their ability to protect themselves and others. Don't you dare let them hear you say they need protection, or they'll never let you hear the end of it?" Jamie gave a huge sigh and said, "You're correct again, wife. I misspoke. Come, let's finish our journey to the Sacred Grove of Dragons, and hopefully, we can get there before our wayward daughters and their enabling companions do."

Chapter Three

The Darkness was inside the Elf woman Hilda but didn't make his presence known to all. Looking at Hilda, you would see a beautifully dressed, stunning Elven female with long silver hair and icy blue eyes. Not much different from any other female Elf walking along this remote village's sidewalk. Hilda curled her lip up at the terribly quaint and modest village, at the boring and modest dress of the Elven villagers. This small village wasn't anything like the Castle Village. There weren't many shops lining the main street, and the people along the sidewalk had their heads down and were walking quickly to and from their necessary errands. There was an air of caution and hyper-awareness among the residents of this small village. Nobody wanted to be out of their magically protected houses for any length of time since the Darkness had come back to Marqueria.

Even though there are very few Elven children born in Marqueria per century, this village had an abnormally high number compared to other villages. The past ten years had seen two dozen new births, but the children living in this village were not out playing in the magical park at the end of the main street today. In fact, there wasn't one child amongst the half dozen villagers who were either brave or desperate enough to be out and about. While walking along the sidewalk, they all were giving Hilda a wide berth. They didn't know the Darkness was inside her, but they sensed that she was somehow wrong and abnormal. Their fear fed the Darkness and gave him a little burst of energy. As Hilda strode slowly down the almost deserted street of the village, with each step she took towards the children's playground, the Darkness began to take her over.

The sky grew dark and grey, and the wind increased, blowing snow around the now deserted street. Lightning streaked across the sky, and the loud boom of thunder shook the windows of the little village's houses and shops.

The Darkness was smolderingly angry that Kenna and Jamie had escaped from the attack near the Sacred Grove of Dragons. While Hilda's vessel was adequate, he wanted one with more powerful magic, like the Elven Princess Kenna. She, or one of her daughters, would fuel him for millennia. He would prefer the mother, but if he had no other choice, he would take one or both of the daughters, having never felt such power in ones so young and tender before. He didn't care what would happen to Hilda after he left her body; she meant nothing to him. She was just the tool he needed now, and her hate and anger were aligned with his own.

He had hidden within the borders of Marqueria for eons, quiet and dormant, waiting for one who would awaken the discord and darkness in this land. When Hilda was born, her anger at being set aside by the Goddess grew with each passing year, unknowingly feeding and strengthening him. The birth of Princess Kenna was the tipping point, allowing him to come almost to his full strength. Now, he needed that very same Princess. He wasn't doing this for any personal reason like Hilda was; this was just his nature. He was the personification of evil, and he couldn't abide joy, love, or light. His goal was to make Marqueria full of darkness, and all that entailed before moving on to the next realm. It was his drive, with no reason or rhyme to it. It was just him, the Darkness.

Hilda, with the Darkness almost fully in control, had just reached the playground the village had built for their younglings. Within the magical playground, fairies and gnomes lived amongst the many trees and winter flowering bushes, with their tiny, colorful homes mostly hidden. It was a bright and cheerful spot, one which the Darkness couldn't abide. She stopped just outside the protective circle in which the playground was enclosed. The Darkness had fully taken her over now, with her hair and eyes turned jet black and her nails and lips just as dark. The Darkness terrifyingly and completely consumed Hilda. He bent down and laid his hands on the ground, just touching the circle. A fog of blackness began to crawl around the circle before seeping up to cover the entire playground in a black, foggy dome. Standing up, the Darkness within Hilda grinned evilly and gave a chilling laugh. Then the Darkness suddenly disappeared, along with the black fog, leaving nothing but a huge empty smoldering crater, where the magical playground and all its magical creatures had lived but were no more.

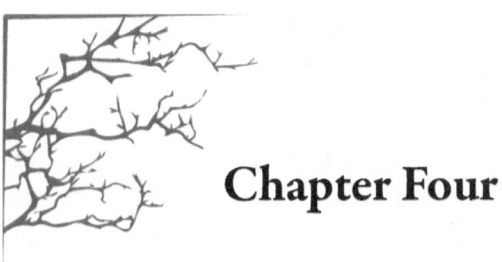

Chapter Four

With AirPods in, Kenna was following the faint trail through the trees, up the mountain towards the Sacred Grove of the Dragons, with Jamie walking just behind her. She was busy looking around and had stumbled a few times; Jamie was laughing and catching her before she could fall, so he was following rather closely, knowing he would have to catch her again soon. This time, though, he ran into her when she stopped suddenly, almost toppling them both off the trail. "Kenna, you need to warn me when you're going to stop, or we both are going to fall," Jamie said, chuckling quietly. Kenna, taking out her AirPods, whispered in excitement, "Jamie, look! There's a gnome! Right over there, under that little bush. Shhhh, don't scare it away." Kenna had always adored gnomes, only finding out they were real a couple of weeks ago. At their home in Montana, she had at least two dozen gnomes in her garden, but the inanimate kind purchased at the local gardening shop or online. Jamie laughed softly at her excitement; he, however, did not share her fondness for gnomes, as they were extremely mischievous. They were known to sneak into homes and camps to steal food and supplies; they would often hide one boot and leave the other in the oven or steal other articles of clothing. Switching the sugar and salt canisters was one of their many irritating tricks.

The gnome, who looked to be waiting for someone, finally noticed them standing on the trail. He quickly jumped off the large mushroom he was sitting on and scampered to within five feet of Kenna. He was small, about twelve inches tall, with a long white beard, bright blue eyes, and walnut-colored skin. The gnome was dressed in a tunic and leggings, in muted shades of brown, similar to the ones the Elves, Bears, and Wolves wore. His pointed hat was leaf green in color, and the tip drooped off to one side. He blended in with the undergrowth quite well. He bowed deeply to Kenna, then said in a rather deep voice, "The woodland gnomes welcome you to our forest, Princess Kenna. We have been watching for you since the news reached us of your quest. We are greatly pleased you were able to survive the attack by the Darkness and his followers." Kenna slowly sat down in the middle of the trail, making it easier for her to converse with the gnome. Her expression was what one would have when meeting an adorable puppy for the first time; she was completely taken with him. "I am pleased to meet you....um..what is your name?" she asked softly, smiling gently at the gnome. With great dignity, the gnome removed his hat and gave another bow, saying, "Finnegan, at your service, Princess Kenna." "I'm pleased to meet you, Finnegan. I simply adore gnomes, I must tell you," she said, grinning back at Jamie and saying, "Isn't he adorable?" Jamie grunted, shook his head, and said, "Wait until we camp tonight and wake up to all our food gone and a boot missing."

"We would never steal from Princess Kenna! Besides, you won't need to camp tonight anyway, as the Sacred Grove of the Dragons is but a hop, skip, and jump along this trail. If you'd quit dallying, you will be there long before dark, with plenty of time to spare," Finnegan said, bowing again to Kenna and turning back towards the forest and saying over his shoulder as he walked, "Goodbye, Princess Kenna and Prince Jamie. We wish you health and victory in the war to come." He then faded into the forest and disappeared from sight. Kenna stood up and turned to Jamie. "See? Adorable!" She said, grabbing his hand and tugging him forward along the trail.

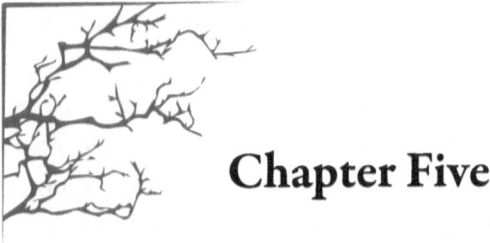

Chapter Five

Kenna and Jamie soon found themselves at the end of their journey. They were standing at the entrance to the Sacred Grove of Dragons. The trail ended at the entrance to the Grove, which was a huge arch one hundred feet tall and twice as wide, made out of live trees and vines. The Grove itself was round and immense. "How is this huge round grove hiding on this mountain? The physics of it doesn't make sense to me," Kenna said to Jamie softly. "Kenna, I think you're forgetting the magic of it all. This isn't Montana or the Mortal realm. This is Marqueria, and we are surrounded by magic," Jamie said laughingly. Kenna nodded her head and continued to look around the Grove. There were Dragons of every imaginable color and size here, all coexisting peacefully. Kenna could just make out the protection circle and dome over the Grove by the slight silver shimmer it created. "Can we enter, or do we need to wait for them to invite us in?" she asked Jamie. Jamie shrugged, pointed his thumbs at himself, and said, "Bear, remember?"

"You need no invitation to enter the Grove, Princess Kenna and Prince Jamie. You are free to come and go as you wish," spoke a grumbly voice from somewhere within the Grove. Kenna grinned at Jamie and, grabbing his hand, pulled him into the Grove. "Dragons!" she whispered to him, practically vibrating with excitement. He chuckled at how adorable she was but also admitted to himself that he, too, was excited to meet his dragon, something he never in his life thought he would be able to do. After stepping through the protection shield, the Grove became even more vibrant and magical. The huge trees were an array of many different colors, leaves of blues and greens to reds and orange, with trunks in black, red, white, and blues, along with the normal browns and grays. There were flowering bushes and fruit trees, Fairies of all shades flying around, and Gnomes scampering underfoot here and there. It was truly a magical grove, something out of a dream.

The Dragons were breathtakingly beautiful and were many different sizes. Some were a foot long, and several were over one hundred feet in length, with many others in between. The color variety was endless, but among them, Kenna found her Dragon immediately. She remembered her vividly from her dreams as a child when her Dragon would come to her the only way she was able, and most often, it was in times of Kenna's greatest pain and sorrow. Dropping Jamie's hand, Kenna began to stride across the Grove, making a beeline for the huge black iridescent Dragon with golden horns, claws, and spikes. She was just as Kenna remembered her. Reaching the magnificent black Dragon, Kenna stopped just a scant few feet from her giant golden claws. Looking up with tear-filled green eyes, she met the shining golden ones of her Dragon. "Oh, little one. Do not cry; this is a most joyous occasion. I have been waiting many years to finally meet my chosen Elf in the flesh. I have missed our dream walks, child. As soon as our mates join us, we can perform our bonding ceremony, my little Elf," spoke the black Dragon in a deep but melodious voice. "I believe your name is Nyx if I remember correctly," Kenna said softly, leaning her forehead against Nyx's head, which was resting upon her large claws on the ground and the perfect height for Kenna to reach. "Yes, little one. I am Nyx. Ahh, here come our mates now," purred the Dragon.

Kenna turned to find Jamie, amazed at the magnificent Dragon at his side. "He is your mate? Jamie is to bond with your mate?" Kenna asked Nyx. "Yes, little one. Our family will be bonded to your family, as the Goddess intended," responded Nyx, with a chuff and chuckle at the end. "Your family? The green dragon sisters are your daughters?" Kenna asked. This time, Nyx gave a growly chortle and chuff, then replied, "That is correct, little Kenna. Our younglings are bonded to yours. Our families will help defeat the Darkness together, as the Goddess has decreed. They all should be here before next nightfall. Now, Kenna, I'd like to introduce my mate, Sika." Kenna stared at the huge male dragon, amazed at the sheer mass of his body. His coloring was the opposite of his mate's, Nyx. He was a soft, dull gold everywhere, but for his chest, claws, horns, and spine spikes, which were black. His eyes were the shining gold of all the shifters and Dragons. His huge gold wings had intricate black designs peeking out from their folded position against his body. "Oh, he is magnificent," breathed Kenna softly. This caused Nyx to chortle loudly, and she said, "Yes, he is a beautiful male specimen, isn't he?"

Jamie reached Kenna and pulled her into his embrace, holding her close and breathing in her scent, which never failed to soothe him. He whispered into her hair, "I have a Dragon, and his name is Sika. It was never in the realm of possibilities for me to become bonded to a Dragon. I am still overwhelmed by this honor." Kenna had wrapped her arms around his waist and, at this, gave him a tight squeeze. "There's more to this than we realized, husband," she whispered. Leaning back, Jamie looked down into Kenna's dark green eyes, his own shining gold ones questioning. "What do you mean, wife?" he asked. A deep baritone voice said, "We will explain it now, brave Bear." They both turned towards the pair of Dragons, who were sitting side by side now. They were truly a wondrous sight to behold, their stunning opposite coloring and immense size almost overwhelming the senses. Nyx gave a chuff and spoke in her deep but melodious voice, "I am pleased to meet the Bear who has been watching over my Kenna all these years. It brings joy to my Dragon Heart that she has found such a brave and caring mate."

Kenna turned to Jamie and said, "This is Nyx, the Dragon from my dreams. Nyx, this is my husband, Jamie." Jamie gave a bow and said, "Well met." He then turned to Kenna and said, "This is to be my bonded Dragon to be, Sika. Sika, this is my wife and life mate, Kenna." The huge golden Dragon gave a chuff and said in his very deep baritone voice, "Well met, Princess Kenna. My Nyx has spoken of you often and shared your past connections with me. She doesn't want to wait much longer for your bonding, so we should complete it now before our younglings arrive."

COMES THE DARKNESS

The Dragons lowered their heads so they were almost level with Kenna and Jamie, and without any instructions, they touched their foreheads to the Dragons' right between the two horns on their heads. The four stayed that way for several minutes, with a faint shimmer around them. When the shimmer began to fade, Nyx and Sika raised their heads and sat back, watching their newly bonded riders. Kenna and Jamie slowly opened their eyes, gazing up at their bonded Dragons in awe. "I can hear you in my mind, Nyx, as if it was in my dreams. Your mind seems so vast, and your knowledge endless. I have so much to learn," Kenna said, a tear escaping from her glistening eyes to run down her cheek. Jamie reached up and gently wiped the tears away, saying, "I know these are happy tears, wife, but I still don't like to see you cry." He pulled her into his arms, gentling her as he rubbed her back softly.

Kenna asked Jamie, "Did we get tattoos on our wrists like our daughters?" Jamie pulled back from Kenna, reaching down to examine her left wrist. A Celtic design in black with gold accents wove itself around her small wrist. Kenna whispered, "Oh, it's lovely." She then grabbed Jamie's wrist and gently touched the glowing gold design woven around it. His had black accents mingled with the glowing of the gold. "We're opposites," murmured Jamie, "Just like our dragons."

Nyx gave a chuff and said, "Come, little ones. We shall feed you, and you must rest before all our younglings arrive. My joy is boundless with our bonding, and I wish to share it with the other Dragons." Jamie turned to Kenna and asked, "All our younglings? What does that mean?" Kenna chuckled and said, "The green Dragon sisters are our Dragons' daughters. Our daughters are bonded to their daughters." "Amazing," whispered Jamie. Then Jamie and Kenna followed Nyx and Sika as they led them deeper into the Grove.

Chapter Six

Noelle, Ember, Blaze, Alaric, Tai, and Kai had been hiking up the mountain for hours and were deep within the forest, the trail barely wide enough to allow two of them to walk side by side. Tai was in the lead as usual, with Kai bringing up the rear. Blaze was behind Tai, and Alaric was in front of Kai, which left Noelle and Ember right smack in the middle of the group. The chatter was to a minimum, but Noelle and Ember had obviously been using their mind link to communicate when Noelle said, "Ember and I think we need to take a break before continuing on. We're hungry and thirsty and need to rest." Tai stopped walking and looked around for a spot to rest. To their left was a meadow with a stream flowing through the far side. "That's as good a spot as any. We can refill our water and rest under the fireberry tree," Tai said, indicating the vibrant pink tree with a deep red trunk. Despite the snow-covered ground, the tree was laden with the delicious, glowing red fruit, which the girls adored. "Oh, good! I'm so hungry I could eat ten of those fireberries," exclaimed Ember. They left the trail and started towards the showy tree, Ember and Noelle walking side by side and occasionally nodding to each other. Blaze and Alaric exchanged amused looks, and then Blaze asked, "Care to share what you two are discussing?" The girls glanced back at them and laughed, shaking their heads.

When they reached the tree, Tai said, "Let us do a quick perimeter check, and then we can relax." While Tai and Kai did their thing, the girls turned toward the tree, studying the area underneath it. "I think right there would be best. It's not too close to the trunk and still within sight of the trail," Noelle said, pointing to a spot ten feet from the tree's trunk. "Okay, perfect. Let's do this then," replied Ember. The girls stood side by side, holding hands, and then, with their free hand, they did a graceful wave from left to right. Suddenly, a round table with matching chairs appeared, set for six. There was a large bowl of salad with dressing, a platter of roast beef, bowls of mashed potatoes and gravy, a large tureen of vegetable soup, a bread basket full of steaming rolls, and small bowls of whipped butter.

The girls clapped their hands and exclaimed together, "It worked! Oh, my Goddess, it worked!" Grinning, they turned towards the other four and said, "Let's eat." Tai smiled at the girls and said, "Nicely done." Kai nodded in agreement. Blaze and Alaric both returned the girls' grins and headed for their seats. Ember said, "Wait. We want to cast a circle before we sit down to eat." The girls faced each other, palms touching and began to chant. They began to glow softly, and their hair floated up off their shoulders and back.

By the power of Light and Love
We cast this circle below and above.
A shield of protection, strong and true

Keep out the evil; only good comes through.

So mote it be, this circle is cast.

A twenty-foot-diameter silver, shimmering dome appeared over the table, and the six travelers were encased in a protective bubble. Kai smiled at the girls and said, "You have been practicing. Your parents would be proud. Come, let us eat. I, too, am starving." He gave Ember a wink and joined his brother at the table. The girls each took a seat next to each other, between Blaze and Alaric. "Where did you obtain the ingredient for this feast?" asked Alaric as he took his seat. The girls giggled, and Ember said, "We borrowed them from our grandparents." This caused laughter from around the table, and then there was little talking while they ate their meal.

As their hunger became satiated, the conversation turned to the girls' parents. "Have you tried to mind link with them recently?" asked Tai. Noelle, with a small frown, nodded, then said, "Yes, we have. Just before we stopped to rest, we still can't reach them." "Our Dragons are talking to us, though. They said they would meet us at the Sacred Grove," added Ember. Noelle, with a small frown between her eyes and tears in her eyes, whispered, "Jade said they took a detour when they felt a disturbance in a nearby village. They arrived soon after it had happened, but the Darkness had already left. The Darkness destroyed the village's magical playground for the children. In it lived many Fairies and Gnomes, and they, too, were destroyed. There is nothing left but a giant crater."

The look Tai and Kai exchanged was unreadable, but it was almost as if they, too, could talk to one another with their minds. Giving a nod, Tai said, "We will set up camp here for the night. Princesses, do you think you could cast a large enough circle to encompass a large tent and a fire?" Noelle and Ember looked at each other for a moment, then both nodded. Blaze and Alaric stood up, Blaze saying, "We will go gather firewood. Is there anything else you need us to do?" The Bear brothers looked at the Wolf brothers in surprise. Tai said, "We appreciate that, pups. When you are done, we four can etch a more solid circle around the camp before the girls cast it. We thank you." "Blaze, do you mind if we go with you? You do realize we aren't the fainting Princesses in the human fairy tales, right?" Noelle said loudly. Ember scoffed and said, "Yeah, we know how to gather wood and put up tents. We've been camping and hunting with our father in Montana our entire lives."

Blaze and Alaric looked at Tai and Kai, and Tai laughed, saying, "Don't look at us, pups. The Princesses are quite capable and do not need our permission." Ember grinned at Tai and grabbed her bow and quiver of arrows, which she slung over her back. She strode through the circle and headed towards the edge of the trees. Shaking her head, Noelle rolled her eyes at the Wolf brothers, and she, too, grabbed her weapons and followed her sister. Blaze ran his hand through his hair and whispered, "Damn it." Alaric nodded his head and said, "Yep. We messed up." Then he grabbed his bow and quiver and followed the girls. Kai laughed and said, "Don't worry, Blaze. Noelle will forgive you, but she'll make you earn it." The Bear brothers laughed loudly as Blaze quickly grabbed his weapons and followed the other three to the tree line and on into the forest. "That courtship is going to be entertaining to watch," said Tai to his brother. Kai nodded his head and replied, "Yes, it is. We'll need the amusement through this war." Tai nodded, exchanging a pain-filled glance with his brother as they moved towards the center of the meadow to set up camp.

Chapter Seven

E mber added another piece of chopped wood to the backpack she was holding and asked, "Don't you think this is enough for the night? You've chopped up one entire dead tree, and we are only staying for the night." Blaze and Alaric both shook their heads at her and then Alaric said, "Better to be prepared than not. If, for some reason, we are unable to leave the circle and have to stay here for a few days, we will have enough wood to keep the chill off at night." Ember said, "I see your point."

Not far from Ember and Alaric, Blaze and Noelle were loading another magical backpack with pieces of split wood, seemingly getting along better. "Have you ever traveled this far from your home before?" asked Noelle as she added another piece of wood to the bag Blaze was holding. Blaze shook his head and replied, "No. There was never any reason for us to venture to the Mountain of Dragons. Dragons only bond with Elves, so as much as we are fascinated with Dragons, we knew it was a waste of time to seek one out." He cocked his head, an expression of surprise on his face, then said, "But that's all changed now, hasn't it? You and Ember are half Bear and half-Elf, and you've both bonded with Dragons. Your father is all Bear, and he has gone in search of his Dragon....I wonder..." "Do you think you'll be chosen to bond with a Dragon? You are a Prince of the Wolves, after all. Maybe Marqueria is changing, and you and Alaric will eventually bond with Dragons," Noelle said, her expression one of hope and excitement. Blaze stared into her deep green and gold eyes, his own gold eyes shining with hope as well. "We could fly together, couldn't we?" he asked quietly, his gaze intense and yearning. Noelle returned his look, her cheeks turning faintly pink.

Their moment was rudely interrupted by Ember, who made a loud whistle and then laughed uproariously when Blaze and Noelle both jumped in surprise. "Come on, you two. Enough with the lovey-dovey eyes. We need to head back to the meadow and help set the circle," Ember said, still laughing as she handed the magic backpack to Alaric. Noelle grabbed Ember's arm to stop her and said, "My bracelet is getting hot. Is yours?" The girls rolled the Black Tourmaline and Amethyst gems between their fingers, looking around, expressions worried. "Yes, mine is too," Ember said, looking up and around the clearing. "What does that mean?" asked Alaric. "It's a protective bracelet. It means evil is near," whispered Ember.

Suddenly, a loud crashing sound came from deep within the woods, in the opposite direction from the meadow where Tai and Kai were. As one, Noelle and Ember quickly grabbed their bows and nocked an arrow, facing the direction the crashing was coming from. Blaze and Alaric unsheathed their short swords and stood at the ready. Whatever it was, crashing through the trees was huge and moving extremely fast. The four teenagers could feel the earth vibrating as it moved quickly nearer to them.

COMES THE DARKNESS

With the loud crashes of trees being ripped out of the ground, a huge beast entered the small clearing where they had been gathering firewood. It stood looking around and breathing heavily, steam coming out of its mouth and nose. "What the Hell is that?!" exclaimed Blaze. Ember said quietly, "I believe that is a Manticore. I thought they were myths." "Haven't you ever seen one before?" asked Noelle, standing still and not taking her eyes off the beast. Blaze whispered back, "No, I've never even heard of a beast like that."

The colossal, powerful creature had the tawny muscular body of a lion, large membranous black wings like a bat, and a thick and luxurious amber mane framing its frightening face and extending down its neck and back. It had a long tail, which ended with a cluster of sharp spines and powerful, sharp claws on its paws. On its head were a set of large, sharp black horns, curved backward. But the most frightening of all these features was the face. It had a human-like face, with a wide mouth full of sharp canine teeth. The eyes were a shining bright blue and were definitely human. The combination of animal and human features was so unexpected and eerie that it sent a shiver of fear through the four teenagers.

"Be careful of the tail. The spikes are supposed to be venomous," whispered Ember softly. "Ooohhhh, so you've heard of me, little elf bear? I am flattered," the Manticore's voice was deep and growly like a lion's roar. "Yes, I have heard of you. I've read about your kind in books about myths and legends in the Mortal Realm. I didn't think your kind was real, though," replied Ember. The Manticore gave a bone-chilling laugh and said, "Yes, we are real, and do you know what we eat, little Elf Bear?" Ember nodded. "What do they eat?" whispered Alaric. "Anything we want, little Wolf Prince," laughed the Manticore. "They eat human flesh," whispered Ember. "Shit," whispered Blaze. The girls still had arrows nocked and, at this point, quickly raised their bows and released their arrows at the Manticore. The movement was fluid and in synch, and so fast it was barely discernible by the naked eye. The girls had unknowingly tapped into their Elven blood. At the precise moment the girls released their arrows, the Manticore started towards them, and the arrows hit him just below his eyes. It screamed in pain and rage but didn't stop its forward motion, just reaching up with a paw to break off the arrows, blood now pouring down its grotesquely human-like face and splattering in the white snow.

The girls had each nocked another arrow, but before they could let them loose, the unnaturally fast Manticore was on them. He batted the girls aside with a huge paw, sending them over fifty yards away. The Manticore then swung its tail at Blaze and Alaric, but they were too quick and escaped being crushed by the spiked end. Unable to stop its forward momentum, the Manticore crashed to the other side of the small clearing while the boys ran to Noelle and Ember, who were just standing up, swaying slightly, blood covering their faces and dripping down onto their tunics. "Are you okay?!" cried Blaze as he attempted to examine Noelle for injuries. She batted his hands aside and yelled, "Stop it! We're fine. Get ready; he's coming back for us!"

Suddenly, the two Wolf Princes transformed into huge, black wolves. It had happened instantly; one second, they were standing there, and the next, they were Wolves. They were enormous, standing seven feet at the shoulder, completely dwarfing the girls. Their coats were pitch black, like the darkest of nights, and their golden eyes shone with an intense golden light. The two giant wolves ran at the charging Manticore, teeth bared and snarling angrily. It was a vicious fight, with growling, snarling, claws ripping, and teeth biting. When the Manticore's tail made contact with one of the wolves, there was a loud yip and yowl, and one wolf dropped to the ground and didn't move. "NO!" screamed Noelle and Ember together; then, their eyes connected, and they nodded to each other.

The sisters joined palms and began to chant softly, their bodies glowing brightly and hair floating about their heads wildly.

By the power of frost and cold
We command the ice to take hold
Freeze this being who means us harm
Make it iced and disarmed.

The girls then turned and shoved their palms towards where the Manticore and the lone wolf were still fighting. A silvery-white beam of light pulsed towards the Manticore, hitting it square in the chest as it stood over the lone wolf. The beam blasted it backward off its paws, where it lay ten yards away, now a figure of solid clear blue ice.

The girls ran to where the injured wolf lay and immediately began to examine the large gaping wound in his stomach area. It was pouring blood and a green gooey substance onto the pristine white snow. "This must be the poison from the barbed tail," Noelle said quietly. "Don't touch it, Noelle!" exclaimed Ember. Noelle growled at her sister, "I know!" Then she grabbed Ember's hands, and with one girl standing on each side of the downed giant wolf's head, palms touching, they began a healing chant.

From darkness to light, from pain to relief,
We chant these words to bring healing and peace.
With every breath, let the healing light flow.
In body, mind, and spirit, let the Goddess sow.

The girls, with eyes closed, then laid their glowing hands on the injured wolf, continuing to chant under their breath. A silvery sheen covered the wolf, and the green goo slowly disappeared, along with the gaping wound. All that was left was the blood matting the black coat of the Wolf. Alaric, who was in his human form, had joined them. He was covered in blood, and gaping wounds were scattered over his body. The girls removed their hands from Blaze, still in his wolf form, and Noelle walked around him to join her sister and Alaric. She assessed Alaric's wounds when she reached his side. "You need healing, Alaric," she said as she reached out for Ember's hands. "No! Take care of Blaze first, please," he growled loudly. Ember looked at him in surprise, as he had never shown a temper before. She realized he was just very worried about his brother, so she moved closer to him, taking his hands in hers. She said, "You need to be healed. We have done what we can for Blaze; he just needs rest for now. Let us heal you so you can help us get him back to camp." She reached up and placed a bloody palm on his blood-covered cheek, staring into his pain-filled golden eyes. "Please," she whispered softly. Alaric painfully nodded his head, moving so each girl could hold one of his hands. Ember and Noelle repeated the chant, and after a few moments, Alaric's wounds were completely healed, but the blood remained.

Chapter Eight

The sound of pounding feet on the ground grabbed their attention, and the three turned quickly into attack stances. Alaric grabbed both his swords and the girls had their bows drawn with arrows ready to fly; all this happened in just seconds. From the side of the clearing nearest the meadow where the camp was to be, Tai and Kai came running out of the trees. They stopped suddenly when they saw the three teens covered in blood and facing them with weapons ready; they looked around the small clearing; the shock showed on their faces as they noticed the iced Manticore figure and the giant Wolf lying behind the three teens. "Calm, younglings. It's just us. Please lower your weapons," Tai said in a soothing voice, one hand up with palm towards the three teens. The three slowly lowered their weapons, and the two Bear brothers continued to move towards them, examining the small clearing as they walked.

When they reached the teens, Kai asked, "What happened? We heard trees being ripped up and the sounds of battle and smelled blood. We came as fast as we could." The sight of the two Bear brothers broke something loose in the two girls, who began to shake uncontrollably. Tears started streaming down their blood-stained faces, making rivers of red, which then dripped off their jaws, staining their clothing further. "It was a Manticore. It knew us. How did it know us? I don't understand how it knew us," rambled Ember softly. Alaric turned to Ember and pulled her into his arms, making soothing sounds. Noelle stared at Tai and Kai with a bloody, tear-stained face and said, "It threw Ember and me across the clearing, and then Alaric and Blaze turned into giant Wolves and fought them. Blaze got smashed by its poisonous tail, and then Alaric just started fighting it. It was going to kill him, but Ember and I followed the Goddess' instructions and turned it to Ice. Blaze won't wake up. Why won't Blaze wake up? We healed him." Noelle moved to stand at Blaze's head, still in Wolf form. She laid a hand on his head and whispered, "Please wake up. Don't leave me. Come back, Blaze. Please." She rested her head against his and sobbed.

The two Bear brothers moved quickly to where Blaze lay and examined him briefly. "Princesses. I need you to please pull yourselves together long enough to get us all back to the Meadow. What you're feeling is the after-effects of battle. It's an adrenaline dump and will pass as soon as you're warm and in a safe place. Come, I need you to help me move us all, as I'm not strong enough to transfer this many," Tai told them gently. They watched as the girls straightened their spines, stepped back from the Wolf brothers each had been embracing, and took several deep, calming breaths. Looking towards Tai and Kai, they said as one, "We are okay. We can help you with this." The Bear brothers nodded, then motioned for everyone to grab hands. Alaric placed a hand on his brother's giant Wolf form, as did Noelle. As soon as they were all touching, they disappeared from the clearing and reappeared in the middle of the Meadow.

There was already one tent set up in the center of a large circle etched into the ground, with a fire burning brightly off to the side. Blaze had reappeared in his human form but remained unconscious. "Before you get to rest, Princesses, we need you to cast the circle, please," Tai said gently. Then, he picked Blaze up with no effort and carried him into the tent, Alaric following him closely. Placing the backpacks he had picked up in the clearing on the ground, Kai said softly, "Please, cast the circle. It will be night soon, and we don't want to be caught without it up." Ember and Noelle looked at each other quietly and then nodded, again communicating without words. They joined hands and began to chant.

We cast this circle of protection to hold.
With perfect light and perfect love
We call upon the Spirits above
We call upon the Earth below
We call upon the Air surround
We call upon the Water that flows
We call upon the Fire within
To ward off the shadows and banish the dark.
We raise a shield, protection assured
With each verse we weave, a barrier is formed
A sanctuary of light, our loves it enfolds
By the power of Earth, Water, Air, Fire, and Spirit
We cast this circle of protection to hold.

From the circle that Tai and Kai had etched into the ground, a shimmering silver dome formed over their heads, encasing them in its magical protection. "So Mote it Be," whispered the girls together to finish the spell. Turning to Kai, Noelle said in a toneless voice, "It is done. We need to clean this blood off and change our clothes. Where can we do this privately?" Kai gave a soft chuckle and cocked his head towards the tent, then said, "In the tent, Princess. This isn't a mortal tent; this is a tent made in Marqueria, and you will be pleasantly surprised by the interior." He gestured for the girls to enter ahead of him. After Kai entered, he secured the doorway, which looked like a solid wooden door on the inside, complete with an iron bar as a lock. Kai promptly ran into the two teenage girls, who had stopped and were gazing around in amazement. He quickly grabbed them before they fell and said, "Welcome to our home for the next few days."

"This is freaking amazing," whispered Ember in awe, then continued, "How is it so huge in here? Those doors, where do they lead? Are those bedrooms? Is there a bathroom?" Kai laughed and said, "Yes, those are bedrooms, and each one has a bathroom attached. When the tent was made, it was woven with a spell that allowed it to displace space. This creates a tent which will grow to accommodate as many as is needed." Noelle nodded and said tonelessly, "I need a bath." She then walked through the sitting room and picked a door to open, looking for her and Ember's room. "Is this one taken?" she asked Kai. He shook his head, and she disappeared through the door, leaving Ember and Kai alone.

Ember continued to look around the 'tent' in amazement. 'This is nothing like camping back home in Montana,' she thought to herself. The inside of the tent was comprised of a large sitting room furnished with soft, cushy couches and chairs, as well as large soft rugs. To the right of the sitting room was the dining room with a table big enough for the six of them. To the left was a large fireplace, which took up an entire wall and was giving off a cheery glow and soft heat. In front of the fireplace were two cozy sofas. Through the sitting room was a hallway with four doors, apparently bedrooms ensuite. "Wow," murmured Ember.

Kai turned to Ember and asked, "Are you okay? The wounds that caused all that blood were healed, right?" Ember nodded, then grimaced at the pain in her neck. "Yes, they're healed, but I have some aches and pains which our healing powers apparently aren't strong enough to make go away," she said quietly. "Why don't you go in with your sister and soak in a hot bath? The bathroom is equipped for two, so you can both soak away the pain," Kai said as he gently guided Ember to her room. Ember placed a hand on the door handle and looked up at Kai, saying softly, "Thank you, Kai, for setting all this up." She then entered her room and shut the door.

Chapter Nine

Staring at the closed door for a few seconds, Kai gave a deep sigh and turned towards the door across from the sisters' door. He opened it and strode in, quietly asking, "What can I do to help?" Inside were two large beds placed on opposite sides of the room. There was a fireplace on the back wall, with a roaring fire crackling and emanating heat throughout the room. Next to each bed was a door that led to a private bathroom for each brother. Tai looked up from where he was standing next to the bed on the right, which Blaze was lying on. He was still unconscious but had been stripped down to his underwear. The blood had been washed off his skin, leaving a raw, angry-colored area spanning his abdomen, where the barb from the Manticore's tail had pierced and gutted him. "There's not much we can do anymore but to keep him warm and hydrated. It's up to him to fight this poison now," said Tai quietly. Tai pulled the thick, soft covers up over Blaze, tucking them up to his chin. Then he jerked his head towards the left side of the room and whispered, "The other pup is in there, cleaning off the blood. I'm amazed that they are still alive. Where the Hell did the Manticore come from? I only know of them from the Mythology books I read over the years while in the Mortal realm. How did one get into Marqueria?!"

Shaking his head, Kai said, "I have no idea. I didn't even think they were real. This is above our pay grade, Tai. Maybe one of us should transfer to the Castle and speak with King Otso and Queen Tati?" Tai shook his head negatively and murmured, "We can't leave these four alone, and I'd prefer we stay together for the time being. If Blaze hasn't woken up in two days, we will revisit that idea." Just then, Alaric came out of the bathroom, dressed in clean clothing and rubbing his wet, pitch-black hair with a towel. For being only sixteen, he was as large as a man but still had some years to grow and fill out. Currently standing at just over six feet tall, there was every indication he would be as tall, if not taller, than the Bear brothers, who were 6'5". "You do know I have Wolf hearing, right? I can hear everything you two have been saying, just FYI," Alaric said with a smirk on his face. The Bear brothers laughed softly, and Tai said, "Yeah, I guess we forgot."

Kai asked Alaric, "Is there anything the girls left out?" Alaric sighed and sat in the soft, cushioned chair next to Blaze's bed. Leaning back with his head against the back of the chair and staring up at the ceiling, Alaric said quietly, "I got the feeling it had been sent to find Noelle and Ember. It didn't want to kill them and intentionally threw them out of the way when he charged us. Once the girls were out of harm's way, the attack became deadly. That thing was trying extremely hard to kill my brother and me. It would have succeeded, too, if not for Noelle and Ember." Alaric turned his head to watch his brother as if to reassure himself that Blaze was indeed still alive and breathing. His expression was bleak and worried.

"Do you feel up to eating something yet?" Tai asked Alaric, who shrugged and said, "I could eat." This made the Bear brothers chuckle softly. Kai said, "I'll sit with Blaze while you go and grab some nourishment. I believe the girls have set the table again if my nose is correct." Tai stood up and said, "Come on, pup. Let's go eat, and then you can come sit with your brother while Kai and I sit outside watching." Alaric stood up and gave his brother one last long look before turning towards the door. Tai put his arm around Alaric's shoulder and softly said, "He's very strong and will survive this. Have faith." He then gently pushed Alaric out the door and followed him, closing the door quietly.

In the dining room, the table was set for just five, a stark reminder that one of theirs was unable to join them for the meal. Tonight, the table held a large tureen of hearty beef stew with dark, rich broth and another tureen of just dark broth, which Noelle was spooning into a bowl. She set aside this to cool while she ate her meal of hearty stew, a salad, warm steaming rolls, and hot sweet tea. She was subdued, more so than normal, and there was a haunted look in her eyes. Tai walked up behind her and laid a hand on her shoulder, giving it a gentle squeeze. She looked up and smiled wanly at him before she returned to eating her dinner, which she was doing much faster than usual. Ember was seated next to her, and she, too, was eating abnormally fast, but her reason was hunger. Noticing Alaric, Ember grabbed his hand and pulled him into the seat next to hers. Mouth half full of food, she mumbled, "Sit, eat. It will make you feel better." Noelle said quietly, "Swallow your food before you speak, please." But there was none of the humor or banter behind the request like there normally was.

Ember swallowed her food and turned, watching her sister for a few moments. "Noelle. Look at me, please," she said softly. Noelle set her spoon down and turned to face Ember, her eyes full of tears. "It wasn't your fault. We reacted as quickly as we could, and we saved them. Blaze will be alright, you'll see. Have some faith, sister," Ember said to Noelle, grabbing her hand and wiping her sister's tears with the other one. Noelle took a deep breath and nodded her head but then said out loud, "We should have cast a circle the minute we noticed our bracelets were hot. We should've reacted faster." The sisters were using their mind link now, excluding the others from their conversation. Ember sighed and softly said, "Next time, we will know better." Suddenly, Noelle stood up and grabbed the bowl of broth, which was now mostly cooled, and a spoon. "I'm going to go sit with Blaze and feed him some broth. Mom always said how important it was not to get dehydrated while ill, and I know we need to keep his electrolytes balanced. At least, I think we are, and I don't know what else to do," she said quietly as she walked toward the boys' room.

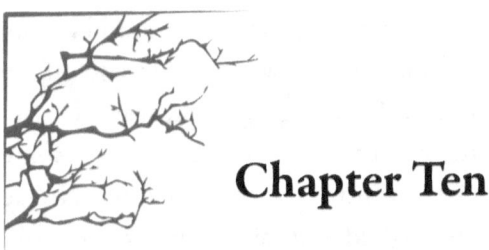

Chapter Ten

The two remaining teens at the table stared at one another, their expressions worried. Tai cleared his throat and said, "You two need to eat. It will help you fully heal. Don't worry about Noelle; she will be fine, especially while spending time with Blaze. Whether she knows it or not, she has bonded with him, and being in his presence, even while he's unconscious, will soothe and comfort her." Ember stared at Tai questioningly and asked, "Bonded? Like our bond with our Dragons?" Tai smiled and shook his head, replying, "No, not like that. Bonded like when you find your mate and accept them."

This left Ember speechless for a couple of moments before she burst out laughing. She laughed so hard that tears were running down her face, and she was breathless. Alaric and Tai patiently waited for her to finish, understanding her quirks. When she was able to control her laughter, she gasped, "Oh my Goddess! She is going to be so pissed when she realizes that little morsel of truth. I hope I get to be there when she finds out." This caused Tai and Alaric to laugh, too, and the mood became considerably lighter.

At the sound of the bedroom door opening, the three at the table turned to see who was coming out. It was Kai who closed the door and came to sit down. "I'm starving. Noelle is going to sit with Blaze for a while, which is good because she needs to be near him right now. So, what's so funny out here, if you don't mind sharing? I could use a laugh," he said as he filled his bowl with stew and grabbed some rolls. Tai said, "I was just informing these two about Noelle bonding to Blaze." Kai laughed and said, "Yeah, she doesn't even realize it yet. Boy, is she going to be pissed when she realizes she's found her mate, and it's the one the Goddess fated for her."

This comment sent the other three into another round of uproarious laughter, while Kai just raised an eyebrow at the three of them and took a bite of his dinner. When Ember could speak again, she said, "That's exactly what I said." Kai raised his hand up for a high five from Ember, who obliged. "Great minds think alike," he said before biting into a roll. Ember's face got serious, and she asked, "How is Blaze doing? Has he woken up yet?" Kai swallowed his food and shook his head, then said, "He hasn't come around yet, but he's holding his own. His heart is strong. If he doesn't wake up by day three, we will contact your grandparents. Both sets." This caused Ember to bite her lip and softly say, "Shit." Both Bear brothers nodded and looked a little worried themselves. Alaric, who looked just as worried as Ember, quietly said, "Oh man. My parents are going to murder me."

Inside the suite shared by Alaric and Blaze, Noelle sat in the chair next to Blaze, who was still lying in the bed, unconscious. She was spooning tiny amounts of warm broth into his mouth and softly telling him to swallow. Amazingly enough, he was obeying her gentle instructions and swallowing what she was feeding him. As she slowly fed him, she also spoke softly to him. "I don't know if you can hear me, Blaze, but I'm going to keep talking just in case you can."

She spooned another small amount of broth into his mouth and said, "Swallow that, please." Which he did, and she continued talking. "I don't know what is going on, but I feel so much better being near you. Calmer," she took a deep breath and continued, "When I saw the Manticore smash you with its tail, I felt your pain. I thought I was going to pass out because it hurt so much. I don't know how I knew it was you who got injured because you and your brother look identical in your Wolf forms, but I knew in my heart it was you. Then I felt the pain, and it was as if you and I were connected. I could feel everything that you were feeling. Let me tell you, I didn't like it. Not one bit. I think this is the Goddess pulling our strings, and it gets my back up. I don't know if you have ever heard that expression, but it means that it makes me angry and makes me want to fight. I don't like to be told what to do, how to live my life, or who I am supposed to marry. This is nothing against you at all, Blaze. I like you, I really do. I enjoy your company, and I feel safe when I'm with you. When I thought you were dead...."

Noelle took a deep, calming breath and continued, "When I thought you were dead, I wanted to die, too. The pain in my heart and soul was more than I thought I could bear. I'm going to tell you this now because you're unconscious, but I don't want to go through that again. I don't want to live without you..... I think I love you. But I don't know if what I feel is romantic love because I've never been in a relationship before or really ever wanted to be in one. The opposite sex never interested me. I've ever only loved my family. And Lucy, I love my dog very much." Noelle sighed, then whispered, "All I know is this: I don't want to be without you, ever. So, you better wake up and be fine. You better not leave me."

Noelle set the bowl of broth down on the table next to the bed. She had been feeding him while she had been talking, so there was just a small amount left in the bowl. Using a napkin, she wiped her eyes and face. She had been softly crying while she was speaking, and her face was wet with tears. Walking to the other side of the bed, she removed her shoes and climbed in under the covers. Putting an arm gently across his chest, then cuddling up close to Blaze and laying her head on his shoulder, she was asleep in seconds.

Chapter Eleven

Back in the dining room, Alaric had just finished speaking when there was a loud yell from outside. The four of them at the table stood up and moved to the door, grabbing their weapons before they opened the door. Rushing outside, where night had already fallen and the fire in front of the tent was still burning bright, the group at first didn't see anything. Then, there was movement on the other side of the fire, and Ember raised her bow at full draw, her arrow nocked. Kai yelled, "Come out where we can see you." There was the sound of scampering feet, and then a twelve-inch Gnome stepped out from the other side of the fire and into the light.

Ember gave a gasp and lowered her bow, then set it aside on the table by the door. With a smile, she started to walk towards it when Tai grabbed her sleeve and stopped her, then said, "It's an asshole, Gnome. How did it get through your protection circle?" Ember rolled her eyes at Tai and said, "Duh, the circle will keep out anyone or anything that means us harm. Obviously, this little guy doesn't." Tai scoffed and mumbled, "Yeah, wait until you wake up with only one boot."

The Gnome had sat down on a small stump and was waiting for them to join him near the fire. Ember sat down close to him, smiling, and asked, "Were you inside the circle when we cast it, or did you walk through?" Ember examined the Gnome, amused by his little outfit, which was very similar to the clothing they were wearing. He had on the tunic and leggings like they did, and they were in shades of brown, too. His adorable little hat, with the point drooping off to one side, was leafy green in color. Ember assumed this was good for camouflaging.

When the Gnome answered Ember, his voice was surprisingly deep. The Gnome said, "I was outside the circle and came in to speak to you. It is a very strong circle, as it gave me a zap even though I mean you no harm." He nodded his head, making his hat slide a little to the right. He then continued speaking in his deep baritone voice, "I was a witness to the attack on the Princesses and the Princes by that horrifying beast. I was sent here to ensure they were in good health and to offer any assistance from the Forest Dwellers." "What is your name? I can't keep calling you Gnome," spoke Ember softly. The Gnome quickly jumped off the stump, then removed his hat and bowed, saying, "I am Finnegan, at your service, Princess Ember." "How do you know who I am?" Ember asked with a raised eyebrow. He replied, "All of Marqueria know you and your sister. We have been watching you since you first began coming through the Tree." Under her breath, Ember whispered, "Yeah, that's not creepy at all." This made the three standing behind Ember laugh quietly.

"No, it's not creepy. We have all been keeping watch over you in case you needed help," he said with a tone of injured pride. Ember bit her lip and then said, "I apologize, Mr Finnegan. I meant no offense." Finnegan stared at her for a few moments as if trying to decide if she was teasing him. Deciding she was indeed not, he nodded his head and said, "Apology accepted. I was sent here by the Dryads to see if you needed anything and if any of you were injured badly." Ember looked up at the Bear brothers, who both had let out a small sound of surprise. "What?" asked Ember. "The Dryads are very powerful keepers of the Trees. It is an honor for them to be asking after you," replied Tai. Kai nodded in agreement. Ember sighed and turned to Finnegan, saying, "We are all fine, but for one. Blaze, the Wolf Prince, was badly injured and poisoned. He still has not regained consciousness despite the healing my sister and I performed. Will you ask if there is anything to be done to speed his healing?"

Finnegan looked worried, then said, "We do not know anything about this creature or its weapons, as it is not a beast from Marqueria. I don't know if we can find a cure here. Your grandmother, the Queen of the Elves, is a great healer. Maybe it is time you connected with her." Ember sighed and said, "I was afraid you'd say that. Nana is going to be so angry with us, but I think you're correct." Ember turned back to the other three and said, "Tomorrow, if Blaze is not awake, we need to contact my Nana." This caused the Bear brothers and Alaric to wince, but they all nodded in agreement.

Finnegan bowed to Ember again and said, "I must return and report my findings to the Dryads. It has been an honor to finally meet you, Princess Ember. We wish you safety and victory in the coming war." He scampered off quickly, and as he ran through the circle, he gave another yell, and the circle gave him a little zap. "Serves him right, the little shoe thief," said Tai quietly, causing Kai to bark with laughter.

"Why don't you two head back inside? Tai and I will be on watch through the night. You can all get some rest," Kai said, gesturing towards the opening of the tent. Ember gave them a worried look and asked, "Can you stay awake all night? I'm a night owl, and I can take a turn." The Bear brothers laughed, Tai, saying, "We've often pulled night duty. Heck, we've even stayed up for several days straight. We'll be fine, Princess. Please, go get some rest." Ember nodded and, grabbing Alaric's hand, pulled him into the tent after her.

Alaric stopped and turned to face the Bear brothers, then said, "Thank you for taking night watch. I am exhausted and would like to stay near my bother." Tai and Kai nodded. Kai said, "We understand the bond of brothers. Go. Get some rest." Ember and Alaric entered the tent and closed the door. The Bear brothers moved to the fire and stood, looking around. They gave each other a nod, then sat down, facing each other. "This has been a cluster, hasn't it?" asked Kai. Tai nodded, saying, "Yep, and we are going to pay a huge price when their parents and grandparents decide to kill us." Rubbing his hands over his face, then through his hair, Kai stood up and said, "I'll do first walk around."

Chapter Twelve

When Ember and Alaric went into the tent, they stood in the sitting room as if not knowing where to go. Ember looked at Alaric and quietly said, "I don't want to be alone just yet. Do you mind if I go into your room and sit by the fire with you? That way, we can be there for Noelle and Blaze if they need us." Alaric took her hand and tugged her towards his and Blaze's suite, saying, "Of course, and I understand about not wanting to be alone." When they entered Alaric's suite, they discovered Noelle sound asleep, cuddled next to Blaze in his bed, and unfortunately, Blaze was still unconscious. The scene surprised Ember and Alaric, who stood still, staring at the occupants of the bed.

"Well, I did not expect to see this when we walked in. Wow. I think Tai and Kai were correct, don't you?" said Ember. "Yep, I do. Come, let's go sit on the sofa in front of the fire; I'm beat," Alaric said softly and took her hand to lead her over to the sofa. Alaric sat down on one end of the sofa, leaning against the back and tall arm, then he lifted his feet and placed them on the ottoman. Ember stood in front of the fire, gazing into it as if in a trance. Alaric whispered, "Ember, come relax. You must be as exhausted as I feel. Come here." Ember turned towards him and gave him a small smile, but her brow was slightly furrowed in worry.

She gave a sigh and walked over, staring down at the sofa, and said, "Where exactly do I sit? You take up most of the sofa." Alaric gave a soft chuckle, then pulled her down next to him, where she sprawled half on his lap. They both were laughing softly as they found a comfortable position.

Ember ended up lying with her back to the rear cushions of the couch and her head resting on Alaric's chest. Alaric was lying down on his back, his head, and most of his torso, which was supported by the thick arm of the sofa. He had his right leg off the couch and bent at the knee, with the foot resting on the floor. He had his left arm around Ember, and with his right, he was absentmindedly playing with her curly cinnamon locks of hair spilling over his stomach. He gave a quiet sigh, leaned his head back, and closed his eyes. Ember whispered, "This is nice. I feel safe here with you." She gave a huge yawn and said quietly, "I'm just going to rest my eyes for a bit." She closed her eyes and, within just a few moments, was asleep. Alaric lifted his head and looked down at her, smiling softly, his golden eyes bright. He watched her sleep for a while, and then he, too, laid his head down and closed his eyes, joining her in much-needed healing sleep.

Sometime during the night, Tai had come in to check on Blaze. He stood in the sitting room looking between the scene in Blaze's bed and the one on the sofa by the fire. He scrubbed his face with his hand and then ran it through his blonde hair to the back of his neck, where he massaged the knotted muscles at the base of his head. "Shit," he whispered, then turned and walked out to speak with his brother Kai.

When he got outside to the fire, he sat in a chair and placed his forearms on his knees, leaned forward, and stared into the flames for a time.

When Kai came back from making his rounds, he sat in the chair next to Tai. Noticing his brother's body language, he asked, "What's wrong? Is Blaze worse?" Tai shook his head and gave a great sigh. "Nope, he's still unconscious but seems to be resting quietly. With Noelle practically glued to his side, it's no wonder he's resting so well. Alaric and Ember are sleeping like the dead, too." "Wait, what?! Are they sleeping together? In the same beds?!" growled Kai softly. "Blaze and Noelle are in his bed; Noelle is fully clothed and sound asleep. Ember and Alaric are on the sofa in front of the fire, fully clothed and asleep. It was rather a shock to walk in and see that, I admit," Tai said, taking a deep breath. Then he said, "They are fated mates, Kai. Being near one another helps them heal physically as well as emotionally. We can't keep them apart; we can only monitor exactly how close they are becoming and make sure they follow the rules of courting." Kai looked at his brother in stunned silence for a few seconds before saying, "I'm surprised to hear you being so reasonable regarding our Princesses. Why the sudden change of attitude?"

Tai stared into the fire as he told his brother, "Who are we to deny them the comfort a mate can bring? Telling Ember about our mates and how we lost them made me remember all the good we had when we were with them, how my love made me feel when I was with her. I want that for Ember and Noelle. Those two boys in there are honorable and good and will protect and love the girls. They are worthy of being paired with our Princesses." Pain flashed across Kai's expression before he smiled softly and said, "Yes, I, too, have been remembering my mate and all she brought to my life. Even with this deep pain in my soul, I remember all the love. You're right, of course. They deserve to feel that, especially with the huge burden they carry at such a tender age." The brothers continued to stare into the fire, listening to the sounds of the night and listening for anything that would threaten the peace within the tent.

"One of us needs to phase to the Castle and let them know what has happened. We need to get Blaze healed, and his parents have the right to know," Kai said, leaning forward and adding another log to the fire. From the fire, orange sparks floated upwards and popping increased while the new log began to burn. Tai nodded and said, "You're right, and I think you should go. I'll remain here and keep watch." Kai stood up and stretched. Then he laughed and said, "Coward." Tai grinned at his brother and said, "You know it." "See you soon, brother," Kai said, then he disappeared.

Chapter Thirteen

The sound of a throat loudly being cleared woke up three of the four teenagers in the room. Noelle opened her eyes and stared at the ceiling as if trying to figure out where she was. Ember slowly opened her eyes and then immediately sat up, looking down at Alaric, who was staring at her with laughing golden eyes. Another throat being cleared grabbed their attention, and the three of them sat up and turned towards the sound. Ember whispered, "Oh, shit."

Standing near the door, gazing at the scene with expressions ranging from amused to worried, were both sets of the girls' grandparents, Bram and Maia, Otso and Tati. Standing next to them were Luna and Ulric, the boys' parents. "We will give you ten minutes to fully awaken, then please meet us at the table for breakfast," murmured Maia, Ember, and Noelle's maternal grandmother. Noelle replied, "Yes, Nana." Ember simply nodded her head. The six adults turned and quickly left the room, closing the door quietly behind them.

Noelle and Ember stared at each other, nodded, and stood up as one. Alaric chuckled and shook his head, amused at the girls' secret communication. They didn't even try to hide the fact they were talking to each other through their mind link. Ember looked down at him, raised an eyebrow, and asked, "What's so amusing?" Alaric said, "You two are. You don't even try to hide it when you talk privately in front of people. If you want people to NOT know you're communicating privately, then don't nod or shake your heads." Ember's cheeks pinked up at that, but then she, too, laughed softly. Shrugging, she made her way to the door and said over her shoulder, "See you at breakfast." After checking on Blaze, Noelle followed her sister out of the room. Gazing at his brother in bed, still unconscious, Alaric gave a sigh. "I'm actually glad our parents are here. We are only teenagers, and what happened to us was traumatic," Alaric said softly to Blaze. He stood up, gave a huge stretch, and then headed for the bathroom to change and get cleaned up before meeting with the adults.

The table had grown to accommodate the added number of diners, so there were eleven places set and one which remained empty. Ember and Noelle came out of their room at the same time Alaric left his. They headed to the dining table together, picking seats next to each other, with Ember in the middle. Kai and Tai sat towards the end of the table, with Tai next to Alaric. The rest of the group made their way to the table, choosing seats across from the teens. Ember cleared her throat and said, "We're sorry we snuck off...." But her Nana raised her hand and interrupted, saying, "No. Not now. Now you are to eat. We will speak about everything after you have had some nourishment." Ember gave a sigh and began to fill a plate with scrambled eggs, toast, bacon, and slices of fireberries. Alaric poured some coffee into two cups and added some cream and honey to it, then set them down near Ember's and Noelle's plates. Ember handed him a full plate, then picked up hers to fill. "Thank you," they whispered to him; then, when her plate was full of delicious-smelling food, Ember picked up her cup and took a large swallow of the hot, sweet brew. She breathed in the comforting scent of the coffee, thinking of her mom and dad, hoping they were okay.

The adults watched the way the three teens served each other, and they all exchanged amused glances but said nothing while everyone ate. "This is so awkward," whispered Ember to Alaric, who just nodded and continued to eat. After a bit, Bram cleared his throat and said, "If everyone has had their fill, we will move to the sitting area." He stood up, not the happy-go-lucky Papa who Ember and Noelle had come to know, but the King of the Elves. His bearing was commanding and firm, his voice was neutral, and his usually twinkling green eyes were somber. He waited for Maia to walk before him, and then he followed her to sit near the fireplace. The rest of the group slowly followed. 'These are not our loving and indulgent grandparents,' Ember thought to herself. Noelle caught the thought and nodded at Ember, agreeing with her.

"Okay, now we can address the sneaking off part of all this," said Maia, the girls' Nana. Noelle and Ember stared at their four grandparents, both still amazed they could be grandparents. They looked the same age as their parents, mid-thirties. Living in Marqueria, their life span was very long, but their appearance would never age past 30-40. Noelle said softly, "We are sorry we worried you and didn't tell you we were leaving. That being said, we knew something was not right with our parents. They would never miss

81

Christmas with us, and it's in a couple of days. Also, they would never NOT communicate with us. You wouldn't listen to me, Papa, when I tried to explain this. You brushed aside our concerns and treated us like small children." Bram stared at Ember and Noelle, eyes contemplative. Finally, he took a deep breath and let it out slowly, then turned and met his wife's gaze. After a few moments, Bram leaned forward and looked to Otso and Tati, the girls' paternal grandparents and the King and Queen of the Bears. Otso gave Bram a small grin and nodded his head. Tati raised an eyebrow, but she, too, nodded.

Turning back to face the girls, Bram spoke quietly, "We apologize for brushing aside your concerns for your parents. We forget that you are not the toddlers who came through the Tree all those years ago and that you are now two very powerful magic wielders on the cusp of adulthood. We haven't given you enough credit or respect. Again, we apologize." When Bram was done speaking, Maia took over, "That being said, from now on, when you have the urge to run away on some grand adventure, please consult us first, and we will try to support you." Otso and Tati nodded in agreement, but Otso also gave his granddaughters a wink and a smile. This caused Bram to give a great belly laugh and say, "I can't say that I'm not impressed with all of you. The future leaders of Marqueria are not afraid and show great courage and strength. We are going to need this in the years to come." Maia lightly elbowed her husband and said, "Husband, you are too permissive. They could have been killed by that beast."

Luna looked at her son, Alaric, and said, "We are unhappy that you didn't feel you could tell us your plans, but we understand and applaud your decision to stay with the girls." Ulric nodded and said, "You followed your protective instincts, and that is all we could ask for."

Ember spoke up now and said, "But we weren't killed. We turned it to ice, and if you want to go see it, we can take you there." Noelle, with a pained expression and tears in her eyes, spoke up now, "Please, first, we need to heal Blaze. I can't bear this pain anymore. It hurts. Why does this hurt so much, Nana?" Maia stood up and went to Noelle, pulling her up and bringing her into her embrace. Noelle, at 5'10", towered over her tiny Nana, who was just 5'3" tall. Despite this, Noelle felt better having her Nana comfort her. From the end of the sofa, Tati said quietly, "This is how the mating works, Noelle. You feel their pain, and it only eases when you are in their presence. It will get easier to handle, I promise you." Noelle stepped out of her Maia's embrace and said, "But we are not officially mated yet. I don't understand." The adults all exchanged surprised looks mixed with confusion.

Luna stood up and came to Noelle, taking her hands into her own. Luna was the Queen of the Wolves, and she was a few inches taller than Noelle; her body was long and leanly muscled. She had the same coloring as her sons: black hair and dusky skin with golden eyes. "My sweet girl, you and Blaze have bonded. That is why you feel his pain and only feel better when you are with him. Were you not aware of this?" Luna asked softly. Noelle stared up into Luna's golden eyes, so like Blaze's. She shook her head and said, "I don't understand. We aren't mated yet. We haven't even really kissed. How did we become bonded?" "It is an unconscious thing that happens between fated mates when they accept that they have found their mates. It means you have accepted that Blaze is your mate," said Luna, studying Noelle's expression.

Noelle's face flushed red, and with a hint of anger, she asked, "So, I have no say with whom I'm going to spend the rest of my life? The Goddess fated it, so it's just going to happen on her timeline, is that it?" Ember leaned forward and grinned at Tai and Kai and whispered, "See, pissed." This caused the two Bear brothers to give a muffled laugh.

Noelle turned on her sister with lightning speed and said between gritted teeth, "This isn't funny, Ember. Did you stop and think about your situation right now? I do believe you're bonded to Alaric, too." Ember's face paled, then went blank. Turning to Alaric, she whispered, "Is it true? Are we bonded?" Not knowing for sure, Alaric looked to his parents for help. Luna and Ulric both nodded, Ulric, saying, "Yes. It is true. Ember and Alaric are bonded as well. It must have been triggered by the violent fight with the beast."

Standing up with hands on her hips, Ember stared down at Alaric and said in a growly voice, "Don't plan a wedding any time soon. Noelle's and my birthdays are next month, and we will be only 16 and 17. We aren't getting married now." Alaric laughed and said, "Good. I don't want to get married right now, either." This seemed to calm Ember down, and her face was a little confused. She gave a sigh and sat down again.

Noelle didn't sit down. She left the room and headed for Blaze's, saying over her shoulder, "Well, come on. We are going to heal him now. I want to know how he feels about this." As one, Mai, Tati, Ember, and Luna followed Noelle into the bedroom. Bram stood up and said to the males who were left out, "Let's go outside and get some fresh air. Then, you boys can tell us exactly what happened with the Manticore."

Chapter Fourteen

The fire in Blaze's room was roaring and crackling, spreading heat and light throughout the room. Blaze was lying in his bed, a blanket pulled down to his waist, with his chest bare. Luna was sitting on the bed with his head in her lap, Noelle and Ember were on the right side of the bed, and Tati and Maia were on the left. "I want you all to place your hands on Blaze. Luna, your hands should be at his temples, with your thumbs across his forehead. Ember and Noelle, your hands will be on his shoulder, chest, stomach, and hip. Tati and I will mirror your hand placements, girls," murmured Maia softly, continuing on, "I want you all to envision the healing light of the Goddess as it enters Blaze. Repeat the chant with me softly and focus on the healing light." Maia began to chant softly, and the others joined in.

With Light from the Goddess, We invoke
Her healing energy, Her healing cloak
With Love and Compassion, She mends and restores
The Body, the Mind, the Spirit, forevermore.

THERE WAS A SOFT, SILVERY glow beginning where the hands touched Blaze's body. As the group of females continued to chant, a gentle breeze floated locks of hair up off their shoulders, and they, too, began to glow gently. This continued for several moments, and then Maia said, "So mote it be." The others repeated it, and the glow dissipated along with the breeze. The five females stared down at Blaze, waiting. Noelle looked up at Maia and, in a soft, pleading voice, said, "Nana, wake him up." Maia said, "It is up to the Goddess now, my child."

Noelle's face took on a stubborn, angry look, and she shook her head, then moved up onto the bed, taking the spot Luna had vacated just moments before. Holding Blaze's head in her lap with her hands on his temples and thumbs on his forehead, Noelle immediately began to glow bright silvery-white, and her hair was wildly floating about her head. She whispered, "Goddess, I demand you heal him. You can't fate us to be mates and then take him away the minute we are bonded. How can you be so cruel? You've been with me all my life and have shown me nothing but kindness. Why have you forsaken me now? Please! Heal my mate!" This last was delivered in a demanding yell and a flash of bright light, which traveled down Noelle's arms and into Blaze. His body arched up off the bed, held that pose for a few seconds, and then fell back down.

There was total silence in the bedroom, and nobody moved. Then, Luna quickly came to Blaze's side and checked his heart and breath. Breathing a sigh of relief, she looked at Noelle and said, "He is still alive." "Noelle, we do not make demands of the Goddess! That is not how this exchange works," said Maia sternly, with an expression of worry. Noelle moved down off the bed and stood next to it. She looked down at Blaze's face and gave a gasp when she saw his bright golden eyes looking back up into her teary green ones.

Tears falling down her face, Noelle smoothed his black hair away from his forehead and whispered, "You came back to me." "I would never leave you, Noelle. I was fighting to come back from the void the entire time. Then, suddenly, a bright flash of light showed me the way out," Blaze said with a raspy voice. He reached up and placed a hand behind her neck, pulled her face down to his, kissed her lips gently, and said, "Please don't cry. It hurts to see you crying." He gently wiped the tears and said, "I could hear you while I was in the void. I heard everything you said." He gave her a soft smile and a wink. Noelle's cheeks flushed red, and she groaned. "We're bonded," Noelle said baldly, watching Blaze closely to see his reaction. Blaze nodded and said, "Yes, we are." He continued to stare into her eyes, waiting. "You're okay with this?" Noelle asked softly. Blaze grinned and said, "Yes, of course I am. It doesn't change anything for us, but it makes us closer. I'm not ready to get married yet, either. Noelle, I heard it all." Noelle grinned at him and bent down to place a kiss on his forehead, saying, "Now, it's time for you to acknowledge the rest of the group, please." This made everyone laugh because they knew she was just deflecting and wanted to move the attention from her and Blaze.

Luna moved forward and placed her hand on Blaze's chest, over his heart. "Well met, my son," she whispered. Blaze reached up, placed his hand over hers, and said, "Well met, mother." Luna leaned down, placed a kiss on his forehead, and said, "I knew you would be okay. You're too stubborn to pass so young." Mai, Taki, and Ember moved forward and told Blaze how happy they were that he was okay, and then Luna said, "Come, everyone. Let's leave Noelle and Blaze alone for a while. Plus, we need you to take us to where the beast is frozen, if you would, Ember." Everyone left the room, leaving the two teens alone.

Chapter Fifteen

Standing outside the tent, near the low burning fire, Maia and Ember were discussing the small clearing. Ember had never seen this side of her Nana before, being so authoritarian, as Nana had always been one to hang back and listen. Now, however, Ember was seeing the Queen of the Elves. Maia gently grabbed Ember's shoulders and pulled her close. Touching her foreheads, Ember showed Nana the small clearing where the Manticore had attacked them. "Got it. Thank you, Ember. You go with Alaric and Tai. I'll show the others where to go. Kai will stay here and guard Blaze and Noelle," Maia said, grabbing Bram's hand and moving to the other leaders of Marqueria. They grouped up and disappeared in seconds. When they all appeared in the small clearing, the Manticore was still there, frozen solid. Maia and Tati both gasped when they saw the beast. It was a massive statue of solid clear ice, tinted faintly blue.

The leaders of Marqueria slowly walked around the frozen Manticore, studying it up close. Face pale, Maia turned to Ember and Alaric, asking quietly, "You fought this creature?" Ember nodded and said, "Noelle and I shot it with our arrows, but we hit it just below the eyes. It had already started forward and was lightning fast. Shooting it just seemed to piss it off. Then it charged and batted Noelle and me away across the field over there." Ember pointed to the edge of the clearing, which was many yards away. Alaric continued with the tale, "When we made sure the girls were okay, Blaze and I shifted into our Wolf forms and attacked. It was vicious and was trying to kill us. What I found strange was that it didn't try to kill the girls; it just wanted them out of the way. Us though? Oh, It definitely wanted to kill us. I gathered from what it said when it spoke to us that it was sent here to get the girls." Bram said, "Yes, Kai and Tai reported that to us earlier. Hmmmm."

Luna and Ulric walked to their son, and they both embraced him, a family hug similar to the one Ember and her family often did. Ulric grabbed Alaric's head and brought it closer to his, touching foreheads. Ulric took a deep breath and said softly, "I am proud of you and your brother. Thank the Goddess you and Blaze weren't killed." Luna reached up and cupped Alaric's cheek with her hand and, in a hushed voice, said, "Thank the Goddess."

Tai spoke up and said, "When we found them, we thought Blaze had been killed. They were all covered in blood, and it didn't look good at all. Thankfully, the injuries weren't serious, but for Blaze's." Otso nodded and turned towards Tai, saying in a low, growly voice, "I am glad you tagged along with my granddaughters on their little escapade, but the more prudent route would have been to notify us of what they were planning." Tati stepped forward, laid a hand on her husband's arm, and said, "It happened the way the Goddess meant it to, husband. Tai and Kai both felt something was wrong with Kenna and Jamie, and they followed their instincts. As for Kenna and Jamie, they still remain missing, so their actions were prudent, for the leaders of Marqueria ignored the pleas of our granddaughters." Around the group, the adults all nodded their heads and looked a little sheepish.

"What do we do with this ice sculpture? Do we leave it, and when it melts, it's gone? Or will it defrost and live again?" asked Ember. "Good question, granddaughter. One I do not have the answer to," answered Bram, her Papa. Tati, queen of the Bears, spoke up loud enough for everyone to hear her, "I believe we can perform a binding spell, which would bind the creature to this location if it should ever awaken." Maia nodded her head in agreement, motioning for Luna and Ember to come closer. The males stepped back several feet and watched as Ember, Maia, Tati, and Luna all joined hands just a couple of feet away from the Manticore, forming a circle.

By the Power of Light and Love
We bind this evil from above.
Neither harm nor pain shall it cause,
Within this binding, no breath it draws.

They continued the chant, glowing brightly until a silver shimmer grew from the ground up and covered the Manticore in a dome. They spoke together one last phrase, "So mote it be," and then released each other's hands and turned to look at the contained Manticore. "Yes, I think that will hold it if it does wake up," said Tati, nodding her head. "I hope so," whispered Ember, eyeing the frozen Manticore with a hint of fear. Alaric draped an arm around her shoulder and pulled her in close, leaning down and placing a kiss on her head. Ember took a deep breath, breathing in his scent to calm herself.

"Can we start looking for our parents now?" asked Ember, turning to look at each one of the adults in turn. Otso met her eyes, his eyes so like her father's that it made her stomach hurt. He said, "Yes, granddaughter. We will start when we get back to the tent. We can gather outside near the fire and discuss what our next move is to be." Ember nodded once, eyed them all challengingly, then reached for Alaric's hand and held the other out to Tai, who grabbed it and Alaric's other one.

The three quickly disappeared, leaving the Royal leaders of Marqueria laughing at her impatience to get started. "Alaric is either going to temper her impulsiveness, or she's going to make him more like her," laughed Otso. Tati shook her head and, smiling at her husband, said, "I believe it will be both. They complement each other and will take on the traits they need to be complete." Luna was watching Tati, and with a smile, she nodded in agreement. The group grabbed hands and disappeared.

Chapter Sixteen

Back at the tent, Ember and Noelle were in their suite, getting cleaned up and changed for dinner. They had met outside around the fire, and an animated conversation regarding the search for their parents ensued. The sisters had managed to make everyone agree that it wasn't normal for Jamie and Kenna to be out of contact for so long.

The six leaders of Marqueria would be returning to the Castle to check on Maxim, Bram, and Maia's nephew and Ulrika, Luna, and Ulric's daughter. They would also continue to prepare the Castle and surrounding villages for battle. Ember, Noelle, Blaze, Alaric, and the Bear brothers would continue their hike to the Sacred Grove of the Dragons early tomorrow morning. So, tonight would be an early dinner and early bedtime.

In their suite, the girls were getting ready for dinner. While Ember sat on the sofa, running her fingers through her mass of waist-length cinnamon-red curls, she asked her sister, "Noelle, do you think about Montana at all since we moved here? Do you ever wish we would have stayed in our Red House in the Country?" Ember gave a sigh and whispered, "Because I do sometimes." Noelle turned from putting on her boots and nodded, saying, "I do, too. Every day, I question our decision to follow Hilda through the

Tree. I miss our quiet life back in Montana and our Red House. When this thing with the Darkness is over, do you want to go back home for a time?" Ember smiled at her sister and nodded. "Yes! After we find Mom and Dad, we can spend our birthdays next month in Montana, like we always have," Ember said, standing up and holding her hand out to Noelle. The sisters left their suite, holding hands and looking better than they had yesterday.

Luna met them before they could reach the others, stopping them just outside their door. She smiled warmly at them and said, "I am so proud of the way you two handled the Manticore. When you first started traveling through the Tree, I always watched you and protected you from afar, and the joy at your discoveries in this world became my joy. Through the years, I have come to care for you deeply and want nothing but the best for you. You are perfect mates for my sons, as no others would have measured up. That being said, you should know this: There is no rush for you to marry. You can wait as long as you want. Into your thirties if need be. It will happen when you say it will happen. You have my word as the Alpha of the Wolves." She bent down and gave each girl a hug and a kiss on the forehead. Then smiled and said, "Now, let us go eat. I'm famished."

Chapter Seventeen

The next morning, Ember, Noelle, Blaze, Alaric, and the Bear brothers were standing in the now-empty meadow, preparing to continue their journey to the Sacred Grove. The tent had been packed into the magic backpack Kai was carrying, and the area where the fire ring had been was back to pristine snow. The leaders of Marqueria had already left for the Castle, leaving the group with the warning, "Don't do anything stupid, and please contact us immediately if you do get into trouble." This came from Maia, back in her Queen roll for a few moments before she hugged her granddaughters close and, with a sheen of tears in her eyes, whispered, "I love you girls so much. Please be safe." She was, after all, at heart, their loving Nana.

"Well, let's get walking. Hopefully, we will be there by the end of the day," said Ember, as she put one of her AirPods in her ear and handed the other to Alaric. She then placed her magical backpack on and slung her bow over her back with her quiver of arrows. Kai started up the trail with Blaze and Noelle right behind him. Alaric and Ember followed them, and Tai brought up the rear. Ember said, "I feel like we should be singing a song as we walk. Something catchy and fast-paced. Anyone want me to put my music on speaker?" Tai growled, "No singing. We need to stay alert and quiet so we can hear anything approaching. Or have you forgotten you two are being hunted?" Ember heaved a sigh and murmured, "No, I haven't forgotten. I just wanted to for just a little while." The group continued on steadily for a few hours before Ember said, "I'm starving. Can we stop and eat?" Chuckling, Tai said, "Don't you remember what happened last time we stopped for lunch?"

Noelle stopped and turned back to stare at Ember. After a few moments, Ember grinned and said, "There's a spot right up there where we can sit and eat a meat and potato pasty. They're in each of your backpacks already, along with a thermos full of hot chocolate." "What's a pasty?" asked Alaric. "Only the best, most delicious portable hand-held meal ever! It's a seasoned meat, potato, and onion mixture encased in a buttery, flaky crust. We grew up in Butte, Montana, and the pasty was a staple meal the miners would pack in their lunchboxes. Most everyone in Butte loves them. They can be served on a plate with gravy or hand-held with ketchup," Smiling, Ember shrugged and said, "I prefer warm and handheld with a gravy container for dipping."

At the front, Kai had stopped and looked back at Tai. Either they, too, could communicate through a mind link, or they were just that in tune with each other; Ember wasn't quite sure yet. She watched them closely as they continued to stare at one another, and Tai suddenly gave a growl and looked rather angry. "Fine!" he said in frustration. Ember grinned at him, gave him a wink, and walked ahead to sit down in the little half-circle of grass just off the trail. It looked as if it had been used often by travelers to rest and refuel during the hike to the Grove. There were stumps made into small tables for setting food and drink on, scattered around the area. Of course, Ember and Noelle cast a protective circle around the group before sitting down.

There was enough room for the group of six to spread out on the ground without touching. Backpacks were taken off, and they all sat down and got comfortable. They then began consuming their pasties and hot chocolate, savoring the food and drink, having realized they, too, were very hungry. They ate in silence, the comfortable silence of companions who liked and enjoyed each other's company and who had been through traumatic events together. When they had all finished their pasties, they continued to sit and sip their chocolate. "I must say, Princesses, that pasty was amazing. It's been several months since I've had one. Thank you for bringing a little bit of Montana to us," said Kai, giving the girls a smile. Tai grudgingly said, "Yes, even though we shouldn't have stopped, I appreciate the meal. I, too, had forgotten how good these are."

"Do you miss Montana?" asked Blaze, gazing at Noelle with a questioning look. Noelle stared off into the trees with a small frown between her eyes. She slowly nodded her head and said, "I do. Ember and I were talking about this a bit ago, and we both miss our quiet life in the mountains. We want to return to Montana for a little while after the Darkness is vanquished, of course." Blaze looked down, his face showing his disappointment. Ember spoke up, "Would you and Alaric like to go with us, Blaze? You could visit and see what the world we grew up in is really like. What you see on the internet is not the entire picture." Alaric and Blaze looked at each other and grinned, nodding their heads.

"Okay, let's get going. We should be there before nightfall if we keep a steady pace," said Tai, standing up and grabbing his backpack. They all gathered up their packs and got back on the trail. They had only gone a few steps when Noelle and Ember both gasped and stopped. They turned to each other and, with tear-filled eyes, said together, "Mom and Dad are at the Grove and are okay!" "What?! How do you know?" exclaimed Alaric. "They just contacted us via our mind link," Ember said. Kai said, "Well, let's get going." The group continued on to the Grove, but at a much quicker pace and with an air of excitement.

Chapter Eighteen

E mber, Noelle, Blaze, Alaric, Tai, and Kai stood at the entrance to the Sacred Grove of Dragons, amazed at the enormous arch, one hundred feet tall and twice as wide, made out of live trees and vines. The Grove itself was round and immense, like a huge metropolitan city with a towering shimmering dome surrounding it. One could make out the protection circle and dome over the Grove by the slight silver shimmer it created.

After the group had stepped through the protection shield, the Grove became even more vibrant and magical. The ancient trees were an array of many different colors, leaves of blues and greens to reds and orange, with trunks in black, red, white, and blues, along with the normal browns and grays. There were flowering bushes and fruit trees, Fairies of all shades flying from flower to flower or simply lounging in the foliage. Ember spotted Gnomes here and there, scampering underfoot in the snow. The air was warm and moist with the sweet fragrance of many flowering bushes and trees. It was truly a magical grove, like something out of a dream.

Ember and Noelle immediately spotted their green dragons, Jade and Sage, way on the other side of the Grove. With them were two huge, massive dragons, one black and iridescent with gold accents, the other a dull, warm gold with black accents. Standing next to the dragons were the girls' parents, Kenna and Jamie.

The girls didn't waste time running across the huge expanse of the Grove. Instead, they grabbed hands and disappeared, only to reappear almost immediately right in front of their parents, who grabbed both girls and pulled them into a family hug. Kenna, Jamie, Noelle, and Ember held on to each other tightly, not yet able to speak.

They only separated when Tai, Kai, Blaze, and Alaric arrived, panting a little from the run they had just quickly completed across the Grove. Tai growled, "A little warning would have been nice, brats." Ember shrugged and said, "Sorry, boys, but we just needed our parents." Ember turned to her dad and asked, "Dad, how in the Hell do you have a full head of hair down to your shoulders?" Jamie laughed and shrugged, then said, "When the Dryads tried to heal me, my hair grew. I rather like it. Makes me look dangerous. At least, that's what your mom said." "Heal you?!" exclaimed the girls together. "We'll explain later, but first, go greet your Dragons," said Kenna.

While the girls reunited with their Dragons, Jade and Sage, Jamie stepped towards the Bear and Wolf brothers, his expression a mix of frustration, gratitude, and relief. He took a deep breath and said, "While I am not happy you allowed the girls to come on this journey, I also understand our daughters are not ones to be told what to do. I am, however, very relieved you all came with them. Come meet our Dragons, and then we can retire to our living area and discuss what happened on both of our journeys."

Jamie then reached out and grasped Tai's forearm with his hand, Tai grasping Jamie's in return. They both said, "Well met." Jamie repeated the same greeting to Kai, Blaze, and Alaric before directing them toward the Dragons and his reunited family.

The group was introduced to Nyx and Sika, Kenna's and Jamie's Dragons. Nyx bowed her head and chuffed before saying, "I am honored to meet the two little ones our daughters have chosen to bond with. My mate and I had been waiting some time for them to choose, and not until you two came through the Tree did they make their minds up. You both are a fitting match for our two younglings." "I am pleased to meet you both and am so excited to get to ride alongside my mom and dad, too," said Noelle politely. Ember, though, excitedly said, "What?! I didn't realize our Dragons were the daughters of our mom and dad's Dragons....was that on purpose?" Sage, Ember's bonded Dragon, gave a chortle and said, "Never one to mince words, are you fiery one?" Ember walked over to Sage and laid her forehead down on Sage's head, right between her golden horns. "I've missed you so much, Sage. It felt like longer than a few days," whispered Ember while she hugged her Dragon's head as best she could. Sage chuffed and said, "I've missed you as well, little Elf Bear. I am so happy you were not seriously injured in the attack by the Manticore."

Jamie and Kenna both gasped loudly, and there were cries of, "What?!! You were attacked?!!" and "When did this happen?" "A Manticore?! What?" Ember rolled her eyes and whispered, "Thanks, Sage. We hadn't told them yet." Sika, Jamie's Dragon, spoke up loudly enough for everyone to hear him. His voice was very low and growly, "Enough! We will retire to our living area and discuss their journey and what we are to do about the Darkness." Nyx chuffed and chortled, amused at all the uproar, and she said, "Yes, Sika is right. We will all go to our area and feed the little ones and their companions. Follow us, honored guests." Kenna's family, the Bear brothers, and the Wolf brothers fell in behind the Dragon family and followed them deeper into the Grove.

Chapter Nineteen

The living area of the Dragon family, or their Dragon's Den, was nestled amidst the foliage, hidden from prying eyes. The entrance to their den was guarded by a massive white stone arch, which had warm gold veins flowing through it. The arch was adorned with intricate carvings in a language nobody in the group could read. There was a silvery sheen between the columns forming the arch, like a force field. Stepping through the arch, the atmosphere was warm and inviting, with soft, green moss carpeting the ground, creating a comfortable and cozy feel.

Ember gasped at the sheer size of the Dragons' home. The den was immense, with massively high ceilings that allowed the dragons to freely move about and stretch their wings. The walls were adorned with shimmering crystals, casting a soft glow throughout the entire space. Sunlight was filtering through the canopy of living trees above, creating a dappled effect of light and shade. Above the den, a network of twisted branches formed the canopy, creating a hidden rooftop garden. Vibrant flowers bloomed in a riot of colors, their sweet scent filling the air.

A sparkling underground river ran through the den, providing a source of fresh water and a serene, bubbling ambiance. Noelle quietly said, "Oh my Goddess! I think I just saw a Mermaid. Ember, did you see it?" The girls stopped walking and looked towards the river. After a few seconds, a stunningly beautiful Mermaid appeared on the large boulder in the center of the river. She had very long, shining, bubblegum pink hair with a matching iridescent scaled tail. Her skin was almost white and had a silvery glow emanating from it. She wore no clothing to speak of, but her hair covered her breasts from sight. Her eyes were disproportionally large in her face and were a deep, sparkly pink.

Staring at the Mermaid in awe, Ember asked, "Do all Mermaids have matching hair, eyes, and tails?" Alaric nodded and said, "Yes, their color schemes match, and they come in any color imaginable. They also have different colored skin amongst their kind. I once saw a rare black iridescent one with black hair, skin, and tail, but her eyes were mercurial silver. She was stunning." As they watched the Mermaid brushing her hair on the large boulder, she was joined by another Mermaid in shades of blue with dark brown skin. "I am just amazed with how lovely they all are," whispered Noelle.

Kenna called quietly to her girls, motioning for them to continue walking, so the teenagers moved on, following their parents and the Dragon family. "What the Hell?" whispered Alaric at the next surprising scene they came upon. There were many piles of treasure carefully arranged throughout the Dragon Den, glittering in the soft light. Precious gemstones of diamonds, emeralds, and rubies were mixed in with ancient-looking artifacts, along with piles of softly shining gold and silver jewelry, creating a breathtaking display.

"We like our shiny things," chortled Jade, Noelle's bonded green Dragon. "It's so overwhelmingly lovely in here," Noelle said to Jade, still staring at the jewels. "Would you like to have some of our shiny things, little one?" asked Jade, chuffing at the end of the question. "Thank you, Jade, but no. I really have no use for jewelry at the moment other than our protection bracelets," Noelle replied. Jade nodded her massive head, chortled, and said, "You'll change your mind," and turned to follow her parents.

As the group continued further into the immense Den, they noticed nooks and alcoves scattered throughout, offering resting spots for the Dragons. Each nook was filled with soft beds of moss and plush velvet cushions, providing a most comfortable place to rest and recharge. Overall, the dragon's living space within the magical grove was a harmonious blend of natural beauty and mystical elements. It provided the Dragons with a sanctuary away from the world, as well as their own kind, yet they still remained connected to it all.

The group stopped a few yards in front of a large tent similar to the one they had slept in the past few nights. Looking back at the way they had come, Ember was amazed at the vastness of the Dragon's Den, and she gently elbowed Alaric so he would turn around and look as well. "It didn't seem as if we walked that far. How does that work? It looks to be about two miles to the arch, wouldn't you say?" Ember said softly to Alaric. Alaric said, "You're right. It felt like just a short walk, but that looks to be longer than the Castle Valley. It must be Dragon magic and some kind of space displacement." Noelle called to Ember, "Come on!"

Alaric and Ember walked faster to catch up with the rest, who were entering the tent. "Go get changed and cleaned up for dinner, little one. We will talk about the troubles you had on your journey during dinner. I'm so happy to be with you again, little Elf Bear," purred Sage as she nodded her head towards the entrance of the tent. Ember went to her, and they touched foreheads for a few moments, then Sage gave her a gentle push towards the tent, "Go, youngling."

Ember followed Alaric into the tent, where Noelle, Blaze, and the Bear brothers were already choosing rooms. Kenna came to her and gave her a tight hug, saying, "I've missed you so much, nugget." Ember returned the hug, burying her face in her mother's hair and taking a deep breath, something she had been doing since she was a baby. Her mom smelled like home and love. "I've missed you too, Mom. Can we talk about what happened to you now?" Ember said. Kenna gently pushed Ember back so she could see her face. She studied Ember for a few moments and then shook her head, saying, "We want you all to get cleaned up, changed, and ready for dinner. We eat outside with our Dragons. We can discuss it when we are all together." Ember sighed and nodded her head. "I could use a bath and some clean clothes, I guess," she said, sniffing her hair and grimacing. Her mom chuckled and pushed her toward the area where the bedrooms were located.

Chapter Twenty

To the right of the tent was a large, lovely round table with softly cushioned chairs at each place setting. The table itself contained many platters and bowls of artfully displayed food, and the aroma wafting through the air was delectable, stimulating the appetites of the group seated around the table. "I didn't realize how famished I was," mumbled Ember around a mouthful of the half-eaten, warm, fragrant roll she was holding. "Ember, please don't talk with your mouth full of food. Honestly," said Noelle, rolling her eyes and giving her sister a gentle jab with her elbow. Ember jabbed her sister back with her elbow, and before it could become an all-out fight, Kenna spoke up, "Enough, please. We don't fight at the table. Besides, we all have tales to exchange." Grinning at each other, the girls sat up straight and turned toward their parents, who were seated across from them. "Yes, mother," they laughingly said in unison.

A few yards away from the table lounged the four Dragons bonded to Kenna and her family. From that direction came a few chortles and chuffs as the Dragons found the girls amusing. Ember looked over at them and sent a wink their way, causing Jade and Sage to laugh outright. Sika gave a growl, causing the Dragon sisters to stop laughing.

"Your father and I will go first," Kenna said, taking a drink from her wine glass and clearing her throat before continuing. Kenna told them how they had been attacked by several members of Hilda's followers and how they awoke in a protected cave, both injured. She explained about the Dryads and their attempt at healing them and mentioned Finnegan, the Gnome. "Really?!" exclaimed Ember before continuing in a more subdued voice after a look from her dad, Jamie. "We met Finnegan as well. He came to check on us after we were attacked. He said the Dryads were concerned but that they couldn't heal us." Kenna nodded and said, "Yes, their healing is meant for the plant life of the forests only."

Jamie had been watching Kenna closely during her retelling of their adventures, and he spoke up quietly, "Kenna. Is that all you're going to say about the attack?" Kenna and Jamie stared at each other for a time before Kenna said softly, "I would prefer if you would tell that part, please?" Jamie took her hand and placed a kiss on her palm, saying, "Sweetheart, you have nothing to be ashamed of. You were protecting us, and the Goddess worked through you to do it. You don't have to carry the guilt for surviving the attack." Kenna nodded and squeezed Jamie's hand before turning towards the others at the table. "Jamie will tell you all that which I have left out," she said, picking up her wine glass and taking a deep drink.

"What happened, Dad?" whispered Noelle, watching her parents with an expression of concern. Jamie took a deep breath and then proceeded to tell them how a giant burst of light and power had exploded out of Kenna and killed all of their attackers. "Oh, Mother, I'm so sorry you had to experience that, but I'm not sorry they were killed. We need you, Mom," said Ember, watching as her mother stared into her wineglass. Kenna looked up at her girls and gave them a sad smile. "It's about survival here, Mom. We have to survive, and if someone has to die to make sure of that, then so be it. This is war, and it's a war we have to win," said Noelle firmly, looking intently at her mother. From the Dragons came chuffs and chirps of agreement, and Jade said, "See, my honored parents? The fire within burns brightly in this one, too."

Kenna took a deep breath and said, "I know you are both right. My mind tells me that it has to be that way, but my heart wants it to be another way. I don't want war; I don't want anyone to die. I want to find a way to defeat the Darkness and Hilda, with no one else losing a life. I just don't know how to do it yet." Ember nodded and said, "I think with everyone at this table, we should be able to come up with a plan to make that happen, Mom. We can find a way to do things the way you want them." Kenna smiled at her younger daughter and said, "Thank you, Ember. I appreciate your understanding."

Alaric, on Ember's left, and Blaze, seated on Noelle's right, had leaned forward a little to better see each other. Their eyes met, and an unspoken agreement passed between them. Nodding, Blaze cleared his throat and said, "I don't think there is a way to fight this war and not have casualties. I believe you need to hear what we have to say about our encounter with the minions of the Darkness before you decide to take that route."

From the other side of Blaze, Kai and Tai were nodding in agreement with what Blaze said. Tai, who was seated directly next to Jamie, turned towards him and said, "My Prince, their tale needs to be heard before any battle strategy plans are made." "Yes, it does," murmured Kai, nodding his head and looking towards the girls, who were quietly watching the interactions of those at the table. He gave them a gentle smile and turned back to Jamie and Kenna. "Princess Kenna, with all due respect, please hear our tale before you put that feeling into a concrete plan," said Kai firmly. Kenna and Jamie looked at each other with concern, then turned to their daughters. Jamie said gruffly, "My daughters, please. May we hear of the ordeals you encountered on your journey here?"

The girls nodded and, holding hands, told their parents what they had experienced on their travels. Taking turns and picking up where the other had left off, the entire story was told. When they had finished, there was complete silence at the table as the others watched Kenna and Jamie absorb what their daughters and their companions had gone through. Kenna and Jamie stared at their daughters for a few seconds, then moved their gazes around the table to the others, studying each in turn.

Kenna let out a loud breath and nodded her head, then she turned to Jamie and raised a questioning eyebrow. Jamie nodded and said, "We would like to see this Manticore. Now that you know the Sacred Grove, you can show us the clearing where the Manticore is and be able to transfer back here." Nyx gave a loud chuff and said in her low, melodious voice, "We will travel there by air but will not land. We will keep watch from above to ensure there are no other attacks." "Can we transfer from here, or do we have to go outside the protective dome?" asked Noelle as she pushed her chair back and stood up. Jade gave a chortle and said, "You may transfer from here, little one. I will be above, keeping an eye on you." Noelle nodded and gave Jade a smile.

Everyone stood up, and Tai and Kai grabbed their weapons, which had been slung over their chairs. Blaze and Alaric, too, had their short swords on in no time at all, and Ember and Noelle both had their bows and quivers slung over their backs. Kenna and Jamie watched them all weapon up and exchanged a surprised look. Noelle caught her parent's exchange and quietly said, "You never know when danger will present itself, and it is better to be prepared than not." Then she grabbed Blaze's hand and gave it a squeeze, staring up at him with a small smile. Blaze reached over and tucked a curl behind her ear, saying, "I'm okay, Noelle." Then he leaned down and placed a kiss on her temple. She nodded and reached for her sister's hand. Jamie and Kenna again exchanged a surprised look; this time, Ember had been watching them, and she gave a loud laugh. "Yep, we have a lot to catch up on, Mom and Dad."

Kenna walked over and placed her forehead to Noelle's, and Jamie did the same with Ember. The girls showed their parents where the small clearing was. Then, everyone joined hands and disappeared. The Dragons rose up and flew through the protective dome so they could meet them there. Dragons could fly extremely fast, so they were only a minute behind.

Chapter Twenty-One

They appeared in the small clearing, released hands, and walked towards the snow-covered ice statue of the Manticore. The binding dome was still active and intact, and there were no footprints anywhere in the clearing, indicating it had been unvisited since they were last there. Jamie and Kenna walked around the giant ice sculpture of the creature who tried to harm their daughters. Turning to Kai and Tai, who were turned towards the tree line, scanning, Jamie asked, "You said it didn't try to kill the girls; is that correct?" Tai turned to face Jamie and said, "Yes, correct. Alaric said it batted the girls out of the way over there," he pointed to the tree line to the left and then continued, "After the girls were out of the way, it attacked the boys with the intent to kill them."

Kenna and Jamie looked over to where the four teenagers were standing. Blaze had his arms around Noelle, comforting her and soothingly rubbing her back, murmuring quietly to her. Ember had her arm around Alaric's waist, her cheek resting on his chest, and his hand buried in her curls at the back of her head. His head was bent down towards her, softly whispering, "It's okay. Ember, it's frozen and contained and can't get at us now. Shhhhhh."

"Well, it looks like we've missed something big here. Something other than the Manticore," Kenna said very softly to Jamie. Jamie was watching the four teens with a frown between his eyes. He suddenly turned to Tai and Kai and growled, "What the Hell is going on over there? What haven't you told us?" Tai met Jamie's eyes and said in an equally growly voice, "Nothing inappropriate has happened between them. Give your daughters and the Wolf brothers more credit, my Prince. Give US more credit." Tai continued to stare at Jamie, his eyes hard. Kai stepped between them and said, "Easy, brother. My Prince, we were given charge of the safety and caring of your daughters. That is what we have done. Alaric and Blaze made a vow to you, and they have done nothing but fulfill that vow."

"Dad, don't you dare be angry at Tai and Kai!" Ember exclaimed as she pushed her way between Kai and her father. She stood toe-to-toe with Jamie, her hands on her hips, and glared up at him from her 5'3" height. "Tai and Kai did everything to protect us and keep us comfortable and safe. Nothing untoward has happened between Alaric and me or between Blaze and Noelle. They would never take advantage of us and have more manners and honor than the boys back in the mortal world we had to deal with." Ember's eyes were glowing green fire with gold sparks, and her hair was slowly lifting up and floating. Noelle laid a hand on Ember's shoulder and said, "Calm, sister. It's okay. This is Dad, not the enemy. Let go of your power. Sshhh." Taking a step back, Ember closed her eyes, took a deep breath, and then let it out slowly.

After repeating that a few times, she opened her eyes and whispered, "I'm sorry I lost my temper, Daddy. I didn't mean to. Tai, Kai, Blaze, and Alaric have become very important to Noelle and me. When I saw your temper just below the surface when you were talking to them, I snapped." Jamie stepped forward and wrapped his baby girl in his arms, saying, "It's fine, Ember. I reacted poorly, and you called me out on it. It's fine, sweetheart. We're good." Leaning back and looking down at his daughter's face, Jamie asked, "Am I forgiven?" Ember gave a small laugh and said, "Of course, Dad. I can't stay mad at you. I missed you and Mom so much. We were so scared when we couldn't contact you." Ember looked up at him with tear-filled eyes, and her father brushed the tears away as they fell. "It won't happen again; I promise it won't," Jamie said, looking at Noelle, too.

Noelle nodded and said, "There's something we need to tell you, but I think you've already guessed, Dad." Jamie nodded and said, "Yes, I believe I have." Kenna walked over from where she had been watching the interaction between her husband and daughters. "Well, I haven't guessed, so why don't you fill me in, girls," she said, raising an eyebrow and waiting.

Jamie gave a great sigh and put his arm around Kenna's shoulder, pulling her tightly into his side. "It appears that our daughters have bonded with the Wolf brothers," Jamie gruffly said. A frown appeared between Kenna's eyes, and she looked a little confused. Looking at her daughters, who were standing with Alaric and Blaze again, she asked, "Do you mean as we bonded with the Dragons?" The four teens shook their heads negatively. Noelle took a deep breath and let it out slowly, then said, "No, more like we've accepted our mates. We admitted that they are our intended mates. It created a bond between us. I feel Blaze's pain, and he feels mine. We feel each other's emotions and need to be together, in close proximity, for any pain or anguish to ease. When I'm not with Blaze, I feel very irritated, almost like I have an itch I can't scratch, and my anxiety increases to the point I can't breathe. I'm told it would be worse if we were separated for a long period of time, and I really don't want to experience that." Kenna just stared at the four teens, saying nothing. Then, she looked up at Jamie questioningly. "Is this normal?" she asked Jamie. Jamie nodded and grimaced.

"I remember when I was apart from you, Kenna. It became unbearable. Why do you think I pushed for us to get married so quickly?" Jamie said, bringing Kenna's hand up and kissing her palm. "Hmmm. I do remember feeling so restless when you weren't with me. Was I experiencing the separation anxiety from the bonding?" she asked Jamie, watching him closely. Jamie nodded and said, "Yes, you were. And now our children are." Kenna turned to Ember and asked, "Is it the same for you?" Ember nodded, her cheeks a little pink, and she stated firmly, "But that doesn't mean I'm getting married anytime soon!" This comment made everyone laugh and eased the tension. Alaric laughingly said, "Good! I don't want to get married any time soon, either." Ember grinned at him, dramatically wiped her hand across her brow, and shook her hand as if shaking off sweat. Another round of laughter ensued.

COMES THE DARKNESS

Suddenly, Jamie, Kenna, Noelle, and Ember stopped laughing and stood eerily still. Then, as one, they burst into movement, grabbing the hands of the rest of the group, and everyone disappeared from the small clearing.

Chapter Twenty-Two

Reappearing in the Sacred Grove of the Dragons, within the protective dome and surrounded by a calm, quiet, and soothing atmosphere, the other four were asking questions on top of each other, "What happened?!" "Why did we leave so quickly?" "Are you okay?" "What did you see?"

Jamie raised his voice and said, "Quiet! We will explain." Kenna and Jamie directed everyone over to the large fire and the chairs, telling them to sit down and hush. When everyone was seated, Kenna began, "Our Dragons mind linked with us and showed us what they were seeing. There was a large group of heavily armed men and women headed our way. The group was comprised of a mix of Elves, Bears, and Wolves. They were just 100 yards from the clearing when we transferred."

There were gasps from the four Weres. "There were Wolves in the group? Are you sure?" asked Blaze, his expression pained. Jamie nodded and said, "Yes, we are sure. There were several Bear among them as well, which I need to let my father know as soon as possible." Jamie then closed his eyes, apparently communicating with his father. Blaze and Alaric exchanged a worried glance, and then Blaze closed his eyes as well, letting his parents know what the Dragons had seen. Kenna said, "We will all return to the Castle in the morning."

Just then, all four Dragons appeared in the sky above them. They were coming in fast, but when they landed, it was very light and graceful despite their weight and immense size. Nyx moved quickly and gracefully to Kenna's side and lowered her head so that it was level with Kenna. She gave a soft chirp and gently nuzzled Kenna, saying, "There was danger close to you this night, little one. It was good we were flying above and were able to warn you of it. From now on, we will be with you just like tonight."

Sika moved to Jamie and gave a chuff before nuzzling Jamie, too. "We will travel to the Castle too. You will not be there alone," Sika said in a low, baritone voice. Ember and Noelle walked over to where their bonded Dragons were, and affections were exchanged before the Dragon sisters turned and headed into their own sleeping chambers. Nyx and Sika said their goodnights and followed their daughters, leaving the eight sitting around the fire.

Ember and Noelle were staring at each other, and then both giggled. Alaric and Blaze both groaned, and Blaze asked, "What are you two up to?" Turning towards the Wolf brothers, with twinkling eyes, Ember asked, "Have you ever had a s'more?" "A what?" asked Alaric. Blaze just shook his head no. Tai and Kai both let out a whoop and together said, "Yes!" Jamie and Kenna laughed at the display of lightheartedness from the group. Noelle said, "You're in for a treat, then." On the table next to Kenna's chair, two large bags of marshmallows, two boxes of graham crackers, and eight large bars of milk chocolate suddenly appeared, along with eight roasting sticks.

For the next while, the group laughed and chatted about mundane, normal things while they enjoyed their overly sweet, gooey desserts. Funny stories about the girls were told, much to their chagrin, but Tai and Kai had a few about Jamie as a child, which had the teens rolling with laughter. They were telling the story of when, on a dare, Jamie tried to ride Raina, Queen of the Unicorns. She then proceeded to pick him up with her horn and carry him home by his pants. "No, you did not!" shouted Ember, tears rolling down her face as she laughed. Looking abashed, Jamie rubbed his face with his hand and nodded his head, saying, "Afraid I did. And my father was not happy about it either. He was so angry I had disrespected another Royal in that manner that I had to chop all the village's wood for a year. As I grew older, I realized what an asinine stunt it was and just how horribly I had disrespected her. I later apologized to Raina. She forgave me and said that the memory of me dangling upside down by my pants all the way to my father makes her laugh every time she thinks about it." This caused another round of laughter from the group around the fire.

As Ember was putting another marshmallow on the roasting stick, Alaric reached over and grabbed another out of the bag and said, "These are crazy sweet, but I can't stop eating them. I've watched Tai and Kai put away at least two dozen each." "Are you saying we are gluttons, young pup?" growled Tai while he took another burnt marshmallow off the stick and placed it on the chocolate-covered graham cracker. He then looked up at Alaric and, with a grin, shoved the entire thing in his mouth. Ember grinned at Alaric and said, "Yep, we introduced the Bear brothers to these back in Montana one night by the fire. Mom usually limits how many we have, but I think she's being more lenient since we almost died."

Kenna just smiled at Ember from across the fire and tossed her another chocolate bar. "There are more important things going on right now than monitoring your sugar intake, sweetheart," Kenna said and shrugged. "Might as well enjoy the little things." Then she took another marshmallow and added it to her roasting stick, and stuck it over the fire, turning it slowly. She had a rather sad look in her eyes as she stared into the flames. Jamie leaned over and whispered, "Are you okay, wife? Do you need me to do anything for you?" Kenna gave him a soft smile and said, "I'm just a little homesick for our Red House in Montana.... Oh, my Goddess!! Christmas is in two days!"

Ember, Noelle, Jamie, and Kenna all looked at each other, their faces showing their dismay that one of their favorite Holidays was almost forgotten. "Can we celebrate it at the Castle?" asked Noelle. Ember started to laugh and soon was laughing so hard she couldn't catch her breath. Everyone just watched her as she tried to say what was so funny, but she couldn't get the words out. Tears streaming down her face, she finally was able to get out, "Santa Clause is our Grandfather."

This sent Noelle and Kenna into peals of laughter, with Jamie hugely grinning as he watched his wife and daughters laughing and happy. "I don't understand," whispered Alaric to the other Weres. Tai smiled and said, "The Mortal world celebrates Christmas, or Yule as we call it, by pretending there's a Santa Claus who delivers gifts to all the world's children on Christmas Eve. The girls knew there wasn't a Santa Clause and that their parents were the ones who got the gifts. The problem is, there really was a Santa Claus, called Father Christmas, and it was King Bram, the girls' Papa." Tai and Kai both joined in the laughter, for having spent many years in the Mortal realm, they understood the humor of the situation. Blaze and Alaric just looked on in wonder and amusement.

When the girls had their laughter under control, Jamie said, "When we return to the Castle tomorrow morning, we can discuss having a Yule celebration with Bram and Maia. I'm sure they would love to host us all for the Yule, with him being Father Christmas and all." This sent the girls into a brief fit of giggles again.

Still laughing softly, Kenna stood up and said, "Okay, it's time for all of us to turn in and get a good night's rest. Go ahead and make your way to your rooms. There's no need for a night watch, as we are well protected by the Dragon magic and the protective dome." Tai and Kai both sighed, and Tai said, "Finally, a good night's rest. It's been a couple of long nights for us. Kai nodded and started for the entrance of the tent.

With a hand on his arm, Jamie stopped Tai and murmured, "I want to apologize for my behavior earlier. I was wrong, and I want to tell you how much I appreciate all the care you've shown my daughters." Nodding, Tai looked down at the ground and said, "Kai and I never got to experience being fathers before our mates were killed. They were both pregnant with our first cubs when they were taken from us. It has been several years, and we are only now able to talk about it, and being around your family has made that possible. Noelle and Ember remind us of what we could have had, but it doesn't make us bitter or angry. It makes us want to protect them all the more."

Tai looked up at Jamie and, seeing his stunned face, said, "It's okay, my Prince. I just wanted you to know that your daughters will always have protectors in us." Jamie nodded his head and whispered, "I never knew you had mates. I just assumed you hadn't found yours yet. I am so sorry for your loss." Tai gave a sigh and said, "It happened the last time Hilda started her war. Her retreating army killed them while they were swimming in the river. That is another reason we will fight Hilda and her followers and ensure they don't survive this time." Jamie grasped Tai's forearm with his hand, and Tai grasped Jamie's in return. Jamie said, "I vow to do everything in my power to make sure Hilda doesn't rise to power again." Tai gave Jamie a nod and then turned and walked towards the tent.

Looking up, Jamie saw Kenna and the four teens watching him. They had witnessed his conversation with Tai. Kenna had tears running down her face, and while the girls and Wolf brothers looked sad, he had the sense they already knew. Jamie moved to Kenna's side and wrapped her in his arms, comforting her. "You already knew about their mates and younglings?" he asked the teens. They all nodded.

Ember, her cheeks a little red, murmured, "I had been rather nasty to Tai about his overprotectiveness towards us when either of us got too close to the boys. He told us what happened, and I felt so terrible. I shouldn't have said what I said, though. But it's ok, we talked, and we are good now." "Having just bonded, I don't want to think about what losing one's mate would be like. It hurts to even think about it," whispered Noelle, cuddling closer to Blaze, who put his arm around her shoulder and gruffly said, "It's not something I want to think about either." Kenna pulled back from Jamie and asked, "Is there a chance they will find another mate, or will they be alone the rest of their lives?"

Jamie stared into the fire as he held Kenna. Shaking his head, he said, "I don't know. I've heard of a few who found another mate when theirs died, and some just find someone to spend time with until that person's mate shows up. Most spend their lives alone or with friends and family." Alaric nodded and said, "It's the same in the Wolf packs. We mate for life, and once a mate passes on, it's extremely rare to find another." He looked down at Ember and gave her a small smile, then whispered, "So, please don't die." She just shook her head, speechless at the thought of Alaric dead. "You better not either," she whispered back.

Jamie said, "Okay, kids. Bed, now. Go on in, and don't worry about this mess. We will clean up here." After saying their goodnights, the four teens entered the tent, leaving Kenna and Jamie alone. Kenna said, "I like those boys. I like those boys with our daughters. What do you think?" Jamie gave a huff and said, "While I'm not ready for our daughters to be so grown up, I will admit to liking them as well. They are good for our girls, and I'm hoping they will temper some of their impulsiveness." Kenna laughed and said, "Not going to happen. If anything, the girls are going to make the boys more impulsive and adventurous." Jamie gave a sigh and said, "You're probably right." With a wave of her hand, Kenna cleaned up the area of all their s'more-making ingredients, then, grabbing Jamie's hand, walked into the tent to find their bed for the night.

Chapter Twenty-Three

The next morning, Jamie and Kenna stood just inside Blaze and Alaric's bedroom doorway, staring at the beds' occupants. Shaking his head, Jamie whispered, "I'm not sure I will get used to this." Kenna said, "It is a bit of a shock at first, especially since the girls showed no interest whatsoever in the boys in Montana." Shrugging, she said, "Should we let them sleep longer? They have been through a lot these past few days."

Nodding, Jamie turned towards the doorway. Kenna followed behind and started to close the door quietly, but then she stopped and stared at her daughters again for a few moments. Noelle was sleeping next to Blaze in his bed. Both were fully clothed and cuddled up close, sound asleep. In the next bed over, Ember was cuddled up close to Alaric, again both fully clothed. Giving a quiet sigh, she quietly closed the door.

Out at the dining room table, which was laden with many different kinds of breakfast pastries and pots of scrambled eggs and hashed browns and bacon and sausage, sat Tai, Kai, and Jamie. All three already had plates piled high with food and cups of hot, steaming coffee in their hands. "Takes some getting used to, doesn't it?" asked Tai, taking a sip of his coffee and watching Jamie and Kenna. Kenna gave another sigh and nodded. "It seems like just yesterday, I was sitting in the Grove by the Red House, teaching them botany. They weren't interested in boys at all in Montana. Now, they're sound asleep next to them." She picked up her cup of coffee and breathed in its comforting scent.

Taking a large drink, she set it down and asked, "So this is a thing, I guess? This is normal?" All three WereBears nodded. "Well, okay then. I'll just have to get used to it," she said as she filled her plate with pastries. Catching Jamie's smirk, she said, "What? I'm eating my worry, so shut it, mister." He laughed and said, "I love you, sweetheart." She winked at him and took a bite of her cinnamon roll.

"So, what's the plan for today? Are we going to the Castle as soon as the kids wake up?" asked Kai before taking a huge bite of a cinnamon roll. Chewing, he gave a groan of satisfaction and, swallowing his bite, said, "These are the best cinnamon rolls I've ever had. Where did you get these?" Kenna smiled and said, "I made them. Cooking and baking always relaxes me, so I magicked myself a kitchen and all the supplies and did some baking early this morning." Tai and Kai looked at the mountains of pastries with wide eyes. Tai asked, "You made all of these?" She nodded and finished the last of her cinnamon roll, then took a deep drink of coffee. She sighed contentedly and said, "I also cooked all the food on the table. As I said, cooking relaxes me and helps me think. I've missed it since we've been in Marqueria."

Just then, the sound of a door opening and footsteps made the adults look toward the bedrooms. Piling out of the one bedroom and heading to the table were Noelle, Ember, Blaze, and Alaric. "I'm starving! Oh goody! You cooked, Mom," exclaimed Ember as she took a seat next to Tai. Alaric sat next to her and began preparing her coffee. Noelle sat next to Kenna, and Blaze sat between Noelle and Alaric. Blaze poured a cup of coffee and added honey and milk, then handed it to Noelle. She said, "Thank you, Blaze," and took a sip, stating, "Perfect." Jamie and Kenna watched in amused surprise as the two couples prepared plates for one another and made sure each other had everything they needed. 'They truly are like mated couples,' thought Kenna to herself as she watched them.

When everyone had eaten their fill, Jamie stood up and said, "Pack your bags and meet us out front in ten minutes. We're transferring to the Castle." "Okay, Dad," Ember and Noelle said together, and they, too, stood up. Blaze and Alaric stood and headed to their room, following the girls. Jamie gave a sigh, much to the amusement of Tai and Kai. Giving them a mock glare, Jamie turned to the door and walked outside to talk to his bonded Dragon, Sika. Kenna chuckled and said, "I think he's having a harder time with this than I am, and he was raised around it." Tai and Kai nodded, and Kai said, "Yes, but he has spent most of his adult life in the Mortal realm. He has picked up many of their misguided beliefs. The longer he is in Marqueria, the more he will be at peace with all of this." Kenna nodded and said, "I'll be outside with Jamie when you are all ready."

Chapter Twenty-Four

The group reappeared in the courtyard of the Castle, which was surrounded by an army of Elves, Bears, and Wolves. Standing in a line to greet them at the entrance of the Castle were the leaders of this army, King Bram and Queen Maia, King Otso and Queen Tati, King Ulric and Queen Luna. From behind them, Lucy pushed her way through and ran for her girls. She stopped right in front of Ember and Noelle, sat at attention, and waited for them to pay her some attention. When they knelt down next to her, her tail was wagging so much her butt followed. She was a wiggling mess, seeking the attention and love of her girls, who had left her behind. "Oh, Lucy! Such a good girl." "We missed you so much, sweetheart. Did you miss us?"....Ember looked up and noticed everyone watching and waiting, so she stood up. Lucy sat right next to her and waited, too.

The leaders of Marqueria all gave welcoming smiles, and Maia said, "We've been waiting. Tati said you would arrive in the morning hours of today. I'm so glad you're all home again." The girls went to both sets of their grandparents and exchanged hugs and greetings. Then they moved down to Luna and Ulric, where Blaze and Alaric were already talking with their parents. Luna gently pushed her sons aside to give the girls each a hug, telling them about the Yule celebration they had been planning at the Castle. "Have you ever participated in a Yule celebration?" asked Luna as she stepped back and took Ulric's arm. Ember excitedly replied, "Not really. We've always celebrated Christmas, though. I'm excited to enjoy the festivities of Yule with all of you." Overhearing the conversation, Maia called out, "We are happy to finally have you here for Yule, my granddaughters!"

Maia instructed everyone to go to their suites and leave their packs, get cleaned up, and then get changed into festive clothing, as their travel clothes were "much too somber for this joyous occasion." Tai and Kai left for their suite, which was in the same tower as Otso and Tati, Jamie, Kenna, and the girls. Jamie and Kenna both started to leave for their rooms when they noticed their daughters standing off to the side with Blaze and Alaric, with Lucy standing guard. The four teens looked worried and a little panicky. Kenna motioned for Jamie to continue to their suite and whispered that she would be right up but had some mom business to take care of. Jamie glanced at the teens, nodded his head, and went up to their tower. Kenna noticed Luna watching the teens as well, so she walked over to Luna and asked her, "Is this an issue with the Bonding?" Luna nodded her head slowly and looked down at Kenna, murmuring, "I didn't think it was this bad for them yet. They will feel pain sleeping apart. What should we do to ease their situation, do you think?"

Kenna looked for her mother and found Maia watching them from the entrance to the Castle. Kenna jerked her head towards Maia, indicating she should come join them. On her way over, Maia snagged Tati's hand, and the two joined Luna and Kenna. The two mothers and grandmothers stood observing the struggling teens for a few seconds. Tati said very softly, "The kind thing to do would be to give them a suite to share, and if that doesn't sit well with Jamie, then maybe add two rooms to the tower suite you share with the girls?" Maia nodded and said, "Yes, it would be cruel to separate them now. What are your thoughts on this, Kenna?" They all turned to look at Kenna, who was biting her lip in contemplation. "Is there a spell of some kind we can cast over them that will allow them to sleep in the same bed but protect their innocence?" The others gave quiet chuckles, and Kenna looked up at them with pink cheeks. "What?!" she asked, sounding slightly offended. "Your Mortal upbringing is showing very strongly in that question. That is all. We do not mean to offend you, Kenna," said Luna softly, taking her hand in both of hers. Luna continued, "The Bonding itself prevents the couple from consummating their union. Until both parties are ready to go through the mating ceremony, there will be no intimacy beyond cuddles and a few kisses." The others nodded in agreement. Kenna's mother, Maia, said kindly, "If you and Jamie had met here in Marqueria, we would have given you a suite of your own to reside in until the mating ceremony could be completed. The Bonding is simply a way for the couple to get to know each other and strengthen their mating bond."

Kenna gave a sigh and said, "Okay. I will go speak with Jamie while you three go talk to the kids. They can have their own suite. I'm sure Jamie will agree since he was raised here, too." Kenna left for her suite to go find Jamie and have the discussion. 'Oh, Goddess, give me strength,' she thought to herself, smiling wryly.

Luna, Maia, and Tati quietly joined the teens and waited while they listened in on what they were saying. "I don't want to be separated. Can you just come live in our suite?" Noelle was saying to Blaze, holding onto his arm tightly. Blaze shrugged and said, "I don't know if your parents would be okay with that." The three Royals cleared their throats together, startling the four teens, who turned around and stared in silence. "Nana, YaYa, do you know what we should do?" asked Ember softly. Luna gave the four a smile with eyes twinkling and said, "Your mother has come up with a solution, and she is off to tell your father about it now." The girls gave pleased exclamations, and the boys exchanged a relieved glance.

"What is mom's solution?" asked Noelle. "You are to be given your own suite within the tower your parents are in," said Tati, smiling. Ember and Noelle stared at their grandmothers and Luna, stunned. "And father is okay with this?" whispered Ember softly. The three adults exchanged amused looks and nodded. Tati said, "Well, he should be, anyway. This is the way of the Bonding, and he will abide by our traditions, no matter how long he spent in the Mortal world." She said this rather sternly, showing she was Bear Queen and Mother to Jamie. The four teens all looked more relieved and settled, so Maia said, "Come. I will show you to your suite." "But, Nana. You said there were only seven floors. All the suites are taken!" cried Ember. The adults all laughed, and Maia explained, "I am the Queen of the Elves, my sweet. I can make another floor and suite whenever and wherever I want. Or did you forget who we are?" Ember grinned at her Nana and said, "Yes, I briefly did forget." "Come, let us go see your new suite. Luna, Tati. If you want to come join us?" said Maia. They both declined, saying they had some things to do to ready the Yule celebration. "Come on, Lucy!" called Ember as she walked into the Castle.

Chapter Twenty-Five

When the four teens entered their suite, they all gave a surprised gasp. "Naaannaaaa....You're amazing," whispered Ember, staring around the suite. "How did you know about all this?" asked Noelle. Maia laughed, gently pushing the two boys further into the room. "Do you like it? Did I get it right?" asked Maia, watching her granddaughters closely. "Perfectly," both girls said in awe. Ember turned to her Nana and asked, "But how did you get all this in this tower? The tower doesn't look this large from the outside." Maia gave a chuckle and said, "I used a space displacement spell. We want this to be your sanctuary, away from all the war talk. When it gets to be too much, you can come here and have your choice of distractions," she gave each of her granddaughters a hug, then said, "I love you both so much, and I'm happy you're staying here with your Papa and me. Well, I'll leave you to it then." Maia walked out of the suite and got onto the elevator, waving at the teens as the door slid shut, leaving the four of them alone in their teenage paradise.

Their suite contained everything a teenager could wish for when on house arrest. To the right of the door, on the curved wall, was a massive stone fireplace with a roaring fire already burning cheerfully. In front of the fireplace, a collection of soft, cushy furniture was artfully arranged, and the floors were adorned with thick, lush rugs, all in deep jewel tones.

Following the curve of the wall brought one to the bedroom area. There were no doors to bedrooms in this suite. No, Maia had built four large, rounded niches within the wall. Each niche had a built-in king-sized mattress and an area with small doorless cubbies for storage. On each bed sat their gaming laptops. 'Goddess bless our Nana,' thought Ember to herself. Between the middle two niches was a smaller niche with LUCY written across the top. Lucy went and flopped down in her bed, gave a huge sigh, and closed her eyes, causing the others to chuckle.

There were wrought copper wall sconces in each cubby, providing soft, glowing light within. The beds were covered with luscious green velvet bed coverings. The large, rounded openings were made of dark walnut-colored wood and were accented with copper hardware. There were vines containing fragrant blooms growing up and over the walls in this area of the suite, along with small trees. The ceiling was a forested canopy, and there was a small waterfall between the bed areas and two doors to the left. Maia had created a hidden, forest-like atmosphere around the bedroom area. "This is amazing," whispered Noelle.

Continuing on and following the wall past the waterfall, there were two doors. Opening one, Ember peeked in and exclaimed, "Nothing but the most amazing bathroom ever!" She grinned at Noelle, who peeked her head in and said, "Holy cow! With the sparkling stone walls, it looks like a cave in here, but a luxurious cave, and there are plants everywhere. There are two huge clawfoot tubs and two walk-in showers, plus two water closets. That one must be yours." This last was directed at Alaric and Blaze, who opened the door and showed the appropriate level of appreciation. They closed the bathroom doors and moved on around the outer wall, coming to the enormous flat-screened TV mounted on the wall. Below the TV was a table containing one Nintendo Switch, an Xbox, and a PS5. "Your Nana is amazing," murmured Blaze, examining the gaming systems in awe. In front of the table were four gaming chairs, one for each of them. "Come on. The best part is over here," exclaimed Ember, practically vibrating in excitement as she almost ran to the next area. It contained two fully automatic 10-pin bowling lanes, complete with a large, rounded booth and table to sit and watch the action. An automatic scorer screen was above the bowling ball return, and there were lights down the sides of each lane. "What is all this?" asked Alaric. Noelle and Ember laughed with joy and yelled, "It's a bowling alley!" Alaric and Blaze just stared at them in confusion. "I'll teach mine, and you teach yours," laughed Noelle as she moved to the side where the bowling shoes were placed neatly in shoe cubbies, one for each, with their names neatly written in copper.

There was a separate shoe area with the names of both sets of grandparents and all their parents, as well as Tai, Kai, Ulrika, and Maxim. "I guess Nana thought we'd have a bowling night or two," Ember said to Noelle, who laughed and nodded her head. "But don't we want to go see what's behind that large copper door over there?" asked Alaric, nodding his head over to the door. "Huh. I didn't even see that door!" exclaimed Noelle.

The four teens walked over to the wide door, Noelle opening it when they reached it. "Is that what I think it is?" breathed Blaze. "A movie theater! I've seen these on the internet," whispered Alaric. They all moved further into the area, which Maia had transformed into a sixteen-seat movie theater, complete with reclining, tall-backed theater chairs with footrests. Off to the side was a full-service concession counter, fully stocked with candy, popcorn, and soda. "This is the best!" exclaimed Ember as she looked at the list of movies ready to play. "Okay, boys. Prepare to watch some of the best movies ever. There's the Star Wars collection, Indiana Jones, oh, and this will amuse you. The complete set of The Hobbit and Lord of the Ring." This last made them all laugh. "I vote for Star Wars," yelled Ember. The others nodded in agreement, and they all went to gather their refreshments.

Chapter Twenty-Six

"Jamie, you haven't said anything for five minutes. Are we going to discuss this, or are you going to continue to give me the silent treatment?" Kenna said to Jamie, standing in front of him with her hands on her hips. Jamie was seated in front of the fire on a sofa in their suite. He had been staring into the flames for several minutes after Kenna had given him the news pertaining to their daughters and the Wolf brothers and their current living situation. "You were raised in Marqueria and really should be okay with this. It's a simple solution and is the tradition here. There's nothing inappropriate about it. Completely platonic," Kenna continued as she sat next to him and began to gently rub his back with one hand.

Jamie gave a grunt and said, "Yes, I understand the tradition of it all and the reason behind it. Spending the past fifteen or so years in the Mortal realm, I've picked up some of their quirks, I guess. I know it's not like they're living together as mated couples. I understand that. I've just realized that our baby girls are growing up, and it seems like it happened overnight." He suddenly gave a deep chuckle and pulled Kenna into his lap. "I guess this will give us more time for just us, wife," Jamie said, kissing Kenna softly on the lips. Kenna sighed and melted into Jamie's embrace. "Come on! Put a 'Do Not Disturb' sign on the door, please!" Jamie and Kenna stopped kissing and turned to look over towards the door, only to find Noelle and Ember watching them and laughing. The girls moved over to sit in the chairs by the sofa, watching their parents with shining eyes.

"What do you think of your new room?" Kenna asked the girls as she got up off Jamie's lap and sat beside him. Jamie put his arm around her and pulled her in close. "Amazing. Stupendous. Stunning. I could go on, but I think you get the idea," answered Noelle, smiling. Ember laughed and said, "We may never leave! It has everything, Dad. You should come up and take a look around. Nana put another level on the tower so we could have the top floor and access to the roof garden and patio area. There's a hot tub up there, Mom. We could all use it." Jamie and Kenna smiled, content to see their girls so happy, especially after what they had gone through. "That would be lovely, sweethearts," said Jamie softly.

The girls studied their parents for a few moments, then looked at each other. They knew their dad wasn't one hundred percent on board with their living arrangements, 'but it's not like we are shacking up with the Wolf brothers,' Ember said to Noelle via their mind link. 'Yeah, but Dad is having a hard time with this. We need to make him see it will be okay,' replied Noelle.

"Dad, this situation and our living arrangements....it's not as if we are living together in the boyfriend/girlfriend way. Think of it like this: the tower is a big dorm, and you and Mom live in married housing, same as YaYa and PawPaw.

Tai and Kai are in dorm housing like me, Ember, Blaze, and Alaric. Our dorm doesn't have bedrooms, though," said Noelle. "What do you mean there are no bedrooms?" asked Jamie. "Oh, Daddy. Just come and see it. Please?" asked Ember. Both girls were looking at their dad with such pleading looks that Jamie couldn't deny them. He laughed and said, "Okay. I give up. Come on, Wife. We have rooms to explore." He pulled Kenna up, and the four of them headed to the elevator.

Jamie and Kenna stood inside the teens' room and looked around in utter amazement. Then Jamie went to inspect the sleeping area and nodded his head in approval. Kenna had followed and exclaimed, "Oh! This is lovely. I want a hidden sleeping nook, Jamie." "Wait until you see the bathrooms," laughed Noelle. When Jamie and Kenna entered the girls' bathroom, Jamie groaned, and Kenna jumped up and down, clapping her hands. "Yes! I want this, too!" Kenna said as she entered and explored the enormous bathroom suite. "Thanks a lot, girls. Now, I'm going to be sleeping in a jungle nook and bathing in a cave," said Jamie, grinning broadly.

"You haven't even seen the best parts. Come on!" cried Ember, tugging her dad's arm towards the gaming area. Kenna and Noelle followed Jamie and Ember to the gaming area, and Jamie said, "Your mom thought of everything, didn't she?" Kenna replied, "Yes, she did. She asked my opinion on a few items, but she ran with it." Jamie laughed and nodded his head as Ember led them to the bowling lanes. When Kenna and Jamie saw the shoe cubbies with their names on them, he turned to Kenna and said, "Be on my team?" Kenna stood on tiptoe and gave Jamie a kiss, then said, "Always."

Noelle and Ember stood watching their parents, appreciating how much they loved each other. In the Mortal world, divorce was common, but it had never crossed the girls' minds that their parents would ever separate, unlike many of the kids they had been acquainted with. Jamie and Kenna turned towards their daughters, and Kenna asked, "Is this the last of it?" The girls shook their heads negatively and led them to the large copper door tucked to the side. "Get ready for awesomeness," crowed Ember. She then opened the door and ushered her parents through.

The girls stood in the doorway, watching as their parents turned stunned faces towards them, then walked to the concession counter to examine what it held. "It has everything!" whispered Kenna. Jamie walked to the movie list, which had 'NOW PLAYING' on the top of the page. "Yes! Indiana Jones," said Jamie. He turned to his daughters and said, "This is amazing. Don't be surprised if everyone congregates here most nights." The girls grinned at their parents and said, "That's the plan." Kenna tilted her head to the side as if listening to something and then said, "My mother says we are all to gather in the library this evening for the beginning of Yule. We are to wear fancy clothes she had put in our closets, she said. Oh, girls. I didn't notice any closets. Where are those hidden?" The girls grinned, and Noelle said, "In the amazing cave bathroom. That way, we can have privacy when we get dressed." Jamie breathed a sigh of relief, which made the females in his life laugh.

COMES THE DARKNESS

"Before we dress for Yule, we need to go to the Dragon Stables for our first riding lesson. Nyx says we have clothing in our wardrobes, and they expect us in fifteen minutes. Go get changed, and we will meet out front," said Kenna as she walked towards the door with Jamie. "Yes! Dragon riding!" Ember shouted and ran for the bathroom to change. Noelle chuckled at her sister's enthusiasm but walked at a more sedate pace, even though she, too, was over the top excited.

Chapter Twenty-Seven

Kenna, Jamie, Noelle, and Ember left the Castle and headed towards the Dragon Stables. It was to be their first riding lessons, and the girls were bouncing with excitement. They were all dressed in clothing similar to their travel wear, but this time, it was in the same color scheme as their Dragon. Kenna wore black with soft gold accents, and Jamie was attired in a soft, dull gold color with black accents. Noelle and Ember were dressed identically, in dark green with gold accents. An added feature to these outfits was the hoods attached to the tunics. The girls said it was the best feature because it was like the hoodies they wore in Montana. In addition to the hoods, the sleeves were long and ended in partial gloves. There was a thumb hole, and the sleeves ended at the second knuckle on the fingers. Ember called them 'built-in half gloves.'

The material was the same as their travel gear. It was practically indestructible, rip-proof, and fireproof, but it had an added spell of being cold-proof. It would maintain their body temperatures at the high altitudes they would be flying in, which would ensure they wouldn't freeze to death flying that high up.

When they reached the Dragon Stables, their bonded Dragons were already in the massive courtyard waiting for them. The girls ran to their Dragons, giving them enthusiastic hugs and pats, chattering the entire time, telling them about their new suite and all it contained. Kenna and Jamie approached their Dragons at a slower pace but gave just as much affection to their Dragons and received it in kind.

"Are you ready for your first rides, little ones?" asked Nyx in her low, melodious voice. There were enthusiastic responses indicating they were appropriately excited. "Let's proceed. You are going to transfer up onto our backs, sitting on what you would call our shoulders, where the neck meets the body. We have arranged our spines and scales to provide a seat and handholds for you. Once you are seated, our scales and spines will rearrange again and form a protective barrier around you. This will help prevent any arrows, spells, or other weapons from hitting you. Are there any questions?" Nyx asked and gave a chirp and chuff, lowering her head to look into Kenna's eyes. Kenna shook her head and disappeared, reappearing on Nyx's shoulders. "Oh, Nyx. This seat is amazing and comfortable. However, did you manage this?" Kenna exclaimed when she was seated on Nyx's back. Nyx gave a chortle and murmured, "Dragon Magic, little one."

When all four were seated upon their Dragons, the Dragons launched into the air and, with strong pumps of their wings, were almost instantly far above the Castle. "Whhooooo Hooooooo!!!!" cried Ember and Noelle, much to the amusement of their Dragons. "We will now switch to mind links to give instructions if there is a need for any," yelled Sika loud enough for everyone to hear.

Kenna had a huge grin on her face and was nodding as Nyx gave her instructions through their mind link. From the top of one of the towers of the Castle came whistles and shouts of encouragement from those gathered. Looking down, the Riders could see their family gathered on top of their tower. Everyone was there. Bram and Mai, Otso and Tati, Ulric and Luna, Maxim, and Ulrika, Tai and Kai, and the Wolf brothers, Blaze and Alaric. All cheering them on and showing how happy they were for Kenna and her family.

Nyx was in the lead, Jade and Sage flew behind their mother, and Sika flew behind the group as rear guard. Kenna chuckled at this because it was so familiar. 'Where do we store our weapons?' asked Ember through her mind link. 'When you have weapons with you, we will provide a place to store them with easy and quick access, should you have need of them,' answered Sage, who then communicated this to her parents and sister so they could pass it on to their riders.

Looking down, Kenna was mesmerized by the beauty of the vast land of Marqueria. It looked so different this far up, but she knew exactly where they were. They were flying towards the Tree and the Grove in which it was contained. The girls and Jamie must have realized it at the same time because they all communicated with each other, and all they said was, "The Tree." There was a hint of longing in all their voices, something their Dragons picked up on. Nyx said,

"Don't be sad, our little Elf Bear family. You will return soon to your Montana for a visit." Nyx had projected her voice into all their minds, ensuring the family understood.

Nyx made a wide turn, and the rest followed. She was flying over land Kenna, Ember, and Noelle weren't familiar with, but Jamie was. It was the main Village and land of the Bears. Far below stood a huge stone fortress, not like the Castle of the Elves, but a rectangular, sturdy stone fortress. There were no fairy tale towers but functional towers made for guarding and scouting the terrain. Within the Fortress walls was a large pond and a large stone mansion with many smaller stone houses surrounding it. About a mile away was a large Village with similar stone houses, all built to be strong, not pretty. 'Is this your childhood home, Father?' asked Noelle via their mind link. 'Yes, it is. I haven't been back since I left all those years ago,' Jamie replied. 'It looks so military-like, except for that huge stone house,' said Ember. Jamie chuckled and replied, 'After the wars began when I was very young, my father, Otso, had this built for his people and our family. When it seemed the war was over, the people built their own Village outside the walls.' 'It looks strong, husband,' said Kenna.

As Nyx flew on further away from the Elf and Bear territory, the forests below became older and thicker, dotted with small lakes, streams, and waterfalls. Suddenly, below them, a huge log castle-like structure came into view. 'Oh, that log castle is gorgeous!' exclaimed Noelle through the mind link. 'It's a good thing you like it, little one. It is your mate's home. This is Wolf territory,' chirped Jade. Below them was a Village on the banks of a small river. The houses here were built from logs, and each one was different. It looked to be as populated as the Castle Village, but more spread out. The log castle was breathtaking, with towers, huge windows, and many stone fireplace chimneys. There were several large decks, and in the back courtyard area, there was a very large swimming pond with what looked to be a grilling/BBQ area next to it. 'I could live here,' stated Noelle. "Same,' said Ember.

"Are all those people headed to the Castle?" asked Ember out loud. Nyx chortled and replied, "Yes, youngling. All the villages are coming to your Papa's Castle for the Yule celebration and to welcome you all home." Looking down, they could see all the small roads and trails, and they all contained people walking towards the Elven Castle. 'That's a lot of people,' murmured Noelle via the mind link. Ember replied, 'It will be okay. It will be fun to see everyone we've met over the years again. I honestly can't wait to try all the food. Alaric said the feast would be amazing. And you know me, I'm all about the food!' This made everyone, even the Dragons, laugh out loud and chortle.

Nyx turned the party of Dragons and riders back towards the Elven Castle, saying, 'It's time for you to get ready for the celebration. We have gifted you some of our shiny things and would be honored if you would wear them tonight.' The appropriate amount of gratitude was shown, and then the group fell silent as they enjoyed the views and the feeling of flying free.

When the Dragons had all landed and their Riders had dismounted, there was a moment of reverent silence amongst them. It was finally broken when Ember turned to Sage and laid her forehead between Sage's golden horns. "Thank you for choosing me to be your Bonded Rider, Sage. I have never experienced anything like that before, and I greatly look forward to continuing our flying lessons," said Ember softly. Sage chirped and chuffed and replied, "It was my honor, little one. You were worth the wait." Nyx said, "Now, be off. Enjoy the party and forget about the war for a while. We will be patrolling the skies to ensure your safety." Goodbyes were said, and the family headed towards the Castle and the Celebration waiting for them.

Chapter Twenty-Eight

"Oh, sissy. You look so beautiful," whispered Ember in awe. The girls were in their bathroom, getting ready for the Yule festivities. Noelle's dress was dark green and gold, with a sweetheart bodice and a nipped-in waist. The dark green velvet was shot through with gold thread, and there were intricate gold Celtic designs covering the sleeves and bodice. The velvet sleeves were long and ended in a V, the point of the V reaching her middle finger on each hand. The velvet was form-fitting through the bodice, waist, and sleeves, but the skirt was silky and diaphanous, made of a green and gold sheer gossamer and free-floating material that flowed like water when she moved. Due to the many layers, it wasn't sheer enough to actually see her legs, just the impression of them.

On her feet were delicate gold slippers with a soft cushioned sole. Her hair was flowing about her shoulders and back, shining and curly. It was no longer short like she wore it in the Mortal realm, as it had been growing very quickly since they had come to Marqueria. Noelle did a twirl and laughed as her skirt fluttered out and flowed around her.

"I never thought I'd enjoy wearing a dress! Me, in a dress!" she said as she gave her sister a hug and continued, "Now, we need to get you dressed."

Ember's dress was exactly the same as her sister's, but for the color. Ember's sleeves, bodice, and waist were form-fitting amber gold velvet, and the intricate Celtic designs were done with shiny dark green thread. Her skirts were just like Noelle's, sheer green and gold gossamer. Her slippers were gold as well. "Next, we need the jewelry the Dragons gifted to us," said Noelle softly, then continued, "The only jewelry I've ever worn is my protection bracelet. Should we still wear them or take them off?" "Yes, I think we should keep them on. They're hidden under our sleeves so nobody will notice," replied Ember. "We will open Nana's chest before we see what the Dragons sent us. Is that ok?" Noelle asked Ember, who nodded her assent. Noelle opened the large dark chest on the counter and gasped. Ember leaned over and whistled, reaching over and taking out one of the tiaras contained within.

"Huh. I kinda forgot we were Princesses. What about you?" Ember asked. Noelle nodded, picked up the other tiara, and, using the mirror, placed it on her head. It was made of gold, with what had to be diamonds and emeralds. The gold had been worked into delicate wires, the intricate design echoing the ones on their dresses. The diamonds and emeralds were set into the gold so closely that the tiara looked to be encrusted with the precious gems. "This is gorgeous, isn't it?" Noelle said as she looked at herself in the mirror, wearing the tiara. "It is," whispered Ember, placing her's on her head as well. The tiaras sat partially down on their foreheads so that they were halfway between their eyebrows and hairlines and then curved down into a point just above the middle between their eyes. Where the two sides curved down and met in the middle sat a large oval emerald. It was a bezel set, about one inch long, and absolutely stunning.

Turning to the other chest, Ember opened it, and again, she gasped. "Oh my. Noelle, these are gorgeous," Ember said, moving aside so her sister could see what was inside. Noelle reached in and pulled out a gold necklace with emeralds set all along the thick chain. "It's lovely," whispered Noelle as she turned to face the mirror, holding it up to her neck. "It's a choker, isn't it?" asked Ember. Noelle nodded and asked, "Will you please put it on for me? Then I'll do yours." Ember reached up and latched the necklace. It was half an inch wide with round, deep green emeralds set every quarter inch along the chain. Noelle helped Ember put hers on next.

The girls stared at themselves and each other in the mirror. "We're a long way from Montana, aren't we?" asked Ember as she studied herself in the mirror. Noelle nodded and, taking her sister's arm, pulled her towards the door. "Come. Let's go celebrate our first Winter Solstice in Marqueria and the beginning of Yule. I'm sure there's going to be delicious food and treats," Noelle said, and she dragged her sister out of the bathroom and into the main area of their suite. "Yeah, trying to control me through food again. Of course, it works, so you're pretty smart, sis," Ember said and laughed.

The girls turned and stopped laughing, for it was then they noticed Blaze and Alaric were waiting for them. The boys were dressed in the formal wear of Marqueria. Both were wearing form-fitting black velvet tunics with gold accents in intricate Celtic designs and form-fitting black leggings along with black boots. They, too, were wearing gold circlets across their foreheads, but theirs were one thick band and had Celtic etchings. The boys hadn't moved since the girls had entered; they just stared in silence. "What?" demanded Ember, putting her hands on her hips and raising her chin in the air in challenge. This broke the spell, and Alaric laughed and teased, "Oh, it is you, Ember. I wasn't sure, with you being in a dress." Ember glared at Alaric for a few seconds, and then she, too, laughed.

"You clean up nice, Alaric. Come on, let's go. I'm starving," Ember said as she looped her arm through his and pulled him towards the elevator. Blaze said to Noelle, "You look absolutely stunning, Noelle. I'm speechless." Noelle's cheeks pinked up a little, and she smiled at him. Taking a page out of her sister's playbook, she looped her arm through Blaze's and pulled him towards the elevator. smiling up at him, she said, "You look very nice, too, Blaze." The four got on the elevator, and the doors closed.

Chapter Twenty-Nine

The four teens entered the Library, and everyone present turned as one to look at them. "Oh, I hate this part," whispered Noelle. Blaze laid his right hand on top of hers, which was threaded through the crook of his left arm, and leaning down, whispered, "Take a deep breath. They are here to pay you homage as the Princess of the Elves and the Bears. They have waited many years to meet your mom, and having you both here with your parents is momentous. Remember, you know everyone here. They are the villagers you've visited with for the past decade or so." Noelle looked up at Blaze and gave him a glowing smile. "You're right. I know everyone here. Thank you, Blaze," she whispered back.

One of the Elves who was standing on the right side of the door stepped forward and loudly announced, "The Princess Noelle of the Elves and of the Bears has arrived with The Prince of the Wolves, Blaze," he then waved them through to the enormous library, which had enlarged to accommodate the entire villages of the Elves, Bears, and the Wolves. "It's like a football stadium back home. It's huge!" whispered Noelle as she walked further into the room with Blaze. The Elf on the other side of the door loudly cried, "The Princess Ember of the Elves and of the Bears has arrived with The Prince of the Wolves, Alaric." He then waved the couple further into the room. "This is amazing!" murmured Ember as she looked around in awe.

The Library had been transformed into a Christmas winter wonderland. There were many lavishly decorated live Christmas trees placed strategically throughout the vast interior of the room, and they looked to be growing directly out of the floor. Near the ceiling, thousands upon thousands of crystal snowflakes that looked as if they were made of diamonds floated and sailed slowly around. The effect was sparkling rays of light dancing around on the walls and floors and the people milling around beneath them. At their feet, a foggy silver mist floated about twelve inches above the floor. This created a soft, dreamlike setting for the Yule.

As the two couples glanced around at the decor, they were interrupted by Angelique, the Elf who ran the bakery and tea shop in the Village. She was attired in a splendid Amethyst-colored gown, with her curly silver hair piled high on her head. "Angelique!" shouted Ember, rushing forward and giving her a warm hug. "Oh, no, Princess! Protocol must be followed here," Angelique exclaimed, pushing her gently back and curtsying. "Pashaw! I've missed you, and I will hug whomever I want to," laughed Ember. Noelle came forward and, taking Angelique's hand in both of hers, smiled warmly at her and said, "Ember is correct. We have missed you and want you to know how important you have been to us all these years." Angelique bowed her head and said, "You two have brought me nothing but joy, and I miss your visits.

Do come down to the Village when you are able, when this war business is finished." Ember and Noelle said, "We will." Then, Angelique moved on.

After Angelique left, she was replaced with seven amazingly gorgeous females who moved as gracefully as a soft breeze. They resembled trees with skin-like bark but soft like silk. Their eyes were huge and very lovely, in shades matching their foliage-like hair, which were the vibrant colors of Autumn. One stood out more than the others. She had glowing silver-white skin with black marks like a Birch tree. Her hair was vibrant reds, yellows, and oranges. Her eyes were huge and sparkling, with swirling orange, yellow, and red irises. The seven females stopped in front of the teens and bowed their heads slightly towards them all. "It is lovely to meet you in person, Honored High Ones of the Elf, Bear, and Wolf clans. Finnegan sends his regards. He is running around outside, as he prefers not to come into the Castle, something about two Bear brothers who are out to get him," a melodious voice said with amusement to the four teens. It was the female resembling the Birch tree who had spoken. Blaze and Alaric both bowed at the waist, and Blaze said, "It is an honor to have you notice us, Esteemed Dryads." The silver Dryad gave the boys a stunning smile and said, "Yes....you two are a good match for my little Tree climbers." Ember gasped loudly and exclaimed, "You're our Tree! The Tree we travel through between Montana and Marqueria." "Oh, you're lovely!" Noelle whispered as she stared in awe. The silver Dryad nodded her head and said, "Yes, I live in the Tree. I have watched you grow from tiny little saplings. You are younglings on the cusp of adulthood, and I am proud of how well you've turned out. If ever you are in need of me, you may use the mind link I am about to give you." The Dryad of the Tree leaned down, then touched her forehead to Ember's, and a soft silvery light briefly surrounded the two. She then turned to Noelle and performed the same magic. "You both have access to me anytime you need it. Use it wisely, my little Tree climbers." She then turned and drifted away, with the other six Dryads following her closely. Blaze and Alaric were watching Noelle and Ember in awe, their faces showing just how amazed they were. "What?" asked Noelle. Blaze shook his head and said, "That has never happened as far as I am aware. Ask your grandparents. I'm sure they will tell you just how amazing this is." The girls bit their lips and shrugged, looking a little uncomfortable.

The girls spent the next hour getting reacquainted with the villagers they had met through the years, both from the Elf villages and the many outlying Bear and Wolf villages. The sisters had met so many of Marqueria's residents over the years that it took quite some time, and Alaric and Blaze hadn't left their sides the entire time they were visiting.

From the area in front of the fireplace came a long, loud, melodious whistle. Everyone stopped talking and listened as Bram said, "Queen Maia, and I welcome you all to our Yule Celebration. This year is very special to us, as our stolen daughter and her family have returned to us. Many of you already know our granddaughters because they came through the tree when they were little more than babies. Their visits gave us all hope that our Kenna would be returned to us, whole and healed. This has since happened, and we invite you to rejoice in this Yule season. Now, since I can see our Ember eyeing the tables of food, I will end with, 'Let us eat and be merry!'"

While King Bram was speaking, tables laden with every kind of food one could imagine suddenly appeared scattered throughout the stadium-sized room. Ember pulled Alaric towards the nearest one, grabbed a plate, and began loading it with one of everything. The four teens were looking for a place to sit when Ulric appeared next to them. He said, "Follow me," and turned towards the fireplace. There, they found their families at a large round table, already sitting with full plates.

"Oh, sweethearts! You look gorgeous," cried Kenna softly as she came forward and gave them each a kiss. "Come, sit with us," she said as she led the four to the table. The males at the table stood up until the girls were seated, and then everyone returned to their seats. Jamie said, "You both are stunning. I love the color scheme and how it matches your Dragons. So clever." "Thanks, Dad. I notice you and Mom did the same thing," laughed Ember, examining their formal wear. Jamie was dressed in black velvet with gold accents, matching Kenna's gown of black iridescent with intricate gold Celtic designs. They also sported symbols of their Royal houses on their heads. Kenna's was very much like her daughters' tiaras but larger. Jamie's was a thick gold circlet with Celtic symbols and designs, similar to the ones Blaze and Alaric wore.

Tai and Kai were seated near the four teens. The Bear brothers were wearing their formal dress of deep brown velvet with gold accents. Much to Ember's and Noelle's surprise, Tai and Kai each wore a thick gold circlet like their father's. "Why are you wearing those? Are you royalty as well?" asked Ember, taking a huge bite of beef Wellington and chewing, watching them and waiting for the answer. The brothers grinned, and Tai said, "Yes, we are. Otso is our uncle. Our father was his younger brother, so your father is our cousin." Ember stared, then said, "No way." This caused everyone at the table to laugh. Noelle asked, "Why has no one told us before now?" Kai shrugged and said, "Being Royal never really sat well with us. It's not a comfortable cloak for us to wear, so we don't often advertise it." Ember smiled warmly at Tai and Kai and said, "I always felt you were like family. Like our older brothers. Our much, much, much older brothers." Tai and Kai both laughed at this, and Tai said, "You are the little sisters we never had, and I'm glad you feel the same."

Maxim and Ulrika appeared across from the four teens, and they both nodded and gave them welcoming smiles as they took their seats. Maxim was dressed in dark green velvet, and he was also wearing a gold circlet, but not as large as Jamie's or the other Weres'. Maxim was Hilda's son, after all, and he was a Prince by birth. Ulrika was wearing a light silver-gray velvet gown, and her tiara was a matching silver instead of gold like the others. Ulrika was Blaze's and Alaric's older sister and was to be mated to Maxim after the new year. The table was filled with laughter and love, with many stories exchanged. Tai reveled in retelling how Jamie had insulted Raina and the consequences of that. Nobody gave a second thought to war.

Chapter Thirty

The evening continued with excellent food, drink, and conversation. When everyone had their fill, the food was magically cleaned up, the tables disappeared as well, and then the music and dancing began. The music reminded Ember of that which was played during St Patrick's Day back home in Butte, the old Irish jigs and reels and the sad ballads. Noelle and Ember both jumped up, and Ember cried, "We know how to dance to this!" Then, the girls grabbed the hands of their bonded Wolves and dragged them out to dance. The girls and their partners danced and danced, enjoying the carefree music and atmosphere, not a thought given to the Darkness or the danger they had faced.

Outside the Castle, it was loud and raucous, with many of the Villagers choosing to move out of the Castle to celebrate Yule. Large, brightly burning fires with huge Yule logs were scattered around the courtyard of the Castle, and even outside the protection of the circular wall, many more fires were to be found. The stunning Dryads had moved outside to be closer to the natural world and the trees and were now sitting amongst several Fairies and Gnomes, including Finnegan. Most of the inhabitants of Marqueria stayed within the protection of the Castle walls, with only a few of the braver souls wandering to the outer fires for a little privacy.

One by one, the stars disappeared from the sky. It happened so subtly and slowly that everyone inside the Castle walls enjoying the Yule celebration didn't notice it at first. Not until the wind began to blow the flames of the fires wildly higher and the fires outside the outer circle and the Castle wall were gradually being extinguished did the revelers take notice. The sounds of happy celebration faltered and then ceased. Total silence encased the outside grounds of the Castle but for the sound of the fierce wind and booms of thunder. The night sky was covered with black clouds, and frightening streaks of lightning screamed across the sky.

The silence of the party outside eventually caught the attention of the inside celebrators, who soon gathered in the courtyard, joining the silent crowd. Everyone was turned towards the giant gates of the Castle wall, staring at the inky black fog that was crawling up the domed protection circle. Suddenly, there came a woman's scream from outside the wall, down in the field where the extinguished fires lay smoking. It was gut-wrenchingly terror-filled and anguished and could be heard above the wind and thunder before it was suddenly cut off.

Within the Caste wall, directly in front of the opened gate, the leaders of Marqueria appeared out of nowhere. Maia raised her voice so everyone could hear her and said, "Find a circle etched into the stones and make sure everyone is safe within a circle." She then turned and grabbed Kenna's hand, who in turn held Noelle's, then Ember, Tati, and Luna joined hands and formed the circle. Almost immediately, they began to glow brightly, and together, they began to chant.

By the power of Light and Love

We cast this circle below and above.

A shield of protection, strong and true

Keep out the evil, allowing only good through.

So mote it be, this circle is cast.

There was a large 'whoosh' sent outward from their circle, and every circle within the Castle walls was cast. The circle and dome enclosing the Castle grounds shone brightly with silver and pearlescent light, chasing the inky black fog down the dome and a few feet away.

Kenna murmured softly, "I feel the Darkness. It has come. It is waiting out there for us." "Mom, can you hear the Goddess? She's telling us what we need to do to protect all these people. Shhh, listen," whispered Noelle, then she moved away from her grandmothers, pulling her mom and sister with her. The three cinnamon-haired, glowing females walked to the gate and stood just inside the outer circle. Kenna was in the middle, with Noelle on the left and Ember on the right. They began to chant.

Malum Discede, Locum istum relinque.

Malum Discede, Locum istum relinque.

Tenebrarum Et abierunt, apage! Apage!

Tenebrarum Et abierunt, apage! Apage!

The last part of the chant was delivered in a shout, with an emphasis at the end. At the same time, they shoved their hands out fast and firm towards the Darkness, which was trying to swallow the Castle and all within it. Beams of sparkling light shot out of their hands straight into the black, foggy Darkness, tearing holes and macerating the ink-like fog. There was a long, guttural scream of rage and hate emanating from the black fog as it was forced back and as it shrank from the light. Inside the inky blackness, a form could just be discerned. It looked to be Hilda but with long black hair, black eyes, nails, and lips. Her head was thrown back, and she was screaming with rage.

As one, Kenna, Noelle, and Ember walked, with hands out, radiant light flowing from their hands, towards and into the evil. They walked out of the Castle walls, chasing the Darkness, ethereal white hot light beaming into it. With one last scream of hate, the Darkness was gone. They completed their chant with:

Dea amoris et lux
Vigilate super nos omnes

While the light had slowly faded with the coming of the Darkness, its return was sudden and intense. The fires roared with heat and cheerfully danced with warming light, and the stars twinkled bright again, with the Winter Solstice full moon and the Cold Moon hanging low in the sky.

Kenna and the girls turned around to face the Castle and found Jamie, Blaze, Alaric, the Bear brothers, the two sets of grandparents, and the Wolf Alphas standing just on the other side of the protective circle. "It's safe to come out. The Darkness is gone," Kenna called. Jamie's intense golden glare and his hands on his hips were the first indications that something was wrong. "We would love to join you, Wife. The problem is, we are locked inside," Jamie replied, raising an eyebrow. Ember and Noelle burst out laughing and holding onto each other for support; they laughed until tears were falling down their faces. "You locked them in, Mom! Oh, my Goddess! The looks on their faces!" Ember cried, laughing harder. Noelle, still laughing hard, said, "I can't breathe....stop laughing, Ember," then she looked over and spotted Blaze, and another bout of laughter erupted from her.

Watching her daughters, Kenna let a giggle out, and then she too was holding onto them, joining in on their almost hysterical humorous explosion of mirth. "Son, you need to get your wife and daughters under control. We need to get out to assess the damage and make sure there aren't any casualties," growled Otso loudly. This caught the attention of the three vastly amused females as nothing else would have. They stopped laughing and turned to Otso as one. "Oh, you're in for it now," whispered Tati as she inched away from her husband, with a smirk on her face and her gold eyes shining with suppressed mirth. As if it had been rehearsed, everyone took a few steps away from Otso. "You messed up big, Dad, and you're on your own with this," Jamie said softly and, shaking his head, stepped a few yards away from Otso.

Finding himself on his own, he turned to his daughter-in-law and his two granddaughters. "Crap," he whispered when he spotted them walking slowly towards him. Their cinnamon-red hair was floating about their shoulders, and their eyes were glowing, Kenna's fiery green and the girls' green with gold heat. "Did you just say what I think you said, Grandfather?" asked Ember softly, a deep growl in her voice, her Bear surfacing. There was an emphasis on 'grandfather,' bringing to his attention that she hadn't called him Ukki or PawPaw, which were her pet names for him. Noelle growled low in her throat, "Get us under control, I believe is what he said, sister." Kenna nodded and murmured, "Yes, that is what he said, daughters." The three now stood right in front of Otso, separated by just the protection circle and dome.

"Do you think we need to be controlled? Really, Grandfather?" asked Ember, hands on her hips and staring up at her Ukki. Otso shook his head, ran a hand through his hair, and said, "I misspoke. I do not think you need to be controlled. I only wanted to get out of this cage you've trapped us in so that we could look for the wounded." Otso looked contrite, and the three nodded, somber now that he had mentioned wounded. Kenna nodded, and with a casual sweep of her hand, the protection circle and dome dimmed a little. "You should be able to come through now," she said, and then, as one, she and her daughters walked towards the fires outside the wall, intent on looking around for injured Villagers.

Chapter Thirty-One

Once everyone was able to leave the Castle grounds, the four teens searched together, along with Tai and Kai. Jamie and Kenna joined Ulric and Luna. Bram and Maia grouped up with Otso and Tati in search of any wounded. The Villagers were joining in as well, but they were sent in the opposite direction from the royal group.

"What language were you three speaking earlier? What did it mean?" asked Blaze as they were walking the outer fields near the tree line. "Latin. I didn't even know I could speak it, but I guess the Goddess decided we needed to use Latin on the Darkness this time," answered Noelle, shrugging; then she continued, "The chant roughly translates to: Evil, Depart, leave this place. Away, Be Gone." Ember stopped walking and stared at Noelle until everyone noticed and stopped walking, waiting to hear what Ember had to say. "Do you think it's because the Darkness originated in the Mortal world and it is Biblical? Latin is the language used in exorcisms by the Catholic Church. They use it to extract a demon from a human. Do you think the Goddess knows this and is steering us in that direction?" Ember asked, head tilted, meeting Noelle's eyes. "Crap," breathed Noelle, nodding her head. "That makes sense. The

Darkness has taken over Hilda's body. For years, it has been influencing others. Sounds like a Demon, a very strong Demon," said Tai, agreeing. "We may need to do more research on the Mortal realm and their history with evil creatures," Kai added, hands on his hips, as he continued to look around. "Maybe speak with some priests and nuns," murmured Ember.

"Didn't you all look into this Bible thing already?" asked Alaric, a small frown between his eyes. Ember nodded and said, "Yes, but after we discovered the oral history on the Evil One who preys on the Five-fingered beings from the Native Americans, we kinda left the Bible alone." Blaze sighed and said, "That means back to Montana, doesn't it?" Ember and Noelle nodded, both looking a little sad. Tai chuckled and said, "You boys can come to Montana with us, I'm sure." This made the four teens all smile, and then they turned to continue walking along the tree line.

The group walked, scanning the area for several more minutes before Noelle and Ember whispered together, "Stop!" They all stopped as one and waited for the girls to explain as they continued to scan the area. "Our Dragons are above us, searching. They say there is someone over near that small bonfire. On the other side of it. We can sense the life force, but it's weak," murmured Noelle softly. Before anyone could respond, Ember began walking towards the fire to the right of them, in the middle of the clearing in front of the Castle. Tai and Kai quickly caught up and moved to the front. Alaric silently appeared at her side, taking her hand in his. "How are you so silent? I never hear you approach, and I have Elf and Bear hearing," Ember grumbled quietly. Alaric chuckled softly and said, "Wolf. That's all I need to say."

"Kids, stop walking. Stay there, please," called Tai from the other side of the fire, twenty yards away, his voice full of worry and pain. Tai and Kai had knelt down next to what they now could see was a female in a silver-grey velvet formal gown. Alaric and Blaze moved so quickly that they joined Tai and Kai in a split second. "No! Oh, Goddess, NO!" yelled Alaric, his voice was filled with anguish. The girls transferred the twenty yards to where the males were, which was quicker than walking. They both gasped and covered their mouths with their hands. Lying on the ground with her legs akimbo and her dress shredded and covered in blood was Ulrika.

Ember and Noelle moved quickly to her side, pushing through Tai and Kai. Kneeling next to her, they placed their hands on her and began to glow. "I've already contacted Mom, Nana, and YaYa," said Noelle quietly. Then, the girls began to chant softly.

By the Power of Earth, Air, Fire, Water, and Spirit.

We call upon the forces of Healing and Grace

To mend these wounds at a swift pace.

Oh, Goddess of Healing, we honor your name,

With trust and faith, we invoke your power,

To bring forth Healing this very hour.

Within just a few seconds, Kenna, Maia, and Tati had arrived and knelt around Ulrika's body, placing their hands on her and joining the girls in their healing chant. After some time, they stopped as one, leaning back on their heels.

By this time, Ulric and Luna had arrived, and they pushed their way through to kneel next to their daughter. "Tell me," demanded Luna quietly, staring at Maia. Maia nodded and began to speak softly, "She had many cuts over her body and has lost a lot of blood. She will survive this attack, Luna, Ulric. Ulrika is strong, and we have healed her wounds. For now, we need to transfer her to the Castle and get her cleaned up, then put her to bed. She needs warmth and rest." In the next instance, Luna, Ulric, Blaze, and Alaric disappeared with Ulrika.

Standing up, Ember put her arm around Noelle's waist. Noelle slung her arm around Ember's neck and pulled her in to hug her. The sisters stood like this, tears falling down their faces until their parents wrapped them in their own arms. "She will be ok, sweethearts. Ssshhhh," Kenna whispered as she held her daughters. Jamie had his arms wrapped around his wife and daughters and murmured, "We need to get back to the Castle's protection now, my sweethearts." Tai and Kai were standing near them, keeping an eye on the tree line. Tai said, "Let's transfer to the Castle's courtyard together now." Kenna nodded and said, "Just touch a shoulder and let me know when you're ready." The Bear brothers said, "Ready," and the next thing they saw was the enormous Castle doors.

In the short millisecond it took them to transfer, the girls had gathered themselves and were calm. They stood and looked around the courtyard, which contained all the inhabitants of the villages who had decided to come to the Castle and join in on the Yule celebration. "Where will all these people sleep, father?" asked Ember. "Bram and Maia have had tents set up in the garden area to accommodate the overflow from the Castle. The Castle will usually grow to house as many as is needed, but even this is more than it can contain. The Library is back to its normal size to accommodate the added bedrooms and bathrooms. So, the ones who don't find a room within the Castle can use one of the tents like the one you used when you traveled to the Sacred Grove of the Dragons," Jamie answered.

The girls nodded, and then Noelle said, "When we were out there looking for the injured, Ember had an amazing epiphany. When the Goddess had us use Latin to send the Darkness away, Ember thought maybe it was a way to let us know that the Darkness is like the evil from the Bible. They use Latin in Exorcisms to banish Demons." Kenna gave a soft exclamation and said, "Holy Cow! I think you're correct, Ember."

"We need to find Maxim and let him know Ulrika is injured," said Kenna. The girls exchanged a stunned look, and Noelle said, "Last time I saw Maxim, he and Ulrika were leaving the Castle grounds to walk amongst the fires of Yule." Kenna closed her eyes and began to glow brightly. She remained still for several seconds before opening her tear-filled eyes and saying, "He's nowhere on the grounds of the Castle or within the Castle. He's simply gone."

Chapter Thirty-Two

After everyone who needed to know was notified of Maxim's disappearance, Ember and Noelle made their way to where Ulrika had been taken, Luna and Ulric's suite. When they entered the suite, Blaze and Alaric met them just within the room. "How is she doing?" asked Ember, taking Alaric's hand and pulling him close so she could wrap her arms around his waist. His arms went around her, and he held her quietly for a few moments, breathing in her scent. Then he said, "She woke up briefly and told us what had happened. She and Maxim had been walking amongst the fires and playing with the fairies when they were attacked. Ulrika said it was so fast, crazy fast, that she didn't smell anything, she didn't hear anything, and she was unable to shift fast enough."

Alaric gave a deep sigh and continued, his voice gruff and low, "She said the lights and fires were just suddenly gone, and the light was totally absent out there. Then, Maxim's hand was yanked out of hers, and something attacked her. She said a blade of some kind slashed and slashed. She could hear Maxim screaming, and then it was suddenly cut off. She remembers little after that until she awoke in the bed." "Our Papa has forbidden anyone from searching for Maxim tonight. He said we have to wait until morning light before we can start the search," Ember murmured against Alaric's chest.

Luna came out of a bedroom and stealthily walked to them. Her Wolf was close to the surface right now, and this was evident in her mannerisms and movements. Ember released Alaric and turned towards Luna. Noelle asked Luna, "Is there anything we can do?" Luna said nothing and gave each girl a strong hug before stepping back to say, "You have done more than enough. Because of you and your quick thinking, our Ulrika is alive. You started healing her as soon as you found her, and that was what saved her. She said she was floating towards the mist when suddenly a silver light found her and began to pull her back. It was the two of you. She said she could smell you both, and so allowed the light to bring her back to us. We are forever grateful, daughters of my heart." She gave them both a kiss on the forehead and said, "Now, please take my sons and go to your suite. You need to rest after the energy you've expended, and my sons need to be near you to heal emotionally. Go. Get some rest, my darlings." She ushered them to the door, and the four of them left, saying their goodnights over their shoulders.

The four teens began their walk to the tower they all shared with the girls' family, Kenna and Jamie, Tai and Kai, Otso and Tati. When they reached the elevator to go up to their suite, it opened and out stepped Tai and Kai. "Where are you going?" Ember asked the Bear brothers. "Making our rounds. Then we will assign sentries from our Bears to stand watch," replied Tai. Kai said, "Please, go directly to your suite and activate the charms that lock the doors. Those are your dad's orders, by the way." The girls nodded, as did Blaze and Alaric. "Goodnight. Please stay safe," said Ember softly. Tai leaned down and gave her a kiss on the head and said, "We will be fine, Princess. The Dragons are guarding from the sky, and after we do our rounds and assign the watch, we will return to our suite. Now, go get some rest. You must recharge after the healing you performed." The four teens got on the elevator, and the door closed. Kai was watching Tai with a small smile on his face. He said, "We aren't going to sleep a wink, and you know it, brother." Tai shrugged and nodded and said, "Come on. We have a Tower to guard."

Chapter Thirty-Three

The next morning, when the four teens went down for breakfast, they found the Castle nearly deserted. Kenna, Jamie, Luna, and Ulric were obviously waiting for them at the breakfast table. The four teens took their seats, with Noelle and Ember seated in the middle and Blaze and Alaric sitting next to their bonded mate. "Where is everyone?" Ember asked as she filled a plate with scrambled eggs, bacon, hashed browns, and fruit and then passed it to Alaric. Alaric, who had fixed her coffee just the way she liked it, took the plate and handed her the cup of coffee. Kenna was watching the teens with a small smile on her face and said, "They are searching for any signs of Maxim. All the Villagers from all the villages are out with your grandparents, combing the nearby wooded areas. We wanted to speak with you before we joined them." The teens all paused in eating and looked up at their parents. "What has happened?" asked Noelle. Blaze asked, "Is Ulrika still doing okay?"

Luna nodded and said, "She is resting quietly and healing. I'm afraid that until Maxim is returned to her, she will not completely heal. They had bonded, and she needed him by her side to heal completely. For now, she will remain in our suite to heal and rest." Ulric gave a sigh and growled deeply, "We must find Maxim. I will not lose our only daughter to this Darkness." Luna placed a gentling hand on his and gave his hand a squeeze. Their eyes met, and he gave a slight nod. Luna brought his hand up to her lips and pressed a soft kiss to his palm.

Kenna said, "We have been discussing an idea we have and want to share it with you. We want your opinions." Ember took a large swallow of coffee and said, "Lay it on us." This caused soft chuckles from all present and broke the somber mood a little. Jamie laughed and said, "Ok, Ember. Here it is. We want you to travel through the Tree and return to Montana." Noelle and Ember each gave a cry of distress, and Noelle said, "No! We can't go alone." Luna spoke up at this, saying, "You misunderstand us. We want all four of you to go through the Tree. We would never separate bonded pairs." This eased the stress and tension coming from the teens, and they all sighed. "Mom, Dad....will you be going with us?" asked Ember softly, a worried look showing her thoughts.

The four adults all exchanged glances and slowly shook their heads. Ulric answered, "We are needed here as rulers of this land. We need to ensure the safety of our clans." He looked to his sons, obviously speaking to them via their mind link. Blaze and Alaric both gave a quick nod and said nothing. "We don't want to leave you. Mom, we are safer with you than away from you," whispered Ember. Kenna shook her head and said, "Not in this situation. No, you're safer on the other side of the Tree. We are sending Tai and Kai through with you to ensure your safety and to keep the authorities in Montana away since you are under eighteen.

Tai and Kai are the appointed guardians of all four of you and will have the paperwork in case anyone comes snooping around." This seemed to calm the girls somewhat, and they gave slow nods.

"That is not the only reason we want you to go through the Tree. While you are in Montana, we want you to investigate and dig into anything you can find about the Darkness. There has to be something in the Bible we missed or something a priest knows, which will help us fight this Evil," said Jamie quietly, scrubbing a hand over his face and through his now long dark hair; he gave a sigh and continued, "I don't like the idea of being separated from you, my girls. But having Tai and Kai there will help ease my worry somewhat." They sat in silence, breakfast forgotten and appetites gone.

Ember gave a soft sigh and then took a deep breath as if she were getting ready to speak. Suddenly, she was eerily still, her eyes out of focus, and her head tilted to the side. Noelle appeared to be experiencing the same. "Ember! Noelle!" cried Kenna, trying to get their attention. The girls slowly came out to their semi-trance and looked at each other. Then, Ember said, "Come on. Let's go get our stuff together. Good thing we have those magic backpacks, huh? We need to get this done now and be ready to go in one hour. The Dryad of the Tree just contacted us and said there's a large army gathering with the intention of marching on the Castle. She said we need to be through the Tree before it marches." Noelle nodded in agreement.

Looking around, their parents and Ulric and Luna were staring at the girls in stunned silence. "What?" asked Noelle. "The Dryad of the Tree is mind-linked to you both?" asked Luna in a soft voice that couldn't hide her amazement. "Is this true, daughters?" asked Jamie, his expression showing his surprise at the news. The girls both nodded, and Blaze spoke up, saying, "Last night at the celebration, the Dryads came to us. The Dryad of the Tree said she was going to mind-link with Noelle and Ember to ensure that if they ever needed her, they could find her." Ulric and Luna exchanged stunned looks, and then Ulric said, "I've never heard of this ever occurring before now. This is truly an honor she has bestowed upon you both." Luna slowly nodded in agreement.

"Okay then. Better hurry up and get packed," said Kenna, smiling at the four teens when they stood up and headed towards their tower to pack what they needed. "This is a huge deal, isn't it?" Kenna asked Jamie. Jamie nodded and said, "It is, and I'm not quite sure what it means." "Why? What could it mean?" asked Kenna. Luna leaned forward, resting her forearms on the table. She said, "Dryads are like Goddesses. Not THE Goddess, but more like her little cousins. They have some talent for foretelling, and if they felt the girls might have need of them one day, enough to give them a mind-link, then they probably had a vision." Jamie gave a great sigh and said, "Luna is correct. This is what worries me. I'm going to go have a few words with Tai and Kai about this. Give them a heads up." He leaned over and kissed Kenna's head, nodded to Ulric and Luna, then left the room. Luna stood up and said, "Come, Kenna. Time for us to seek out Tati. She may have some information we need." She kissed Ulric and left the room with Kenna. Ulric looked around the empty room and shrugged, then reached out and snagged a sausage link.

Chapter Thirty-Four

Luna and Kenna had just entered the courtyard of the Castle when Tati appeared right next to them. Kenna gave a start, Luna gave a laugh, and Tati grinned, then said, "I had a feeling you would want to have a chat with me this morning. Is this about the Dryad mind linking with the girls?" Kenna nodded. "What do you know of it?" Tati motioned over to a table and chairs under a blue-leaved tree, "Come, let us sit and chat comfortably." The three moved to sit at the table, whereupon a tray with a teapot and three cups appeared, along with some lemon scones.

Tati poured three cups of tea and placed a plate containing a scone in front of each of them. "What do I know of it? Well, I knew it would happen. The day the girls returned from their journey to find you, I had a vision of the Dryad of the Tree passing the mind-link to the girls. Now, as for what that might mean? Any number of things. What do I think it means? I believe the Dryad has had a vision, and in that vision, the girls had great need of her. Therefore, she gave them a mind-link so that they could connect with her no matter where they were. Even in the Mortal realm, in Montana." Kenna set her teacup down and asked, "You mean they will be able to communicate with her when they are in Montana?" Tati nodded and asked, "Is the Tree not contained in Montana as well as in Marqueria?" Kenna nodded, picked up her scone, and took a bite. Chewing, she had a thoughtful look on her face. Swallowing her food and then taking a sip of tea, she asked, "Will the girls be able to mind-link with us while they're in Montana?" Luna perked up and asked, "Will our sons be able to as well?"

Tati took a drink of tea and then set the cup down. A small frown appeared between her eyes, and she shrugged. "I'm not sure. The girls are very powerful, as are you, Kenna. It is possible. As for the Wolf Princes, I'm just not sure. It is possible, as they aren't normal Wolves." Luna's and Kenna's gazes met, and both showed frustration at the non-answers they were receiving from the Queen of the Bears. Tati reached out and placed a hand on each of their hands. She gave them a gentle squeeze and said, "I know this isn't what you want to hear, but it is all I know for sure. My only advice is to go back to the prophecy I had about them. They will protect each other. As long as they are together, they will be fine." The three women sat quietly for a time and finished their tea, then Tati said, "It is time." They stood up and walked towards the front of the Castle, where they found the four teens gathered with Tai and Kai, Ulric and Jamie, Bram and Mai, and Otso.

Kenna walked straight to her daughters and enveloped them in her embrace. She held them tightly, their faces buried in her hair, breathing in the calming scent of their mother. Jamie joined them in their family hug, wrapping his long arms around his wife and daughters. Nobody spoke.

After a few moments, Tati cleared her voice and said, "They need to leave now. Say your goodbyes and let them transfer to the Tree." The Wolf family had been in a family embrace as well, but at Tati's words, they, too, stepped apart. Ember and Noelle gave their two sets of grandparents hugs and kisses, then gave their parents another before moving to stand in a circle with Tai, Kai, Blaze, and Alaric. Holding hands, the six disappeared.

Kenna had tears streaming down her face, as did Luna. Their respective husbands held them and tried to soothe their anguish at the leaving of their children. "When you are ready, Kenna and Luna, we will be in the Library. We have much to discuss and plan," said Bram softly; taking Maia's hand, he headed into the Castle. Tati laid a hand on Kenna's shoulder before she, too, took her husband's hand and followed Bram and Maia, leaving the grieving parents alone.

Chapter Thirty-Five

The six appeared in the Grove near the Tree. Standing under its canopy of vibrant leaves was the Dryad of the Tree. She glided over to stand in front of Ember and Noelle, inclining her head. "You must hurry through the Tree. The Army of the Darkness has begun its march towards the Castle," she said in a low, melodious voice. "Do our parents and grandparents know about this army?" asked Noelle. The Dryad nodded and said, "Yes, little sapling. They are aware. Even now, they are preparing the area for battle. They are strengthening the protective circles for all in the area. But you younglings must travel through the Tree. The Darkness is hunting you and must not find out you passed through." She urged them towards the Tree. "Will we be able to communicate with you when we are in Montana?" asked Ember. The Dryad nodded, continuing to herd them towards the Tree.

Ember explained to Blaze and Alaric how they would pass through the Tree. The Dryad spoke up and said, "You do not need the chant anymore, little saplings. You are now strong enough to pass through with as many as you want to carry." The girls nodded at the Dryad, and Ember said, "Thank you for helping us. Please be safe." Noelle said,

"Don't let them catch you." The Dryad gave them a soft, radiant smile and said, "I will be fine, little ones. Now go." This last was said rather sternly and with some urgency. Tai said, "Now, Princesses." They all touched the tree and disappeared. The Dryad gave a sad sigh and, with tears in her large, beautiful eyes, walked to her tree. She began to chant.

Close this Doorway; let it be sealed

From this realm, it is concealed.

Until the Evil is destroyed

The Darkness sent back to the Void.

Close this Doorway and let it be sealed.

From this realm, it is concealed.

The Dryad glowed brightly for a few seconds, then stepped into the Tree. The Tree and the Dryad were gone in the next instant.

Chapter Thirty-Six

The six travelers appeared in the Grove next to the Tree in Montana. Stepping away from the Tree, they turned to observe the Grove and the Red House below. They had been gone for a couple of months, according to Marqueria Time. They had left at the end of Autumn, and now the ground was covered in snow, and all the leaves were off the trees except the Tree. "It feels wrong coming home without Mom and Dad," whispered Ember. "Yes, it does. I wish Lucy could've come with us. Mom said she would age significantly if we brought her back to Montana. Better to leave her there, but it's not the same without her here," Noelle said softly, staring down at their house. Tai started down the trail to the house and said, "Come on, let's get things in order." The others fell in behind him, and Kai brought up the rear.

They walked down the trail until they reached the back patio with the fire ring and seating area. It, too, was covered in snow. "Is this where you make your s'mores?" asked Alaric. Ember smiled and nodded, then said, "Yes, it is. Dad built this for Mom ten years ago so she could sit out here and watch the sunsets. It was when her disease was very active, and she couldn't walk very far." "Your mom was sick?" asked Blaze, his face showing his astonishment. Noelle raised an eyebrow and said, "Yes, she was. She has a disease called

Rheumatoid Arthritis. Her kidneys were shutting down; she couldn't walk far due to pain and joint swelling. Then it attacked her bone marrow, and she couldn't fight off any simple viruses or bacteria and was always sick. She spent some time in the Hospital due to it. Why are you so surprised?"

Kai turned from the back door and said, "We don't get sick in Marqueria. We can heal ourselves of most minor injuries and have healers for the major ones. But we don't have disease in Marqueria. Haven't you noticed that your mother hasn't been ill since she's been in Marqueria?" Ember and Noelle exchanged a look and nodded. "Will she get sick again if she comes back to the Mortal realm?" asked Ember with a frown. Tai came from around the front of the house and heard Ember's questions, and he said, "Yes, she will become ill again if she returns here. Although it depends on how long she stays, is what your YaYa, Queen Tati, told us." He turned to Kai and said, "The front of the house looks undisturbed. In Mortal time, we have been gone for just a week or two, not the months that have passed in Marqueria time." Kai nodded and said, "Okay, younglings, let's get settled and then make a plan to search for more information regarding the Darkness."

Kai opened the back door, which hadn't been locked in their rush to follow Hilda with the Darkness inside her through the Tree. Despite not being locked, the house hadn't been bothered. They lived several miles from town, out in the mountains, and few people traveled this road. Plus, all the neighbors keep an eye on each other's houses and report or check out any strangers in the area.

COMES THE DARKNESS

Kai entered the house first, followed by Ember and Noelle, Blaze and Alaric, and lastly, Tai. Noelle immediately went to the freezer and checked to see if the frozen spell jar was still there. She picked it up and said, "This is what keeps The Darkness contained within Hilda." She placed it back into the freezer and closed the door. Ember said, "Come on, boys, we'll show you where our room is, and you can put your gear away." "What about our weapons?" asked Blaze, looking at Tai and Kai with a frown between his eyes. Tai gave a sigh and said, "You can't walk around with your short swords strapped to your hips, not here. You can maybe get away with carrying a bow, but only around here in the mountains, not in town. Kai and I have on occasion carried a gun, but you four will not."

Ember and Noelle both scoffed, and Ember said, "We happen to own our own guns, Tai, and we know how to use them. Dad made sure we knew our rifles and handguns inside out. We can disassemble them, clean them, and put them back together accurately. We use rifles for hunting when we aren't using our bows. The handguns are for protection, but we've never needed to use them. Dad has always been around, and nobody messed with us; I mean, have you seen the guy?" Ember gave a laugh, and the others chuckled.

Kai, still smiling, said softly, "We realize you both are proficient with firearms, but there isn't going to be a need for you to use them. You can access the Goddess and the magic in this realm, correct?" Ember slapped her hand onto her forehead and said, "Duh. I forgot." Noelle laughed and said, "Oh yeah. Okay, you're right. Our defensive magic is better than firearms." "I'm not used to being weaponless. I don't like the feeling of not being able to defend myself or Noelle," stated Blaze with a stubborn look on his face. Kai and Tai exchanged a resigned look, and then Kai said, "Okay. We understand. We will get you both a dagger with a hidden sheath so you can wear it at all times." Noelle spoke up quietly, her voice a little sad, "Dad has all the weapons downstairs, next to his office. All the guns are in the gun safes, and the other weapons are in the locked steel cabinets. He has short swords, daggers, ankle knives....just go down and take a look at what there is and choose what you want. I'm sure he wouldn't mind. The combination is our birthdays. January 13th and 14th, and the day they got married was January 24th. So, 01131424." Tai, Kai, Blaze, and Alaric all nodded their heads, and Blaze put his arm around her and pulled her in for a hug, sensing her sadness over her parents' absence.

Alaric had been looking around the kitchen and breakfast area and, with a quizzical look, asked, "What is this room called?" Ember chuckled and said, "Looks like you're getting a crash course in mortal cooking. Come on, boys, Ember and I will give you the tour. This is called the Kitchen and breakfast nook. This is where the food is prepared, and this is an oven. Over there is the microwave and dishwasher." Ember pointed out each appliance and showed them how they worked. She opened the refrigerator to show them the food inside, much to their amazement. "Hmmm, looks like we need to hit the supermarket and get some food. After we get Blaze and Alaric settled and changed into mortal clothing, we can drive in and go shopping. Does that work for you two?" Ember said, looking at Tai and Kai. "I'm driving!" exclaimed Noelle. The girls each grabbed their Wolf brothers and pulled them out of the kitchen towards their room. Tai and Kai stared at each other for a few seconds, shrugged, and then Tia said, "Let's go down and check out the weapons room."

Chapter Thirty-Seven

Tai and Kai stood in the middle of the weapons room, amazed at the array of available steel. "I guess our cousin didn't completely conform to the Mortal world, did he?" stated Tai, grinning at Kai and picking up a gleaming, beautifully crafted dagger. The blade was made of blue steel, with Celtic symbols etched along the blade. The hilt was crafted of what appeared to be an Elk antler. The pommel, in the shape of an old Finnish Bear's head, was carved out of the Elk antler hilt, and the grip was wrapped in fine leather. A straight guard, made from the same blue steel as the blade, sat below the hilt. Testing the edge, Tai cut his thumb but quickly healed it. "I believe Jamie made all of these himself. I've never seen more finely crafted blades," murmured Kai, examining and handling the matching dagger to the one Tai held. Tai nodded and said, "These will do nicely for us. Let's find a couple for the Wolf brothers."

"Huh...would you look at this? He made some with Wolf head pommels, and there are even a few in the Elven style. I think he must have been a little homesick," said Tai softly. "I know how he was feeling. It was not easy living here all those years, disconnected from Marqueria and our Clan," replied Kai, gathering the four blades and their sheathes, which were made of soft but strong leather. As Tai was locking up the weapons cabinets, he said, "We also need to see if the Wolf brothers can shift here, in the Mortal realm. We know we can, but it took us some practice. We can spend a little time every day having them tap into the magic of this land and shifting. Also, Ember and Noelle need to practice their defensive magic. Kenna had it instinctually, but the girls may have to work on accessing it while here in Montana." Kai nodded and headed out the door towards the stairs, with Tai following.

Chapter Thirty-Eight

Ember opened the door to their bedroom ensuite, entering ahead of Noelle, Blaze, and Alaric. Their bedroom took up half the upstairs, measuring thirty by twenty feet, so 600 square feet. It was huge, but it gave the girls each their own space and doubled as their classroom. Ember walked to her side of the room and placed her pack on the king-sized bed. Jamie had made hers and Noelle's beds out of logs, but they sat on the floor. It was essentially mattresses tucked into a log platform bed. The headboards were carved from a huge old slab of wood, which was eight feet across and five feet tall. Carved within the headboards were depictions of animals. Wolves, Bears, Unicorns, Elk, and Deer, along with a river and a couple of mermaids. If you looked closely, there were Gnomes and Fairies hidden within the foliage carved into the wood. It was a gorgeous piece of artwork and something the girls treasured. There were two nightstands per bed, carved out of the headboards, on each side of the bed.

"This is my bed, and that one is Noelle's. There's a bathroom through that door, over there next to the closet doors. There is also a bathroom down the hall. The upstairs is all ours. At the end of the hall is another bedroom and bathroom, but we have it set up as our studio for painting and practicing our hand-to-hand combat," explained Ember. Ember sat on her bed and watched as Alaric and Blaze examined the girls' space. "There's no magic here, is there?" asked Alaric. Noelle chuckled and replied, "There is, but it isn't as easy to access as it is in Marqueria. Here, we do our own cooking, cleaning, and shopping."

The Wolf brothers nodded their heads, their faces showing their unease. "It feels different here," stated Alaric. Ember said, "Alaric. Please come here." Alaric walked to Ember's bed and placed his pack on the floor next to it. Then he sat next to her and put his arm around her, pulling her close. "I'll be okay; just give me a minute to adjust. It just feels different here and will take me some time to get used to," he said softly, giving her a slight smile. Ember leaned in and gave him a soft kiss on the cheek, then she leaned her head on his shoulder, and they just sat quietly for a time, soaking up the calmness they gave each other naturally, thanks to the Bonding.

On the other side of the room, Noelle was getting Blaze situated, and then they, too, sat on the bed, cuddled up, and sat in silence. Blaze said, "This isn't as easy and exciting as I pictured in my head. We've never been away from our parents for any length of time despite being taught to be independent and self-reliant. We are Wolf, and we need our pack, no matter how independent we seem. Lone wolves don't last long without a pack." Noelle leaned back and grabbed his chin, turning his face towards her so he could see her. She said, "You are not alone. You still have a pack. We are your pack: Ember, Tai, and Kai. You and Alaric are not alone." Blaze stared at Noelle for a few seconds, then leaned down and placed a soft kiss on her lips. "Thank you," he said simply. Noelle smiled softly and nodded.

After they sat for some time, they heard Tai yell up the stairs, telling them to come down. The teens got up and headed downstairs to see what the Bear brothers wanted. Once they joined Tai and Kai in the front room, they sat on the sofas and waited. Tai handed Blaze and Alaric each a magnificently crafted dagger contained within a beautifully tooled leather sheath. The Wolf brothers gasped and examined their new weapons. "Oh, I remember those. Dad made those about three years ago. I always loved the Wolf head pommels," said Ember softly. Noelle stared at the daggers for a second and then gave her head a nod as if accepting that it was okay for the boys to have them. Blaze had noticed, or maybe he felt it, but he knew she'd had a moment of being unsure if they should be holding her father's daggers. "Are you okay with this, Noelle? If not, I will find another weapon to carry," Blaze said quietly, watching her closely to gauge her reaction. Noelle stood up and went to stand next to Blaze. She took the blade out of his hands and held it gently, examining the fine craftsmanship. "I'm okay with it, Blaze. I believe my father would think it appropriate for you both to be carrying these. Almost as if they were made for you, with this Wolf head pommel, isn't it?" Noelle said softly, handing the blade back to Blaze. He re-sheathed it and held it casually in his hands.

"I thought you were going to change into clothing more appropriate for the Mortal realm," Kai asked, looking over their Marqueria clothing. "We don't have anything the boys can wear. We will have to borrow something from Dad's closet. Come on, I'll show you dad's closets," Ember said, tugging Alaric towards her parents' room. Noelle and Blaze followed them.

Twenty minutes later, the teens were back in the kitchen, dressed in jeans, hoodies, and hiking boots. The clothes were just a bit loose on Blaze and Alaric, as Jamie was over 6'5" and outweighed the boys by at least fifty pounds of muscle. At sixteen and seventeen, Alaric and Blaze were tall for their ages, at least in the Mortal realm anyway. Alaric was around 6'1" now, and Blaze was 6'2" and they both weighed in about 190 pounds. If it weren't for the way they held themselves, they would have looked just like any other teenage boy in Montana. The two Wolf brothers moved with a stealthy and deadly grace not seen in the high school boys in Butte, Montana.

"You'll do," said Tai, who was dressed in some of Jamie's clothes as well, but he and Kai were wearing t-shirts and flannel shirts with their jeans. On their feet were leather work boots. "You look like lumberjacks," crowed Ember, laughing as she looked over their outfits. Tai and Kai looked at each other, and Tai asked, "What is wrong with what we are wearing?" Noelle and Ember were laughing, and Noelle said, "Nothing, really, but you could change out of the work boots. There are some insulated hiking boots in the closet by the front door." The brothers looked down at their boots and shrugged. "Fine!" growled Tai, and he walked to the closet near the front door. Grabbing two pairs of boots, he returned and handed a pair to Kai. They quickly changed their shoes, and Kai asked with mild sarcasm, "Is this to your liking?" Ember and Noelle both nodded, and grabbing the hand of their Bonded Wolf, they started for the garage.

In the garage was a black Toyota Tundra Crew Cab, a black Toyota Sequoia, and a black Toyota Highlander. "Your parents like Toyotas and black, don't they?" asked Kai. "Mom says they have the best safety rating, and they last the longest, according to Dad," replied Ember. Noelle walked to the Sequoia and climbed into the driver's seat. Blaze climbed in the front passenger side, Ember and Alaric climbed in and sat in the third-row seat, and then Tai and Kai sat in the middle captain's chairs. "How does this...car?...move?" asked Blaze, looking around the interior of the SUV with great interest. Noelle chuckled and said, "This SUV has a motor, which is fueled by gasoline. Just watch and observe." She gave him an impish grin and then pushed the garage door button and waited until it was opened; Noelle then backed out of the garage and headed into town.

Chapter Thirty-Nine

The black Sequoia arrived at the local Safeway, and after parking, Noelle and Blaze, Tai and Kai, and Alaric and Ember climbed out. Blaze and Alaric stood still for a few moments as if trying to get their bearings. "Riding in a vehicle is quite the experience," Alaric said quietly to Blaze. Blaze nodded and said, "We've seen this on the internet, but it is an entirely different experience in person, isn't it?" Then, they both looked around in utter amazement. "Is it always so loud and busy here?" Alaric asked, grimacing. Ember shrugged and said, "This isn't even a large town. Butte has less than 35,000 people, I think." Blaze and Alaric stared at the girls, completely gobsmacked.

"What?" asked Noelle, head tilted questioningly. Blaze shook his head and murmured, "There aren't 35,000 people in all of Marqueria." "Ohhhh," whispered Noelle. Tai came around the Sequoia and said, "We need to go in and get what we need, then get back to the house. We are attracting too much attention." Ember laughed and said, "Oh, don't worry about the stares. It happens all the time, and you'll get used to it. I've recently realized that they can sense there is something different about us." Alaric laughed at this, shaking his head, then asked, "You think they are staring at you because they sense you are different?" Ember nodded and said, "Why else would they stare?" Blaze and Alaric looked at Tai and Kai in utter amazement. Tai smirked and said, "Boys, they don't understand. They don't see themselves as any different from the humans they grew up around." Noelle and Ember were watching the four Weres with questioning looks. Kai laughed and said, "Girls, listen closely. You have always been stared at because you are devastatingly gorgeous, and yes, while they can slightly sense that you are different, they chalk it up as you being beautiful." The girls both blushed a little and rolled their eyes. "We are more than our looks," said Noelle softly. The four Weres nodded, and Blaze said, "We know that. Everyone in Marqueria knows that." This seemed to appease the girls, and they smiled slightly. "Well then, let's go shopping, boys!" exclaimed Ember, grabbing Alaric's hand and pulling him towards the store. The rest of the group followed them into the store, ignoring the many looks they received on the way.

Ember, Noelle, and Kai each grabbed a cart. On the drive in, they had decided to divide and conquer the grocery shopping. Ember and Alaric would shop for fruits and vegetables, Noelle and Blaze would shop for dry goods, and Tai and Kai would hit the meat, dairy, and frozen sections.

Ember and Alaric were in the produce section, inspecting potatoes, when Alaric became aware he and Ember were being watched. His Wolf instincts honed in on three males near the bakery section, which flowed into the produce area. They appeared to be in their late teens or early twenties, watching Ember and chatting amongst themselves. Their eyes held a speculativeness that Alaric wasn't keen on.

He became eerily still and stared at the three males until they became aware of him. As Ember obliviously continued to chat and pick through the potatoes, Alaric telegraphed his dominance with just his body language and eyes. All three males paled a little and quickly looked away from Ember, then turned as one and walked in the opposite direction. "Don't you think?" Ember was asking Alaric. Alaric turned towards Ember and said, "You know best. This is all new to me. We don't have stores like this. Our food comes from the source, not stored in large buildings." Ember looked closely at Alaric and asked, "Are you okay?" Alaric leaned down, gave her a soft kiss on her forehead, and nodded. "Just a little overwhelmed, is all," he replied and moved to the bin which held the oranges.

On the other side of the store, down the paper goods aisle, Noelle was tossing paper towels, toilet paper, and other much-needed paper products into the cart, with Blaze looking around, seeming to be on guard. "You don't have to be on high alert in here, Blaze. Nothing ever happens in the grocery stores around here. We're not in danger, so why not try and enjoy this new experience?" Noelle laughingly said as she added another large pack of toilet paper to the cart. Blaze nodded and gave her a smile, saying, "Sorry, I'm not comfortable here yet, but yes, you're right, and I will try to relax and take it all in."

The two continued down the aisle and turned to enter the next one, which happened to be the soda aisle. "Is this the soda pop I've seen on the internet?" asked Blaze, picking up a six-pack of Pepsi and examining it. Noelle chuckled and said, "Yes, it is. We don't usually buy it, but I thought you and Alaric would like to try some. Pick out whatever flavors you'd like to try." Blaze grinned and started putting several different varieties in the cart, taking up most of the area on the bottom, while Noelle looked on with amusement.

After Blaze had put the last six packs in, he suddenly became still, lifted his head, and sniffed the air. Noelle, noticing the change in him, touched his arm and asked, "What is it?" "I smell a Dragon," Blaze whispered. "That's impossible!" exclaimed Noelle in a whisper. "Follow me," he replied as he stalked slowly down the aisle, nose elevated slightly. When they reached the end of the aisle, they met Tai and Kai, who seemed to be having the same thoughts as Blaze. "You too?" asked Tai, and Blaze nodded. With Blaze and Tai in front, Kai and Noelle followed as they sought out the supposed Dragon.

The next aisle over, they encountered Alaric and Ember, with Alaric sniffing the air and heading up the aisle away from them. "Hey!" whispered Noelle, catching Ember and Alaric's attention. The six gathered in the middle of the deserted aisle, exchanging surprised glances. "Noelle, do you sense the Dragon?" asked Ember softly. Noelle closed her eyes and tilted her head as if listening. Her eyes popped open, and she exclaimed, "Yes! How is this possible?" Ember shrugged and said, "I felt it over near the produce, and Alaric followed the scent here. He says it has faded, though." "Let's go check out and load the groceries; then we can explore a little more," said Tai softly as he glanced around. They all nodded and pushed the carts toward the checkout lanes.

They put all three carts in one lane and began loading the goods onto the belt. Noelle and Ember moved to the front and were greeted by the pretty blond checker who appeared to be in her late twenties. "Hi, girls! I haven't seen your mom come in for her usual weekly trip. Is she feeling poorly?" asked the checker with concern. Noelle shook her head and said, "No, she and Dad went on a couples-only trip and won't be back for a month. How have you been, Anna?" As she scanned the items, Anna replied, "Oh, I've been okay, just busy with getting ready for Thanksgiving and Christmas. I can't believe how quickly they seemed to sneak up on me this year."

The girls stared at her in surprised silence for a few minutes, and then they both nodded. "Your parents are going to be gone for Christmas?" Anna asked in surprise. Noelle, thinking quickly, replied, "Yes, they are, but they will be back in time for our Birthdays. My dad's cousins are staying with us until they get back." Anna turned and looked at Tai and Kai with an eyebrow raised. "Hi, I'm Anna. You had better take good care of these girls while their parents are gone. These are two of the nicest girls in town." She stared them down for a few more seconds, much to the amusement of the Bear brothers. Tai nodded his head and said, "Of course we will, Anna. I'm Tai, by the way." Giving a nod, Anna's cheeks got a little pink, and looking away, she continued to scan the groceries.

When Anna was done scanning all the groceries, they had been bagged and loaded back into the carts, and she said, "Okay, your total is $375.63." Kai grabbed his wallet out of his back pocket, took out his credit card, scanned it, and waited for the receipt, all the while giving Anna a charming smile. Cheeks pink again, Anna handed Kai his receipt and said, "If you need any help with the girls, they have my number. I used to babysit them on occasion." Kai nodded his head and said, "Thank you, Anna." Then, he gave her a wink and followed the group out the door, his mind turning to the Dragon they were searching for.

When they reached the SUV, Ember was a little peeved and said, "Don't flirt with Anna. She is a wonderful person, and I won't have her played with." She glared at both Tai and Kai, hands on hips. The brothers burst out laughing, and Tai said, "Ember, it was harmless flirting. We would never strike up a relationship with a human." Ember watched them for a few more seconds and then nodded and relaxed her stance, turning to help load the bags into the back of the SUV. When the last bag was loaded and the carts returned, they all climbed into the SUV so they could chat in private.

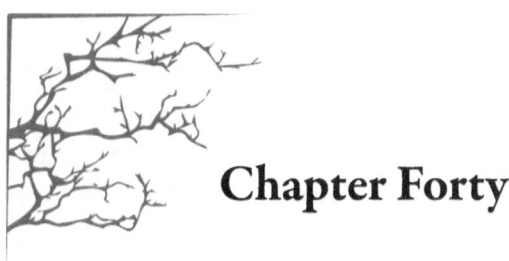

Chapter Forty

"Is it possible there's a Dragon in the Mortal world?" asked Ember from the far back seat. Kai shook his head and said, "I don't know how it could be. How would a Dragon go unnoticed here? It's not possible." "Then explain the scent and the feeling we all experienced," stated Alaric. "I can't," sighed Kai. "Is anyone hungry?" asked Ember. Noelle laughed and said, "We will take the groceries home and put them away; then we can come back in and get something while we do some walking around in search of our ghost Dragon." Everyone agreed, so Noelle started the SUV and began the journey home.

The groceries had been put away; they had returned to town and were debating on where to eat. "I say we go to the new burger joint. We've only gotten to eat there once, and Blaze and I are all about the burgers," said Noelle, giving Blaze a wink. Blaze grinned at Noelle and said, "I'm all about the burgers. I pick that place, wherever it is." "Fine, it's settled. Burger place. As long as they have other items on the menu?" asked Tai.

The six of them had found a big enough booth and were currently looking over the menu, Noelle and Ember oblivious to the stares of the teenage boys in various booths around the restaurant. Alaric and Blaze weren't oblivious, though, and both had given a low growl in their throats, low enough that only the occupants of the booth could hear. Surprised, Noelle and Ember looked up from the menus they were perusing and cocked their heads in almost identical fashion at the two Wolf brothers. "What's wrong?" asked Ember softly. Tai and Kai knew exactly what was going on and were unsuccessful in suppressing their mirth. "Did we miss something?" asked Noelle.

With a huge grin, Tai said, "The pups are having a hard time suppressing their jealousy over the attention you two are receiving from the youths of this town." "They are being rude and disrespectful towards our bonded future mates," growled Blaze. Kai gave a bark of laughter and said softly, "This is a different world, and the younglings here do not know about mates and bonding and have no idea these two are the Princesses of Marqueria's Elf and Bear Clans. You need to tamp it down, wolf boy." Both Alaric and Blaze closed their glowing gold eyes and took slow, deep breaths. "Better?" asked Ember, her hand on Alaric's arm. Alaric gave her a soft smile and nodded.

The waitress came to their table and took their order, then returned with their drinks. After she left, Ember said, "Let me out, please. I need to use the bathroom." Noelle said, "Me too." After the girls left the booth, Tai leaned forward and whispered to Alaric and Blaze, "You two better keep yourselves under control here. This world is not like our world. Magic and shifters are fantasy and myth here. In all actuality, humans are afraid of what is different, and instead of trying to understand it, their first instinct is to destroy it. I will not have your baser instincts put Noelle and Ember at risk. Get it under control because if you don't, you will remain on their property and not be allowed anywhere else. Understood?" Looking sheepish, Blaze and Alaric nodded.

The girls were stopped by a group of teenagers when they were halfway back to their booth. "Ember, Noelle! We haven't seen you two around much lately. You've missed Muay Thai lessons for weeks. Is everything okay?" asked a smiling, brown-haired teen girl. The girls nodded, and Noelle said, "Yes, everything is fine. Our parents went on a trip, so we've just been hanging close to home. How have you all been?" One of the boys, who had the look of a jock, complete with the letterman's jacket, blond hair, and beefy corn-fed all-American physique, leaned forward and jerked his head towards the booth where Tai, Kai, Blaze, and Alaric were sitting. "Babysitters?" he almost sneered. Ember raised an eyebrow at his tone and replied, "The two older guys are our dad's cousins. The other two are our boyfriends." She stared him down hard. He and another of his friends stood up, almost as if they were trying to intimidate the girls with their meager 5'11" height, and then they moved a little closer. The blonde whispered, "Oh, I see. You were too good for any of us, so you went to the Rez and grabbed a couple of Natives, is that it?" "You prefer red meat?" whispered the brown-haired oaf. Noelle and Ember gasped at the blatantly racist and nasty question; then, they reacted as one.

It happened so quickly the jocks didn't know what hit them. The girls had dumped them on the ground with a lightning speed knee sweep and dump. Standing over the two racist idiots, Ember leaned down and said, "If I ever hear those nasty words out of your mouth again, I'll do more than dump you on the ground." Noelle added, "In the future, don't even speak to us." Then they moved on towards their booth and the amused faces of their companions. Tai flagged down the waitress and said, "We will need to take those orders to go, please. We'll leave a nice tip if you can make it fast." He gave her a wink, and with pink cheeks, she hurried to the Kitchen. Ember and Noelle didn't sit down but instead asked Blaze and Alaric to follow them.

Taking them each by the hand, the girls led them back over to the booth where the two boys were just picking themselves up off the ground. Noelle said, "Hello again; since you showed such interest in our dates, we thought you'd want to meet them. This is Blaze, and that is Alaric. They are from Canada and will be staying with us for some time." The two boys who had been dumped on the floor looked up at Blaze and Alaric, their faces going white as they took in their size and the deadly look in their golden eyes. Blaze stuck out his hand towards the boys, and the blond hesitantly took it, shaking it. Blaze repeated it with the brown-haired boy, and then he said in a very low, growly voice, "Yes, we are native and belong to the Wolf clan. If you ever insult Ember or Noelle again, we will hunt you down and make you regret it. Understood?" The two jocks nodded their heads, and then the blond hastily said, "We have practice," pushing his buddy towards the door to leave.

The girls remaining in the booth were all staring at Blaze and Alaric in fascination and hunger. Ember turned and looked at Blaze and Alaric, too. Studying them, she understood the fascination the Mortal girls were showing towards them. They were beautiful specimens of the male of the species. Ember felt a tiny seed of possessiveness take root and moved to Alaric's side, taking his arm in hers. He smiled down at her in amusement as if knowing exactly why she did what she did. Leaning down, he placed a kiss on her forehead and whispered, "You have nothing to worry about. I am yours." Ember grinned, caught out but not bothered by it.

Noelle, on the other hand, wasn't dealing with her possessiveness in such a productive manner. Her green and gold eyes began to faintly glow, and she moved towards the nearest girl, her intentions clear only to those from Marqueria. Just as quickly, Blaze swept her up into his arms and carried her to the door, quickly exiting the restaurant. Tai and Kai had been standing near the doors, holding their bags of food, and they roared with laughter as they watched Blaze set Noelle down, but only when they reached the SUV.

Ember turned towards the booth of girls, who were still watching the door with stunned looks. "Well, that's our cue to leave. You're lucky Blaze got her out of here before she did something you'd regret. You should never stare at another female's mate with such a hungry gaze. Could land you in the hospital," Ember said with a threatening smile. Then she turned and tugged Alaric to the door, where they met Tai and Kai, who were having a hard time controlling their mirth. "Not a word," said Ember in a growl as she exited the restaurant, Alaric in tow with a huge grin on his face.

Chapter Forty-One

The drive back to the house was quiet for the first few minutes until the guys couldn't contain their laughter anymore, and they laughed until tears were streaming down their faces. "And to think we thought it was the boys we needed to worry about!" exclaimed Tai, still laughing. "That takedown move was sweet!" cried Kai as he went into another burst of laughter. "The looks on those boys' faces when they found themselves on the ground...Priceless!" said Tai, still chuckling.

The girls allowed the four of them to wind down enough so that they could ask some questions. Ember spoke up from the rear seat, "What happened to us? It was as if I wanted to stomp those girls into the ground. And I certainly didn't want to stop with just a takedown on those two racist oafs. What they said was disgusting." Noelle said, "Yeah, I wanted to pummel them and the girls, too. I couldn't control myself and felt my magic coming to the surface. What happened?"

Tai took a deep breath and let it out slowly, calming his laughter. He then replied, "The bonding that occurred between you and Blaze triggered your possessiveness, and you were just naturally marking your territory. The Elves aren't as territorial, and I didn't think you two would react this strongly. It appears the Bear part of your DNA is dominant in this instance." The girls both nodded and said, "Aahhh."

When they got back to the Red House in the country, as the girls called their home, they sat at the breakfast counter and ate their now lukewarm burgers and fries. "I think we should stay on the property for a while. At least, until we can control our Bear side," murmured Noelle when she was done eating. Ember nodded and said, "Yeah, you're probably right. We can do most of the research from here on our laptops. Tai and Kai can go into town and speak with the priests. I was thinking maybe try the Serbian Orthodox Church as well as the Catholic ones."

"That's a tomorrow issue. For now, we stay here, and you two need to cast a circle of protection around the house and patio. Kai, Blaze, Alaric, and I will go out and etch it into the frozen ground," said Tai as he stood up and threw his trash away. Ember spoke up and said, "Noelle and I can etch it in with magic." Noelle nodded and said, "We'll meet you on the patio. Come on, Ember." The girls left the room, going in the direction of their bedroom.

Blaze turned toward Tai and Kai and asked, "Do you think the girls are getting close to shifting?" By the looks on their faces, the thought hadn't even crossed their minds. "Let's hope not. The first shift is painful enough without the magic of Marqueria to help. I don't know if they'd be able to complete it in this realm. Speaking of which, have either of you tried it yet?" asked Kai. The boys shook their heads. Tai clapped his hands together, rubbed his palms, and said, "Looks like we have another task to work on today."

COMES THE DARKNESS

The girls returned, attired in their Marqueria clothing. "These are more comfortable for us to perform magic in than jeans," explained Noelle. Tai shrugged and opened the patio door for everyone to go through, then closed it after him.

Chapter Forty-Two

E mber and Noelle were walking side by side, holding hands. From their handhold, silvery mists of light fell to the grounds as they walked around the part of the property they wanted to enclose in a protective circle. "This is the biggest circle we've ever cast alone. Do you think we will be able to?" asked Ember. Noelle nodded and replied, "Yes, I do. Now concentrate on what our intention is." Where the silver mist was falling to the ground, it etched a ten-inch deep trench through the snow and dirt. They were almost done with the outer circle, which contained the archery range, the back patio, the house, and the attached garage, plus another ten yards out from the farthest point. All in all, it was a giant circle measuring one hundred yards in diameter. This gave them a total of 1.63 acres to run around on within the protective circle.

When the girls reached the point where they had started, they moved to make another circle on the patio, which would be thirty feet across. It would be etched into the concrete permanently. After that was complete, Ember turned to Tai and Kai and asked, "Do you think we should etch one around the Tree in the Grove? It would prevent anyone with bad intentions from passing through to us, but it would also prevent anyone from trying to get through to

Marqueria." "Huh, good idea. Yes, I think you should, but first, cast the large one around the house and archery range. The one on the patio is for emergencies," replied Tai.

The girls performed their chant in their minds, and with a pop sound, a huge clear dome appeared over and around the house and outer areas. You couldn't see it if you didn't know it was there, and if you did know it was there, it took several seconds of searching to see the shimmer. "Well, come on. Let's go up to the Tree," called Ember towards Blaze and Alaric, who were down at the archery range, checking things over.

When they reached the Grove, all of them gave a soft sigh. The Grove was more like the land of Marqueria than any other place in the Mortal world, and the Magic soothed their souls. "Should we contact the Dryad of the Tree before we do this to make sure it is acceptable?" asked Noelle. Ember nodded, as did the other four. Holding hands, the girls closed their eyes and began to use their mind-link to contact the Dryad. After a few seconds, the girls dropped their hands and opened their eyes, turning towards the Tree, where the Birch Dryad appeared. She was just as lovely in the Mortal world as she had been in Marqueria. "You must have great need of me to have used your mind-link so soon after we parted. What can I do for you, my little tree climbers?" asked the Dryad in her soft, musical voice.

Noelle and Ember explained their idea regarding the protection circle around the Tree and also mentioned in passing that they had felt and the others had smelled a Dragon while they had been in town, which had prompted the protection circle around the house. The Dryad closed her large eyes and became completely still as if communicating with someone in her mind. Suddenly, her eyes popped open, and she exclaimed, "There is a Dragon in the Mortal realm. I have spoken with the trees along this mountain range, and they have confirmed this to be true. It is a Dragon and yet not a Dragon, is what they have told me. What this means, I cannot tell you. As for the protection circle, it is not needed. I have shielded the Tree on the Marqueria side from sight. It is undetectable to any in that realm." The girls stared in stunned silence at the Dryad, and then Ember asked, "Does this mean our parents can't get through to us?" The Dryad reached out a long, graceful arm and touched Ember's cheek with her long, slender hand. She then said, "It has to be this way, little sapling. To protect the Mortal world, the way had to be hidden from all, even your parents. You can still communicate with them if you concentrate and use your mind link." The girls nodded, and the Dryad turned to Tai, Kai, Blaze, and Alaric. She said, "Do not hunt this Dragon. The trees whisper and say it is a special one and is to be unharmed. It may seek you out, sensing your difference from the Mortals, and you are to welcome it into your fold. This has been seen." The Dryad tipped her head towards them all and faded back into the Tree.

"What the Hell is that supposed to mean? A Dragon that isn't a Dragon? Also, if she has hidden the Tree on the other side, does that mean we are stuck here?" asked Ember in frustration. Tai and Kai glanced at each other and then shrugged. "Come on. Let's return to the house and begin our search for the Darkness. It's getting late, and the sun sets early now," said Noelle, heading back down the trail to the house. "I still can't wrap my head around the fact that we get to celebrate Christmas again. Time is so weird," muttered Ember as she followed her sister down the trail.

"Speaking of Christmas, are we going to put a tree up and decorate like we do every year?" asked Noelle, glancing back at the group. "I don't know. It feels weird without Mom and Dad, plus we just celebrated it a couple of days ago. We have a few weeks to decide. We have Thanksgiving first, and I can get behind celebrating that food feast," said Ember with a laugh.

Chapter Forty-Three

The next morning, I found the group of six back in the Grove. Tai thought it was the best place for Blaze and Alaric to practice their shifting since it was out of the way, and no one could accidentally wander near due to it being on private property. "Are you ready?" asked Tai, standing next to Kai, both with their arms folded over their chests and watching the two Wolf boys. Ember and Noelle sat on the bench near the Tree and watched in interest. They hadn't really had time to watch the boys change last time, as their lives were being threatened.

"Okay, try it now," called Kai. Blaze and Alaric briefly shimmered silver, and then they changed quickly into giant black wolves. It all happened in just seconds and looked smooth to Ember and Noelle, but Kai raised an eyebrow and said to Tai, "A little slow, but just like we did our first time in the Mortal world." "Okay, change back," hollered Tai. The two giant black wolves glimmered silver, and then.... nothing happened. The Wolves looked at each other and then shimmered silver again. This time, they changed back into Blaze and Alaric, but it took about ten seconds. The two boys sat on the ground and looked as if they had just completed a marathon. "I was afraid we were going to stay stuck as Wolves," muttered Alaric. "Yeah, that one hurt," groaned Blaze.

"It's normal for the shift to take a little longer in the Mortal realm. You'll need to shift twice a day and try to do it faster each time until it becomes second nature like it is in Marqueria," said Tai as he walked over to them, extending his hand and pulling Blaze up, then doing the same with Alaric. "Good job. I'm only slightly surprised you were able to change on your first try," said Kai as he moved closer to them.

"Exactly how do you shift? If Noelle and I are half Bear, shouldn't we be able to shift?" asked Ember from the bench where she and Noelle were leaning back against the Tree. Tai turned to stare at them for a few moments and then said, "If you want to try, now is as good a time as any. Come over here." The girls jumped up and joined the other four. "Okay, so to shift, you need to go deep within your mind. To the part of your mind where your Bear lives," said Tai. The girls just looked at him with confusion. Kai scoffed and said, "Really, Tai? 'Go deep into your mind?' is how you're going to teach them?" Tai shrugged and said, "Then you do it." He, Blaze, and Alaric went to the bench under the Tree and sat to watch the girls try to shift.

Kai directed the girls to sit on the ground and then joined them. They sat in a circle with their knees touching. Kai spoke very softly, saying, "Close your eyes. Take a deep breath in and release it very slowly, then repeat. Now, slowly enter your mind, listen closely, and you'll be able to find where your Bear lives. Follow the whispers of the Bear deep into your mind. When you reach the Bear, you'll need to embrace it fully. Wrap your arms around it and accept it." For several minutes, the girls sat quietly, eerily still. Then they were covered in a silvery sheen, and in the next instance, where the girls had been sitting, stood two massively huge silvery white bears with shining green eyes.

"Oh, my Goddess," whispered Blaze. Alaric said nothing, just stared at the gorgeous silvery white bears dwarfing Kai, who had jumped up quickly and moved out of the way instinctively. Kai, who was 6'5", looked small next to the glowing white bears. Kai shook his head in wonder, looked at his brother, and asked, "But how?" Tai shrugged and continued to stare at the white bears. "I don't know. I have always believed that the Spirit Bear was a myth. We've never had a Spirit Bear in Marqueria. There are stories, but in the thousands of years, one has never been seen," Tai said softly, reaching a hand out and touching the incredibly soft fur of one of the Bears. Then, in the blink of an eye, the Bears shifted back to Ember and Noelle, who looked around and grinned at everyone.

"Not bad for our first shift, was it? I didn't feel any pain whatsoever," said Ember as she walked to where Alaric was standing, still watching her with an amazed look on his face. "Why are you all just standing there staring at us?" asked Noelle, walking to Blaze and gently pushing his chin up to close his mouth. "Did you see the color of your fur?" Tai asked as he plopped down on the bench next to his brother, Kai. The girls nodded, and Ember said, "It was a lovely shade of silvery white that sort of glowed. Why weren't we brown or red, like our hair?" Leaning forward and placing his forearms on his knees, Tai stared at the ground for a few moments before lifting his head and staring at the girls again. He then said, "The Spirit Bear is a bedtime story passed down thousands of years in our Clan. It tells of a silvery white Bear who will come and bless the Land of Marqueria with Peace and Harmony. Nobody has ever seen the Spirit Bear, at least nobody still living."

The girls looked at each other and then back at Tai and Kai. "What does this mean?" asked Noelle. Tai shook his head and said, "I don't know. Are you able to communicate with your parents via the mind link?" The girls nodded, then they sat on the ground near the Tree and closed their eyes. Slightly glowing, they stayed in that position for five more minutes and then opened their eyes and stared at each other. Tired of waiting, Blaze asked, "Are you going to share what you discovered?"

"They haven't found Maxim yet. Ulrika is healed, but for the issues with being separated from her bonded mate-to-be. The Darkness has retreated. The Tree is not accessible from the other side, so Mom and Dad can't come through. Our YaYa told them it was as it was meant to be. She said we had important things to accomplish on this side of the Tree without interference from parents and grandparents. I guess she had a vision about this and the Dragon that isn't a Dragon," Ember said quietly. Noelle picked up where Ember had left off, saying, "They told us to continue to seek information on how to defeat the Darkness, as well as search for the Dragon on this side. As for the Spirit Bears, our dad congratulated us on being able to shift but didn't know what it meant that we were colored the same as the Spirit Bear.

He is going to speak with our Ukki and YaYa, King Otso and Queen Tati, about it and get back to us." The girls sat there and stared at each other, obviously using their mind link.

Chapter Forty-Four

When the group was halfway down the trail to the red house, the scent of Dragon wafted to them from the direction of the Grove. As one, they turned and ran back up the hill in search of the Dragon that wasn't a Dragon. There was no one in the Grove, but the scent was stronger here. Noses lifted slightly, they separated and slowly walked around the Grove, trying to find a trail to follow. "Here!" cried Ember as she ran out of the Grove in the opposite direction from where the house was. They all followed her, Tai moving out in front. As they got to the tree line and ran out into a small clearing, Noelle shouted, "There it is!" She was pointing to an area above a large outcropping of rocks, and flying over it was a pearlescent, glowy white Dragon, just discernible with the naked eye. It was flying away very quickly and was out of site in seconds.

"Damn it!" shouted Tai, running a hand through his blond hair. "Calm, brother. At least we now know that, yes, there is a Dragon. A Dragon like none I've ever seen before," said Kai softly, laying a hand on Tai's shoulder. "There are no white Dragons?" asked Noelle. Kai shook his head and said, "No. White Dragons are like White Bears. Myths." "This can't be a coincidence. A Spirit Dragon appears at the same time we shift into supposed Spirit Bears?" said Ember, turning to head back to the house. Alaric caught up to her and took her hand in his. She looked up and gave him a distracted smile but continued on. The rest joined her, and soon, they found themselves back at the house, sitting on the patio in the soft chairs.

Nobody spoke for a while, and then Ember said, "I'm starving, more so than usual." "Yeah, that's the shifter thing. It takes a lot of energy to shift, especially here in the Mortal world. Tai and I will go in and make some pizzas for all of us. We'll let you know when they're ready," said Kai. The Bear brothers went into the house, leaving the teens alone.

"I'm a little tired of being 'special and the saviors of Marqueria.' Couldn't we just shift into normal huge brown bears or even black ones? That would have been fine. Why did it have to be the Spirit Bear?" said Noelle in a frustrated tone, her expression surly. Blaze watched Noelle for a few seconds and then said, "But you're not normal, Noelle. Your mother is the first in the Elven Matriarchal line. Princess of the Elves and soon-to-be ruler of all. Your father is the Heir to the Bears and their Prince. Never in our history, and remember it is a very long history, has a mating such as your parents' happened. Kenna, Ember, and you have a direct line to the Goddess. The Dryad of the Tree gifted you a mind-link, again, which has never happened. Wishing you were normal isn't going to work, and it shows a lack of respect for the powers that were gifted to you. You're strong enough to bear this responsibility, Noelle." Noelle stood up and stomped her foot, yelling, "Well, maybe I don't want this responsibility! Maybe I want to be a normal teenager and have a normal, boring life! Our mom and dad would never be separated from us if not for these 'wonderful gifts' bestowed upon us! Nobody asked us if we wanted this burden!" Noelle was lit up like a glow worm; her hair was blowing furiously around her head, and her green and gold eyes were shooting sparks.

Ember stood up and went to her sister, laid a hand on her shoulder, and simply said, "Noelle." Noelle turned on her sister with lightning speed and shoved her hand off her shoulder, crying loudly, "Don't you dare! You feel the same way I do. I can read it in your mind, or did you forget?! Don't you dare deny that you feel the same as I do!" Ember nodded her head, and tears escaped down her cheeks. She said, "I do, Noelle. I feel the same as you do right now. I miss our life before we took Mom through the Tree to Marqueria. I miss our quiet life here in this house, where it was just us, our parents, and Lucy. But we can't go back to that, ever. It will never be the same for us here. There is an Evil out there hunting us, trying to destroy the world, every world, Noelle. If not us, then who? Noelle, I'm serious. If not us, then who will fight it? You know Mom and Dad aren't made to hide away from danger. They didn't raise us to run and hide in the safe places either. It isn't who we are." Ember moved closer to her sister and, taking her hands in her own, looked up at her and said, "Noelle. I mean, seriously. We are the granddaughters of Santa Claus, remember?" This last was delivered with a barely contained smirk and a wink. Noelle stared down at her sister for a few moments and then burst out laughing. She wrapped her arms around Ember and pulled her in close, saying, "Damn it, Ember. Can't you just let me fall apart? Granddaughters of Santa Claus? You wacko doo," The girls held each other for a few minutes, and then Ember said, "You've fallen apart; now you pick up the pieces and move on." Then, her stomach gave a very loud grumble. "Come on, let's go eat. I'm starving too," said Noelle as she pulled her sister towards the patio door in search of food. Blaze and Alaric stood there, looking after them, their faces showing their pride in the amount of strength within the girls and their ability to shake it off so quickly.

Chapter Forty-Five

Ember shoved the last bit of pizza into her mouth, chewed and swallowed, then said, "That was amazing! Best batch of pizzas so far, boys." There were nods of agreement while the rest were finishing up. Ember stood up from the table and said, "I'll get started on cleaning the kitchen while you all finish up." Noelle stood up and said, "I'll help." Then, she followed her sister into the kitchen. The four Weres were left sitting at the dining room table, exchanging worried glances.

"What are they up to?" asked Tai, looking towards the kitchen with a frown between his eyes. "Maybe they just wanted a few minutes to themselves," murmured Kai, glancing towards the kitchen with a speculative expression. "No, they're definitely up to something. We saw them communicating via their mind link, and when we asked what was up, they clammed up and wouldn't tell us," said Blaze quietly. "What is Thanksgiving?" asked Alaric.

Tai and Kai looked at him in surprise and then stared at each other. Kai whispered, "Shit." Tai nodded and said, "We need to go back into town and get all the ingredients for a complete dinner." "What? Why?" asked Blaze. "Thanksgiving is a holiday here in the United States which celebrates....well, I'm not really sure what it celebrates. It was initially based on the first supper with the natives of this land and the colonizers. That has changed over the years as the real truth about the colonizers and the genocide they perpetrated on the Natives became more widely known. Most didn't want to celebrate that. Now, it's a day when families all gather together and have a feast. Usually roast turkey, mashed potatoes and gravy, stuffing, corn, and different pies, but especially pumpkin pie," said Tai softly.

As the Weres made plans to go shopping again, Ember and Noelle were in the kitchen talking about Thanksgiving. "Do you think we should go this year? Without mom and dad?" asked Ember as she was wiping down the countertop. After putting a stack of plates into the cupboard, Noelle turned to look at Ember. "I think we should go, even without Mom and Dad. We need to carry on this tradition, at least. It helps so many people," Noelle said quietly. "What about the four in there? Should we ask them to come and help?" asked Ember.

Noelle started walking towards the dining room and said over her shoulder, "Only one way to find out!" Ember followed her, and when the two girls entered the dining area, the four Weres at the table stopped talking and looked a little guilty. "Just what are you planning?" asked Ember, staring at each one in turn. Noelle stared at Blaze and said, "Spill it." The girls waited for a few seconds, just staring. Finally, Blaze said, "We were talking about going back into town to shop for Thanksgiving Day food." Exchanging a glance with Noelle, Ember chuckled and said, "Funny. We were talking about Thanksgiving, too."

Tai nodded and said, "We just remembered that it is tomorrow, and we're sorry you're not with your parents to celebrate." Noelle and Ember nodded, and then Noelle said, "Well, we don't celebrate it in the normal way; that is to say, we don't cook a big feast and sit and stuff ourselves. We volunteer every year to serve dinner to the homeless at the Rescue Mission." Ember nodded and said, "It's something we've been doing since we were little. Mom and Dad have always done it, and when we were born, they just brought us along."

The four Weres continued to stare at the girls, but this time, their faces showed a little awe. "What?" asked Ember. "Your family just continues to amaze us, that's all," said Kai. "Would you mind if we tagged along with you tomorrow?" asked Alaric. Ember grinned and said, "The more, the merrier. Plus, you four strapping males can do all the heavy lifting." Blaze clapped his hands together, rubbed his palms, and then said, "Then it's settled. We all go and help out." Noelle gave him a soft smile and a nod.

"We also need to go through all the closets too and collect winter clothing and footwear. Since we won't be needing it and they need it more than we do, we figured we would minimize our wardrobes and those of our parents. We will leave three sets of clothing for each of us, but the rest should go to the Rescue Mission, along with the camping gear like the tents, sleeping bags, and such," said Ember. "Tai and Kai, do you want to handle our parents' closet? Dad's clothing fits all of you, so leave yourselves some. Ember and I will go to our room and sort our own clothing," said Noelle.

Tai and Kai nodded, and grabbing the large black lawn and leaf bags Noelle handed them, they headed towards Kenna and Jamie's bedroom. Ember grabbed two large bags and handed them to Alaric, saying, "Here, you can hold while I put stuff in." Noelle handed two bags to Blaze and said, "Ditto." "Ditto? What is that?" asked Blaze. Noelle laughed and said, "It means the same. Come on, let's go up." The four teens went to the girls' room and started to sort through the clothing. After an hour, they were done and met Tai and Kai in the kitchen, where they, too, had two full bags.

"If you four would take the bags out and put them in the Sequoia, we will go downstairs and start on the camping gear. You can meet us there," said Noelle as she and Ember started toward the basement. The four Weres grabbed the bags and headed out to the garage.

Chapter Forty-Six

The next morning, I found the six of them at the Rescue Mission, unloading boxes and bags of clothing, camping gear, and outerwear. When that was completed, they went to the kitchen of the Mission to find their assignments. The Director was there handing out assignments, and when he saw the girls, his face lit up. "Noelle, Ember! It's so good to see you here. Are your parents on their way?" he asked, looking around. "Hi, Joe. No, our parents won't be able to make it this year; they're on a couples-only retreat and are gone until after the New Year. I'd like to introduce you to their replacements, though," said Noelle, and she made the introductions. Joe's face showed his joy at having four such brawny guys to help with the heavy lifting. "Where do you want us this year?" asked Ember.

Joe gave her a grin and said, "As always, I want you and your sister out on the serving line. You both are so nice and talkative; you are just a joy to be around. So when the food is ready, you'll be out there with the other teens. As for you four, I could really use your help getting the turkeys out of the oven and sliced up, and then the serving bins are taken out to the serving area." Tai, Kai, Blaze, and Alaric all nodded and followed Joe to the Kitchen.

Following the routine from prior years, the girls went to the dining room and began stacking plates, setting out silverware, folding napkins, and setting the cornucopias on each table to give it a festive look. Behind them came a timid "Noelle, Ember," and the girls turned around to find two of the girls from the restaurant fiasco the other day. "Oh, hi Cindy, Jessica. Are you volunteering here, too?" Ember asked.

The girls' faces turned red with embarrassment, and they both shook their heads. "No...well, yes, but we stay here, and it's one of our assigned duties. To help in the kitchen," stuttered Cindy, the brunette. She shrugged her shoulders and said, "Our dad lost his job when the mine shut down and wasn't able to find one that paid as well. We lost our house and had nowhere to go, so we ended up here until our dad can save enough money to rent a place we can afford. It's been a hard year." "Yeah, mom is in and out of the hospital with her Lupus, so she can't work. We've applied at all the restaurants, but no one is hiring. So we help out here when we're not in school," said Jessica.

Noelle and Ember said nothing at first, but then Ember said, "I'm sorry about the other day. I didn't mean to be so aggressive." Jessica laughed and said, "Are you kidding? Seeing those jerks put on their asses was the best thing I've ever seen!" "They shouldn't have said what they did; it was disgusting," said Cindy softly. The four girls all nodded at each other. They were interrupted by Joe, who came out of the kitchen hollering, "Time to get the serving line going, folks."

The four teenage girls were joined by several older ladies who looked like school lunchroom ladies. They seemed to be in charge and placed the girls where they wanted them. Ember and Cindy were on mashed potatoes and gravy, and Noelle and Jessica were on stuffing and corn station. The line was long, out the door, and down the street because the Mission served anyone in need of a hot meal, not just the people staying at the Mission.

For hours, the girls loaded plates with food, and the four Weres carried platters and platters of food to replace what was given out. It was nothing but nose to the grindstone for at least four hours. That didn't mean it wasn't fun, for the girls were laughing and joking and engaging the diners as they went through the food line. Sometimes, they came back for seconds and thirds. When the last dinner was served and the last piece of pie was handed out, the girls looked at each other and grinned. "That was fun. I miss Mom and Dad, but I'm glad we did this, Noelle," said Ember softly. Noelle nodded and smiled at her sister.

Cindy and Jessica fixed two plates and took them to a middle-aged couple sitting in the corner. They gave them a hug and then returned to help clean up. "Are those your parents?" asked Ember. The girls nodded as they wiped down one of the tables. "Yeah, they didn't want to eat until everyone had been fed at least twice," said Cindy with a shrug. Ember and Noelle stared at each other, obviously using their mind-link, but only to those who knew them. "We'll be right back," said Noelle, and they walked to the back in search of Tai and Kai.

Chapter Forty-Seven

"Can we do anything?" asked Noelle, watching Tai and Kai. Kai and Tai exchanged glances and nodded. "Yes, I think we can. Nobody knows this, but Kai and I own a couple of houses in Butte. We bought them several years ago and held onto them so that we could have a place to stay when we were looking for your father. Plus, we wanted to be near the Tree," Tai said. "They're nothing fancy, but one is currently empty, and the other is rented. Why don't we go out and sit down with them to discuss this?" said Kai.

The girls smiled at the two Bear brothers and nodded. Alaric and Blaze followed the girls out to the dining room, with Tai and Kai behind them. Ember went over to Jessica and Cindy and then followed them to where their parents were sitting. Introductions were made, and when everyone was seated, Kai leaned forward and said, "We understand that you've had some hard times recently. Having been homeless a few times ourselves, my brother and I understand. We have a house that is currently empty. It's not much, but it has three bedrooms, two bathrooms, and a fenced yard. It's down on the flats, south of town, so it's harder to get around town. Do you have a vehicle?" Jessica and Cindy's dad, Ben, shook his head and said, "No, that was repossessed, unfortunately, but I do have a license. I usually take the bus to work."

The girls' mom, Audrey, said, "How much is the rent?" She looked very worn and tired, and Ember thought she had the same look her mom got when she was in pain. Tai and Kai both smiled, and Tai said, "Nothing. It's yours for as long as you need it. The lights and water are paid for automatically, as are the cable and internet, so you don't need to worry about that. There's a Toyota 4-Runner parked in the garage that is yours to use as well. Don't worry, it's insured." The family of four sat there speechless, their faces showing how amazed they were.

"But why?" asked Audrey, looking from Tai to Kai and back again. Tai said, "Why not?" Then he stood up and said, "If you would gather your things together, I will be back with the 4-Runner and the house keys." Ben stood up and held his hand out; Tai shook it, and then Ben turned to Kai and shook his hand. Ben said, "I don't know what to say other than thank you." Tai nodded his head and said, "When you're able, pay it forward. That is all we ask." Audrey spoke up and said softly, "But we don't have any furniture, Ben." Kai said, "The house is fully furnished. We rented it out as a short-term rental, so everything is stocked. Towels, bedding, dishes. It's all there." Then he turned to Ember and Noelle and said, "Will you drive us out to the house?" The girls nodded and stood up. Cindy and Jessica hurried over to them and gave them each a hug. With tear-filled eyes, Cindy said, "Thank you. You have no idea what this means to my parents. What it means to us." Noelle nodded and said, "We do. We understand. Go get your stuff packed, and we will be back to get you." Noelle gave her a hug and grabbed Blaze's hand. She walked towards the door, Ember and Alaric following, Tai and Kai bringing up the rear.

When everyone was in the SUV, Tai and Kai were in the front, with Tai driving. From the third-row seat, Ember said, "They need groceries, and it's late on Thanksgiving. I don't think anything is open." "Damn," whispered Kai. "If anything is open on the way, we will stop and grab a bunch of stuff. Maybe a gas station convenience store is open," said Noelle from the middle seat. The SUV headed down from uptown Butte, driving the main road headed south. The uptown Safeway was already closed, and every grocery store they passed was closed.

"There!" shouted Ember from the back. Up ahead, on the left, was a large convenience store. Tai pulled in and parked, and they all got out and went into the store. "Divide and conquer, people," said Ember as she headed back to the milk section, Alaric in tow. Alaric had grabbed two baskets from the stack by the door and handed one to her. When they got to the milk coolers, Ember and Alaric loaded up on what dairy they could find. Turning back towards the front of the store, they walked up the aisle Noelle and Blaze were shopping in and helped them get cereal, bread, peanut butter, crackers, and canned soups. When the four baskets they had were full, they went to the checkout, meeting Tai and Kai, who each had a basket full of frozen items. The clerk rang them up, giving them funny looks the entire time. After they paid and carried the bags out to the SUV, Ember laughed and said, "That clerk couldn't figure us out at all."

Chapter Forty-Eight

Tai pulled into the driveway of a well-kept brown house in a small subdivision south of town. There was a two-car attached garage and a fenced backyard, and there were tall trees in the front and back yards, giving a sense of privacy. Kai got out a set of keys, and everyone entered the house. Kai led the way to the kitchen and turned the lights on along the way. Ember said, "I thought you said this was a modest house, nothing special? This is really nice, Tai." "I didn't want to scare them away; they might have refused if they knew where it was, thinking they couldn't afford it," Tai said as he started to put the groceries away in the stainless steel refrigerator.

Ember looked out the back patio door and whistled. "A deck with a hot tub. Their mom, Audrey, has Lupus, so this will be good for her pain relief," Ember said, nodding her head. Kai walked in and said, "Okay, the heat is turned up, and there's firewood next to the fireplace if they want a fire." Noelle handed the last frozen item to Tai, who put it in the freezer; then she turned to Ember and said, "I'm going to put in a grocery order to be delivered here tomorrow, along with some other items the girls might need. Want to help me with it when we get home?" Ember smiled at her sister and said,

"Yes, that sounds wonderful. I think we should send them some gift cards to the local clothing stores, too. Being in high school and living in a homeless shelter wasn't easy for them. I think they deserve a treat."

"Okay, I'm going to take the 4-Runner to the Mission, and you guys will follow me. I'll just hand over the keys to the house and SUV and hop in with you," said Tai as they were all leaving the house.

When they got to the Mission, Tai went in and collected the family and brought them out to the blue 4-Runner, handed the keys to the dad, and handed the mom the house keys and a few legal-looking documents. They gave the mother a hug, shook hands with the father, and waved at the teenage girls. Ember lowered the rear window and said, "Goodbye! We'll stop by in a few days after you get settled." She waved and raised the window when Tai jumped in the front seat with Kai. Tai said, "Let's go home. I'm exhausted, but I feel good." "My mom says that's the high from doing good and helping people. You're physically exhausted but also kinda revved up, and your soul is happy and content, right? Yeah, that's the contact high from helping others," said Noelle softly. Blaze squeezed her hand and said, "Thank you for bringing us today. I felt needed and liked that I was making a difference." Noelle just smiled at Blaze and laid her head on his shoulder, closing her eyes. They didn't make it two miles out of town before she and Ember were asleep.

"How can they be so kind and giving?" asked Alaric. Tai and Kai chuckled. "It's in their DNA. Their parents are like this, too, especially Kenna. Because of Kenna's tragic childhood, she wanted Noelle and Ember to be brought up never wanting or needing anything, but their parents also made sure they had compassion, empathy, altruism, and love for their neighbors. It's a fine line to walk, giving your children everything and not raising spoiled brats," said Tai softly. "They will make amazing leaders of Marqueria," whispered Blaze.

Chapter Forty-Nine

The next morning, what would become the teenagers' daily routine began. They woke up, ate breakfast, got dressed, and headed to the Grove. There, they practiced their shifting abilities and hand-to-hand combat. Tai and Kai also added defensive magic to their training. Although Ember and Noelle were relatively new to magic, they excelled. Though Tai, Kai, Blaze, and Alaric had a little skill with the type of magic the girls could wield, the males were in no way experts. The girls were quickly becoming so, though.

They had been practicing casting a circle without using the chants. The chants were said in their minds quickly and pushed out with their innate magic within them. After a week of daily practice, Ember and Noelle could cast a circle without using chants, and it was lightning fast, too. Tai and Kai also taught them how to harness the magic held within the earth and use it for attacks and protection. This was harder than casting a circle and required concentration. After two weeks, this was lacking in all four of the Teens.

"We need a break, Tai. Can we go bowling or watch a movie? Or even wander around the mall? Also, we need to stop by Cindy and Jessica's house. We have Christmas gift cards for the family. Can we do that today?" asked Noelle as they were sitting at the breakfast nook, eating breakfast. Tai and Kai looked at each other, saying nothing. Then, Tai gave a heaving sigh and nodded his head. He said, "Okay, today is a break day. We will all go into town and stop by to check on our tenants, and we can do something fun." "Ice Skating!" shouted Ember. "Yes!" said Noelle excitedly, then continued, "Dad has several pairs of hockey skates downstairs, which should fit you all. There are several skating rinks scattered around town, or we can go to the High Altitude Skating Rink."

"You guys clean up the kitchen, and Ember and I will go down and gather what we need," said Noelle, pulling her sister towards the basement stairs. Blaze and Alaric laughed, and then Blaze said, "Noelle is getting just as good as Ember at dodging chores." Alaric nodded and started loading the dishwasher. Tai said, "I'm going to do a walk around. I feel uneasy for some reason. I have all morning." Kai nodded and said, "Same. Maybe it's just being cooped up here for two weeks; I don't know. I feel on edge, too. I'll come with you." The Bear brothers walked out the patio door to do their walk around the property.

"Do you feel it, too?" asked Blaze, looking at Alaric. Alaric nodded and said, "It actually started yesterday for me. I feel as if someone is watching us, but I can't catch their scent, and I can't see anyone around. It's weird." Blaze nodded and said, "Yep, that's how I feel. It started yesterday. Maybe we just need to get out of here and go do something."

The girls walked into the kitchen, carrying a box full of hockey skates and helmets. "These are all we could find. There are five pairs, and they should fit you all. I'm not sure about the helmets. Dad has a big head," said Ember laughingly. "Do you think it's okay if we wear our clothing from Marqueria? It keeps us warmer, and we can move better in it," asked Noelle, looking between Ember, Blaze, and Alaric. Ember nodded and said, "They kind of look like workout gear, fancy workout gear, but with all the skaters, I don't think they'd look at us twice. There will be people out on the ice wearing speed skating clothes and figure skating, so I think we will be okay."

"Where did Tai and Kai go?" asked Ember. Alaric answered, "They went on a walk around the property. They feel uneasy about something." Ember and Noelle exchanged a look, and Blaze asked, "What? I know that look. What's going on?" Noelle went to him and wrapped her arms around his waist, leaned back to look up at him, and said, "Ember and I have been feeling weird since yesterday. Like someone was watching us in the Grove, we couldn't smell anyone or see anyone, but it felt like someone was there." Blaze leaned down, placed a soft kiss on Noelle's lips, and said, "Alaric and I feel the same, and it started yesterday." From the patio door, Tai said, "Well, that makes six of us. Maybe we need to just get the Hell out of here for a day."

Everyone met in the garage and loaded up into the Sequoia. They had all chosen to wear their Marqueria clothing for their outing. Blaze placed the box of skates in the back of the SUV, closed the door, and walked around to climb in next to Noelle in the middle seats. Tai was driving, and Kai was riding shotgun. As usual, Ember and Alaric were in the third seat. Using her cell phone, Ember called Cindy and Jessica to let them know they were stopping by for a short visit.

It had been snowing all week, and the highway into town was snow-covered and icy. Noelle was glad she wasn't driving and said so. Tai laughed and said, "Ah, this is nothing." Ember spoke up from the rear seat, "You guys do know that it's Christmas in two weeks, don't you? Can we get a tree this week and decorate it? Plan on a Christmas dinner and all that?" After a short period of silence, Kai said, "We can do that, Ember." So, for the rest of the ride in, the talk turned to Christmas and all the yummy food they were going to make.

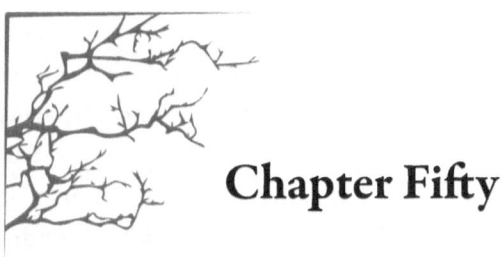

Chapter Fifty

Tai maneuvered the SUV into the driveway of the brown house south of town. Everyone got out and was greeted at the door by Audrey, who looked so much better than she had two weeks ago. Ember noticed that she looked well rested; the pained look was gone from her face, and her hair and makeup were done. Ember thought to herself, 'Mom always said that you can tell how much pain someone was in or how active their disease was by how they looked. Most of the time, hair and makeup were not done when there was a lot of pain present, mom always said.' Ember smiled at the memory, then turned her smile towards Audrey, Cindy, and Jessica, who were ushering them into the house.

Ben wasn't at home, as he was working. He had gotten a job at the county landfill. It had good benefits, and the pay was decent, according to Audrey, who needed insurance coverage due to the high cost of her Lupus medication. Audrey asked if they wanted anything to drink, and they all declined, saying they couldn't stay long but wanted to drop off their Christmas present early. Audrey and her daughters stared at Ember and Noelle, saying nothing. Then, Audrey said, "We don't need Christmas presents. You all have done so much for us, more than we ever could have asked for."

Noelle moved forward, took Audrey's hand in hers, and said, "Our mother was an orphan who spent her childhood in the system, being shuffled around from home to home. She aged out at eighteen and was alone. She had nowhere to go. She came to Butte because she said it called to her. The owner of an uptown cafe gave her a job and a small apartment upstairs above the cafe, which was rent-free. It is our tradition to always help someone during the Holidays. We want to help you, and when you are able, you will help someone and pay it forward. That's how this works."

Audrey had tears in her eyes and said, "I know your mother. We had some college classes together, and then we would run into each other at the Rheumatologist's office. I never knew that about her, but it explains a lot. Such a kind soul." Ember handed a gift card-sized envelope to Cindy and one to Jessica. Noelle handed two to Audrey and said, "These are for you. You can use it for anything you want. It's our gift to you and your family." Audrey leaned up and gave Noelle a hug, then she moved on to Ember and said, "You two are just like your mother. Thank you so much for all the blessings you have brought to us this Holiday season." Goodbyes were said all around, and the six got back into the SUV, pulled out of the driveway, and headed toward the skating rinks.

"Just how much did you put on those gift cards?" asked Tai, looking back at the girls in the rearview mirror. The girls giggled, and Ember said, "We put $1,000 on each card." Tai and Kai laughed, and Kai said, "Well, I hope they have an amazing Christmas."

Chapter Fifty-One

The six of them were lacing up their ice skates at the Clark Park ice rink. They had decided not to go to the High Altitude Center, as it was very crowded, and none of them felt like skating with a bunch of people. Clark Park was an old park with a large ice rink, lit up at night with streetlights along the outer circle. It was surrounded by pine trees and felt more private than the other parks.

Standing up and gliding out on the ice, Noelle turned around and, skating backward, yelled, "Come on, slowpokes!" Then she took off around the link, Ember close behind. The two of them were quick and graceful on the ice, obviously having been skating all their lives. The four Weres finally got the skates on and joined the girls out on the ice. They, too, were comfortable on the ice and glided around, challenging each other to a race. 'This was just what the six of us needed,' thought Ember to herself. She laughed as Alaric grabbed her and twirled her around, and soon, they were dancing across the ice.

After dancing and racing for over an hour, they all sat on the snow banks to remove their skates and put their boots back on. They were all laughing and smiling and tossing around playful insults about how slow the other ones were. After they had their boots on, they started walking for the

SUV parked on the street under a large tree. As one, they all stopped walking and stood perfectly still. Their heads tilted, and noses pointed up in the air; they were all sniffing. "Dragon!" whispered Noelle as she took off running towards the playground, where the scent was coming from. The others quickly followed her and the scent across the park, but it faded fast and then was gone.

The six of them stood together, looking around the playground in the fading light. There were a few people swinging on the big cowboy swings, which were big enough for adults to play on. A young couple with their toddler on one end and a lone figure in a hoodie on another, just swinging quietly. As Ember watched the lone swinger, who appeared to be just a kid, she caught a glimpse of snow-white hair under the hoodie and unconsciously took a few steps toward the swings. Alaric grabbed her hand and asked, "Where are you going?" Ember turned to Alaric and, in confusion, said, "I didn't even realize I was moving. Weird. I just felt this incredible pull towards that boy at the end there. The one with the hoodie." Everyone turned to look at the swings, but there was just the couple with the toddler. There wasn't anyone else on the swings.

"Where did he go? He was right there at the end! I swear!" exclaimed Ember. "I saw him too," murmured Noelle as she walked over and put her arm around her sister's shoulder. The girls looked up to see that the others were looking at them curiously. "What?" asked Ember. Tai ran his hand through his blond hair and said, "We only saw the couple with the toddler. There was nobody else on the swings." Ember and Noelle stared at each other for a second, and then, as one, they began the walk down the hill toward the cowboy swings. Blaze, Alaric, Tai, and Kai followed more slowly, whispering amongst themselves.

When the sisters got to the swing on which the boy had been swinging, the faint scent of Dragon was detected. "I think our boy is the Dragon that isn't a Dragon," whispered Noelle. Ember nodded and whispered in awe, "A Dragon shifter." The four males finally reached them and hadn't heard what the sisters had said. "Damn it! Where did he go?" whispered Tai. "Come on, let's go back to the SUV. I feel exposed out here," said Kai.

They all moved back towards the Sequoia. When they reached it, after looking around, they climbed in, closed the doors, and sat in silence. "How is it possible for a Dragon to be in this world and nobody has noticed? Where does it disappear to? What did the Dryad mean by 'the Dragon that isn't a Dragon'? This is so freaking frustrating!" growled Tai from the driver's. Kai said, "We don't have the answers to any of those questions. For now, I think it best we go back home and do more research on the Darkness. Also, I think looking into dragon myths would be a good idea. Maybe there's something in them about a Dragon that isn't a Dragon." Everyone agreed, but Ember said loudly, "I think it's a Dragon Shifter, and so does Noelle. Is that a thing?" Tai and Kai both shook their heads, and Blaze spoke up, saying, "There are no Dragon Shifters in Marqueria. We have a myth of the Spirit Dragon, but no shifters." Ember and Noelle both sighed loudly, and then Ember said, "I'm starving. Can we hit a drive-through on the way home?"

Chapter Fifty-Two

The boy from the swing sat at the top of a tall pine tree, watching the six people below. They had given up searching for him and were walking back to the SUV they had arrived in. He knew he had to leave now if he was going to make it back to the Grove before they got home to the red house in the country. The boy smiled at the phrase, 'the red house in the country.' He had heard one of the girls use it, and he liked the sound of it in his head. As he watched them drive away, he quickly jumped from the tree and shifted while still in the air, then he turned towards the Grove and flew very fast to make it there in time.

He loved spending time in the Grove. It felt like a home was supposed to feel. Safe. He couldn't remember his parents or even having a home and had spent most of his life alone in the wilderness surrounding this small town of Butte. As he flew towards the red house and the Grove, he watched the traffic on the interstate below him and wondered what it would be like to ride in a car. He had never ridden in a car, a bus, or a plane. The boy chuckled at that thought. Why would he need to ride on a plane when he could fly anywhere he wanted to go? When the boy was very young, around three years old, he found himself alone in the mountains near where the earth boiled and steamed. He knew now that it was called Yellowstone National Park. He spent several years in the Park, hunting and hiding from the humans and searching for the family he couldn't remember. He didn't recall what his family looked like, but everyone comes from a family, right? So, he looked around the park and surrounding communities, hoping to find them. He always came up empty.

Now, his days were spent navigating the bustling streets of the small towns of Montana and sometimes venturing to the larger areas such as Billings, Great Falls, and Missoula. He had particularly enjoyed the trips he had taken up to Glacier National Park. Most days, he lived in the shadows, hiding his true nature from the world. Because the other children teased and taunted him, unaware of the incredible secret he carried within him, he stopped attending school early on. The adults at the school had started to ask too many questions. Questions he didn't have the answers to.

One fateful night, as the full moon cast its silvery glow over the town of Butte, he felt the familiar tingling sensation that signaled his transformation. With a deep breath, he embraced the change and let the dragon within him emerge in all its glory. As a dragon, he soared through the starlit sky, feeling the wind beneath his wings and the exhilaration of freedom coursing through his veins. When he was Dragon, he felt truly alive, untethered from the constraints of his human form.

As he was flying across the sky, he felt a strong pull to an area behind a red house deep in the mountains. Flying closer, he felt a tingling and warmth emanating from the Grove behind the red house. Landing in the Grove, he felt such peace and a sense of safety that he shifted back to his human form and sat on the bench near a giant ancient birch tree. The boy got the feeling that the Tree was alive, and when he sat on the bench and leaned his head back against the silver-white bark, he felt a jolt of energy enter his body, startling him. He stood up and looked at the Tree and watched in amazement as a stunningly beautiful woman walked out of the Tree. She had glowing silver-white skin with black marks like a Birch tree. Her hair was vibrant reds, yellows, and oranges. Her eyes were huge and swirling orange, yellow, and red. The boy had never seen such a lovely creature before, and for some reason, he wasn't afraid of her.

That night, he met the Dryad of the Tree, and she had been his only friend ever since. He would often visit her at night because the mother, the two daughters, and, on occasion, the father, who lived in the red house, would spend hours during the daytime in the Grove. The daughters would pass through the Tree often and only be gone for a few minutes. The Dryad of the Tree told him they were going to a different world called Marqueria and that one day, he too would be able to visit, but first, there were things the mother and daughters had to do to make it safe for him.

So, the boy stayed in the Mortal world, and despite his loneliness, he wasn't sad. He watched the family in the red house often, and their love for each other gave him hope. He hopes that one day, he will have a family such as theirs. He knew they weren't like others in the Mortal world, as he could sense the power in all of them. He knew the father was a shifter and had seen him shift on several occasions into a massive, majestic Bear. He knew the daughters were shifters, but they hadn't shifted until just a week or so ago. Their mother was not a shifter, but she was very powerful, with strong magic inside her.

Tonight, the boy landed in the Grove and looked around. There was no one else there, so he walked over to the Tree and laid a hand on it, hoping the Dryad of the Tree would come to visit him. After a few seconds, the Tree began glowing, and the boy stepped back, waiting for the Dryad to join him. She stepped out of the Tree and smiled at the boy, moving gracefully towards him and taking his hand; she led him to the bench under the Tree and sat next to him. "What have you been up to, my little sapling?" she asked him, still holding his hand in hers. He peeked up at her through his long, snow-white bangs and gave her a mischievous smile. Then he said, "I followed them tonight. All six drove into town and visited the family in the brown house. The house the Bear shifter brothers own and gave to the homeless family to live in, remember?" The boy looked to the Dryad, and seeing her nod, he continued, "They gave the family four gift cards for Christmas worth $4,000. The mother cried; she was so grateful. Then, the six left and went to the park to ice skate and play. When they were leaving, I got too close, and they caught my scent. I sat on the swing, pretending to be with another family. The daughter, Ember, was drawn to me and walked towards me before her Wolf mate pulled her back. I thought it was a good time to disappear, so I did and sat in a tall tree and watched them leave." He finished with a small frown and a sad look in his eyes. The Dryad gently lifted his chin and asked, "What did you learn tonight by watching them, little sapling?"

The boy bit his lip and looked to be thinking hard. Then his face lit up with a shining smile, and he said, "I learned that they are very generous and giving. They take care of each other and love each other, but they also care about others who are not in their family. They are not like most people I have encountered in my travels." The Dryad nodded and pulled him into her arms, giving him a gentle hug and holding on for a few moments longer. Then she said, "The time is nearing for us to introduce you to them, but that time is not now. Please be more careful and do not get caught. I now sense the girls getting closer to their home, so we need to go, my youngling. Please be safe and stay in the shadows." She stood up, placed a kiss on the top of his head, and glided back to the Tree, saying, "Goodnight and sweet dreams, young Dragon. We will speak again soon." The boy said, "Goodnight, Dryad of the Tree. I look forward to our next visit." The boy then shifted and jumped into the air, flying towards the mountains and his secret cave. The Dryad watched as he flew out of sight, then she sighed and said quietly, "You will have the family you deserve, my sweet young Dragon. Soon." Then she walked into her Tree and was gone.

Chapter Fifty-Three

Back at the Castle in Marqueria, Kenna was pacing in front of the fire in the Library as she addressed the Royalty who had gathered. "No! I don't understand why you won't pursue Hilda or the Darkness. The quicker we can contain or destroy It...she...whatever the Hell it is, the quicker I can see my daughters! Not to mention Maxim! We need to find him and bring him back to Ulrika," she said loudly and firmly, her cheeks pink with anger and frustration, her green eyes glowing, and her hair starting to float. Jamie stood up and went to her, pulling her into his arms and trying to soothe her. "I understand your frustration, wife; I do. But we need to wait and see what our daughters and the others find in the Mortal world. They are searching for a way to destroy the Darkness. We need patience," he said as he stroked her cinnamon curls and held her close.

Kenna leaned back, her eyes filled with tears, and said, "I can't do this, Jamie. I need to be near our daughters. Having them a world away, with no way to get to them, is killing me. I feel so helpless." She laid her head back down on Jamie's chest and gave a sob. Jamie looked up and met his father's eyes. They stared at one another for a few moments, and then Otso gave a negative shake of his head and said, "It's not possible, Jamie. We can't find the Tree. It is gone from Marqueria." Tati stood up and came to Jamie and Kenna; laying a hand on Kenna's shoulder, she said, "The Dryad of the Tree has hidden the Tree from Marqueria. She said it was for the Mortal world's safety, and therefore, it is for the safety of Ember and Noelle, Alaric and Blaze, and Tai and Kai. They are in that world to find answers, and it just happens to be the safest place for them."

Kenna stepped back from Jamie and looked at her mother-in-law, Queen Tati. "How did you handle it when Jamie went through the Tree to find me?" Kenna asked her quietly. Tati gave a sad smile and said, "Not very well at first. I had a few temper tantrums, and I argued with Otso about sending him through, too. Then, I had a visit from the Goddess in the form of a prophecy. I knew your daughters would come through the Tree when they did. Why do you think Otso was there, waiting for them? I told him when and where they would come through. That is how we knew Jamie had found you and built a life with you. Your daughters. Now we must put our faith in them again and wait for their findings." Kenna took a deep breath and let it out slowly, then nodded her head. "Okay. I'm okay, I'm fine. Not really, but I will be. I always am. What can we do here? Have there been any sightings of the Darkness or Hilda?" Kenna said in a firm voice, her anger dissipated.

Turning to watch her parents, Queen Maia and King Bram, she waited for their answer. After exchanging a look with his wife, Bram stood up and said, "There was a sighting of Hilda in a remote Elven village. She destroyed, or rather the Darkness destroyed, the magical playground for the children of the village and, along with it, the Fairies and Gnomes who lived within. Then she disappeared." "That's the third village she has hit. What are we going to do to protect the others?" asked Jamie, running a hand through his shoulder-length dark hair.

"I say we get on our Dragons and search for her," murmured Kenna. Jamie stared at her for a moment and then nodded. "I agree," Jamie said. Turning to see what the other leaders thought of the idea, he smiled when they all nodded. "Let's go get changed, wife. We're going hunting," he said to Kenna. They left the room and went to get ready for their ride.

After they had left the room, the remaining leaders all exchanged looks. "Are you going to tell them they can't kill Hilda? They need to know. If she dies, then the Darkness is free and harder to track," said Maia. Bram nodded and said, "Yes, I'll remind them." Ulric stood up and began to pace around the room, then he came back and said, "I agree with Kenna. We need to put all our effort into hunting the Darkness down and finding a way to contain it until our children can come home with a permanent solution." Luna stood up and joined her husband, saying, "I agree as well. Taking the conservative path hasn't yielded any solutions, and I don't like feeling helpless and useless while my children are doing all the work."

Tati and Maia exchanged a glance, and both gave a sigh. Tati said, "There may be a way we can contain Hilda with the Darkness within her. It's not guaranteed, but it might work." Maia nodded and said, "When the girls froze the Manticore, we set a containment circle around it. We checked it yesterday, and it is still there, frozen and contained. I think we can freeze Hilda and contain her within a circle." From the library door, Jamie growled, "When were you going to share this with us?" Kenna, at his side, was glaring at her parents. "You may be the rulers of this land, but it is our daughters who are being hunted by the Darkness. Anything to do with Hilda or the Darkness needs to be shared with us," Kenna said softly.

Jamie and Kenna moved further into the room. They were both dressed in their black and gold dragon-riding gear, but this time, they had weapons. Each had a pair of short swords strapped to their waists, an Elven bow and quiver over their shoulders, and a pair of high-powered binoculars on their chest. They looked fierce.

Luna spoke up, moving toward Jamie and Kenna. "Ulric and I will shift into our Wolf forms and search on the ground. We can track her from the last village she was seen in. We will transfer to that village and shift, then begin our search." Kenna smiled and said, "That's an excellent idea. We will start at that spot, but from the air." Then, Luna and Ulric disappeared, and Kenna and Jamie left the room, heading for the Dragon stables.

The remaining four exchanged worried looks. Bram said, "I feel as if we need to give the leading of Marqueria over to the next Generation. The Elven line is supposed to be Matriarchal now, and I feel it is time for me to step down and pass the crown to Kenna." Maia gave a small gasp and asked, "Really?" Bram nodded his head and gave his wife a smile. "Maybe we could go travel the realms and do some exploring?" he winked at his wife. Tati said, "Hmmm, that sounds lovely." As she turned to Otso and asked, "What do you think? Time for us to hand down the mantle of leadership to the next generation?" Otso slowly nodded his head and asked, "How would this leadership work? Our son, Jamie, is to be the next leader of the Bear Clan, but he is married to the next leader of the Elves. After marrying the Wolf Princes, our granddaughters would be next in line for all three crowns. How would the Wolf, Bear, and Elven clans take to one ruler or, in this instance, two pairs of rulers? This is a matter for another day after the Darkness is contained or destroyed, I think." The others nodded and stared into the fire with contemplative looks.

Chapter Fifty-Four

Kenna loved riding her Dragon, Nyx. She felt carefree and powerful on the back of Nyx, watching the landscape pass by below and seeing the majestic mountain peaks from this height, which was indescribable. Having her mate, Jamie, flying at her side astride his bonded Dragon, Sika, was a dream come true. Throughout her childhood, fraught with violence, neglect, and abuse, Kenna would escape into her dreams. There, she would meet her Dragon, Nyx. Nyx would soothe her wounds, calm her fears, and promise they would be together in real life someday. Kenna would always wake up with her bruises and cuts healed, causing her adoptive parents to look at each other in fear.

If not for Nyx, she didn't think she would have survived her childhood in the Mortal realm. Nyx gave a chirp, and into Kenna's mind, she said, "It does no good to dwell on the past, little one. We are to be mindful and present in the here and now. That way lies the future for you and yours." Kenna leaned down and gave Nyx a kiss on her neck and replied, "I only think of the past so that I remember how good I have it now. Don't worry, Nyx. I'm fully in the here and now. And the now means catching Hilda so that my daughters can come home."

Nyx gave a chirp and made a wide turn to circle over an area below, which was burnt, and at the center was a black crater. It was on the edge of a small village, a quarter of the size of the Castle Village. Jamie and Sika pulled ahead of them and landed quickly, yet gently, on the edge of the crater. Nyx and Kenna both laughed at the protectiveness of their mates. "We let them believe they are protecting us, little one. They need to feel useful, but even they know we are strong enough to handle whatever is thrown our way," chortled Nyx into Kenna's mind.

Nyx and Kenna landed softly next to Sika and Jamie, and then Kenna jumped off and gracefully glided to the ground, landing with knees slightly bent. "You know how to float now?" Jamie asked with a raised eyebrow. "Oh, that's just a little spell I picked up from a book in the library," Kenna replied, giving Jamie a wink. Luna and Ulric came out of the tree line near the crater and walked the perimeter until they were standing next to Jamie and Kenna. "We picked up Hilda's scent on the other side, near the trees. It continues deeper into the wooded area. We will shift and follow from the ground," Luna said as she shifted quickly into a huge black Wolf with glowing golden eyes. Kenna gasped and said, "I forgot how gorgeous your wolf is, Luna." Luna bowed her head and turned with Ulric, also in his giant Wolf form, and headed into the trees. "We should return to the skies and look from above, little one," chirped Nyx. Kenna transferred into the seat Nyx had made for her and stored her weapons in the little niche. Jamie, already mounted on Sika, blew a kiss to Kenna, and he and Sika took off in a swoop of wind. Kenna and Nyx stayed for a few more moments, staring at the black crater. "This once was a magical playground with Fairies and Gnomes living within. Hilda and the Darkness did this. They killed all those Fairies and Gnomes and destroyed this beautiful place for children," said Kenna softly, wiping a tear off her cheek. "I'm going to catch them, and I'm going to destroy them," she growled. Nyx took to the skies with Kenna looking vengeful.

Chapter Fifty-Five

Back in the Mortal realm, Ember and Noelle were seated at the dining room table with laptops open, notepads and pens at their sides. Both had earbuds in, listening to music as they worked. They had been up since 6 AM searching for any information regarding Dragon Shifters without any luck so far. "This is so frustrating. Everything that comes up in my searches is in reference to those stupid romance books or book series about Dragon Shifters. Ugh!" grumbled Ember as she took out her earbuds, then stretched and yawned. She looked at the clock on her laptop and gasped. "It's eight already. No wonder I feel cranky. I'm hungry. Let's take a break and grab some breakfast," Ember said to her sister as she closed her laptop and hurried toward the Kitchen.

Noelle removed her earbuds, gave a huge sigh, and stood up. She stretched and then reached down to close her laptop but stopped when she saw the note scribbled across the bottom of her notepad. "Ember!! Come here!!" she yelled, picking up the notepad; she looked closer at what was scribbled across the bottom. When Ember quickly returned from the kitchen, Noelle asked, "Did you write this?" Ember shook her head and read it. Then she gasped, and she read it out loud, "To find the Dragon that is not a Dragon, you must start in the land of the boiling mud." The girls stared at each other, amazed, and then Noelle yelled, "Hey, Guys! Come here!!" Ember grinned at her, Noelle smiled back, and the two waited.

Tai, Kai, Blaze, and Alaric walked into the dining room, and Ember handed them the notepad without saying a word. They read it, and then Tai read it out loud again. They looked up at the girls with faces full of confusion, Blaze asking, "What does this mean?" Ember grinned and said, "Well, we think it means Yellowstone National Park, but the major deal is….neither Noelle nor I wrote that. It just appeared on the notepad."

The four shifters looked at the girls, speechless for once. Then, Tai smiled at them and asked, "Soooo, road trip?" "Yes!! I was hoping you'd say that. Ember, come on. Let's go get ready. Blaze and Alaric, we're going on a road trip to one of the most awesome places in this state. Yellowstone National Park," said Noelle. Then she grabbed Blaze's hand and pulled him towards the stairs to get ready. Alaric was watching Ember and asked, "What do I need to bring?" Ember smiled and said, "Come on. I'll show you." Then, the two teens followed the other two upstairs.

Tai and Kai smiled at each other, and Kai said, "I always enjoy going through the Park. It's one of the few places where we can be in the wilderness and have entertainment by watching the stupid things tourists do." Tai grinned at him and asked, "Remember that one year when the lady walked up to pet the wild bull, Elk? The Elk that was in a rut? Then he chased her all the way to her car? Yeah, she got lucky on that one." The two brothers laughed for a few moments, and then Tai said, "Well, let's get the Sequoia packed. Road snacks, pillow, drinks coming up."

Chapter Fifty-Six

After an almost two-hour drive on the interstate to Livingston and then another hour driven on the secondary road to Gardiner, the six of them finally arrived at the North Entrance of the Yellowstone National Park. "We can drive through to Cook City from Mammoth Hot Springs, but that's the only road we can drive on during Winter. We could go by snow coach to Old Faithful Geyser and stay at the Lodge. Hopefully, they have openings less than two weeks before Christmas. Otherwise, we will be traveling about in the dark and by foot," said Ember. Kai grinned at Ember and said, "It's all been arranged. I did it online before we left. We park over there and meet the snow coach in a little over an hour. That gives us some time to look around here."

Tai parked the SUV, and they all piled out, heading to the information signs next to the parking lot. "This is beautiful and all, but how are we going to find information on the Dragon that isn't a Dragon? This Park is huge, and we don't even know what we're looking for," said Alaric, looking around and lifting his head to sniff the air. "Also, who the Hell snuck in the house and wrote that note? The writing was old-fashioned and swirly, almost calligraphy. We didn't even look around to see who did it," grumbled Blaze. Tai gave a short laugh and said, "Relax, boys. Kai and I did a sweep around, and there was no one in the house. We believe the note was made by magic. Who do we know around us who contains magic besides Noelle and Ember?" There was silence for a few moments, and then Noelle exclaimed, "The Dryad of the Tree!" The Bear brothers nodded and grinned at the teens.

"So you think the Dryad is helping us find the Dragon...or the not-a-Dragon person?" asked Ember, then nodded and said, "Makes sense." Tai began to walk towards the Mammoth Terraces Trail boardwalk leading to the Mammoth Hot Springs Terraces. "Come on. Let's stretch our legs before the four-hour ride into the interior of the Park. Plus, this is an interesting hydrothermal feature," Tai said to the group. They all followed him, backpacks on. "Wow, that's some strong rotten egg smell," said Blaze, grimacing. "Yeah, it's from the sulfur content in the hot springs," replied Noelle. They walked up the trail leading to Devil's Thumb, which is the hot spring that is actively building up the travertine terraces. When they got there, they were silent for a time, watching the steam rise from the earth and the water flow down the colorful deposits.

A small herd of Elk was walking across the terraces, pawing at the ground and lapping up the warm water. Ice crystals had formed on their coats, giving them a sparkle. The lead cow stopped and stared at the six of them, raised her nose into the air to sniff, and then stomped and gave a loud bark. At that, the entire herd ambled quickly away, out of sight in seconds. "Well, I guess they scented us and took us for predators," grumbled Ember, and, turning to Tai, asked,

"Is it because we shifted? Noelle and I used to be able to watch herds for hours, but they didn't know we were there." Tai nodded and said, "Probably. Your bear scent is stronger after the shifting, plus there are four Bear and two Wolves here."

There was a gasp, and a high voice asked, "There are four bears and two wolves up here?! Where?!" The six of them quickly turned around, and there stood a couple who were obviously not from a cold region and were obviously tourists. She was decked out in a super puffy purple coat with fur lining the hood, matching purple ski pants, and knee-high fur boots. She had on a purple pair of sunglasses and carried a large purple handbag. He was dressed in a red one-piece snow suit with a fur-lined hood, matching red puffy boots, and red sunglasses. They removed their glasses and waited expectantly for an answer.

"Oh, we just said, can you imagine if there were bears and wolves here with the elk?" said Ember with a smile. The couple just stared at them for a few seconds and then smiled and nodded. "Isn't it lovely here?" gushed the woman, continuing on with, "I'm Annabelle, and this is my husband Brad." Ember murmured, "Of course you are." Annabelle asks, "Excuse me?" Ember spoke louder and said, "How are you?" "Oh...yes, we're fine. Are you all related? Such a difference in coloring." Noelle gave a quiet gasp, glaring at the woman, and said, "Seriously?" Then she turned and grabbed Blaze's hand, pulling him in the direction of the boardwalk. "Come on. We need to leave now," she called over her shoulder to the others in her group.

Tai and Kai stared down the couple, not taking their eyes off them. Ember and Alaric followed Blaze and Noelle, and when they were twenty yards away, Tai turned to the couple and growled, "That was an extremely rude question. Learn some manners before the next person teaches you some." Then, he and Kai moved to follow the teens down the boardwalk.

When they reached the area for passengers going into the interior of the Park, a small line was forming at the Snowcoach. "Let's go get in line; it's almost time to check in," said Kai as he picked up his backpack. The four teens followed the brothers to the check-in line. It was going to be a four-hour ride into Yellowstone's interior, so after they checked in, everyone used the facilities. By the time they were assembled back near the snow coach, it was time to board and leave. Part of the drive was going to be in the dark due to the early sunsets, but that was okay with the six traveling together. There were four other travelers, two couples, who were seated in the front when the six got on, one of those couples being Brad and Annabelle, of course. Or the 'purple and red nightmares' as Ember had named them. They moved to the back and made sure there was a row of seats between them and the two couples.

The next four hours were spent looking at the spectacular Winter scenery and wild animals and talking low about how they were going to search for the Dragon. The agreed-upon method was to sneak out at night and have Noelle and Ember transfer them to spots they'd been to with their parents in the past. Many of these were off the beaten path and had to be hiked into, ensuring that they wouldn't run into any humans while searching.

When the slowcoach arrived at the Old Faithful Snow Lodge, the passengers quickly unloaded and entered the lobby to check into their rooms. It was a lovely building made out of large timber. While looking rustic, it was very modern and had everything a vacationer would need. The six travelers weren't interested in any of this, as they were in a hurry to get out and search for signs of the Dragon. After they were checked into their rooms, they headed up to leave their backpacks and refresh before going to dinner. After they ate, the plan was to transfer from one of their rooms to the furthest point the girls had been in the Park. Blaze gave one of his keys to Noelle, Ember gave one of her keys to Alaric, and Tai and Kai shared a two-bedroom.

On their way down to the restaurant, Ember was going on about her room. "It's so charming. I love the warm wood accents, and the view from the window is stunning. What is your log home like, Alaric?" she asked Alaric quietly. Alaric smiled softly and said, "It is warm and inviting, with log walls, giant stone fireplaces, and huge windows that allow the sun to shine in. My mom has brought the outside in by having plants growing everywhere." Ember, holding his arm and walking at his side, said, "Oh, that sounds lovely. We flew over your home, and both Noelle and I said we could live there." They got to the entrance of the restaurant and were seated immediately.

After they had all placed their orders and the drinks were brought to the table, they began to speak in low voices so the surrounding diners wouldn't overhear what was being said. "I think we should be able to get to Mount Sheridan and Mount Hancock tonight. Then tomorrow, we can check Table Mountain and the Tower Falls area," Noelle said softly. Tai nodded and said, "What about around here, Old Faithful area?" Ember shrugged and said, "It's always so crowded here. Don't you think someone would have noticed a Dragon?" Tai raised an eyebrow and said, "Yes, but there are areas around here one could hide." Ember grinned at Tai and said, "We can spend tomorrow checking around here, then. If we don't find anything tonight, that is." They were interrupted by the waiter bringing their food.

The six started to eat, realizing how hungry they actually were. After a few moments of silence with just the sounds of eating and utensils scraping, Ember nudged Tai with her elbow and, not looking up from her plate, whispered, "The nightmare couple from the snow coach is paying us way too much attention." Tai, careful not to look up, took another bite and nodded his head. "Yes, I've been watching them. I felt something was off on the coach, and then they watched us as we went to our rooms," he said, picking up his beer, taking a drink, and looking around the room as if admiring it. Noelle and Ember were looking at each other, using their mind-link to communicate. Noelle gave a slight nod and leaned close to Blaze, whispering to him. Blaze kissed her on the forehead and nodded. Tai and Kai used their mind link, so Kai was aware of this, too. Ember turned to Alaric, but he met her eyes and gave a little nod. The six continued to eat, and when they were finished, the waiter came over to give them the bill. Tai signed it and charged it to the room. The six of them stood as one and quickly moved towards the exit.

As they neared the hotel lobby, the couple got up from their table but were called back to sign their bill before they could follow them. And follow them they did, but weren't fast enough. "Let's go outside and see the geyser erupt at night," said Ember rather loudly. As if they had planned it, they headed for the exit at a fast walk and left the hotel, walking quickly around the building in the opposite direction from the Old Faithful geyser. Once they were out of sight of the entrance to the hotel, Tai said, "Now, girls, we need to transfer now." When all of them had grabbed hands, they disappeared.

Chapter Fifty-Seven

The six reappeared at the base of a large mountain in deep snow. Tai said, "Okay, time to shift." Grinning at each other, they all shifted. If it weren't for their sheer massive sizes, the bears and the wolves would have fit right in. Of course, Ember and Noelle would have stuck out like a white pearl on a black sand beach. They all started up the mountain, noses lifted or pressed in the snow, trying to catch a scent. It was Tai's and Kai's idea to shift and search as their Bear and Wolf forms, saying the snow was too deep in the backcountry and they could cover more ground. They proved to be correct.

The mountain was covered in a matter of a couple of hours after they had split up into three groups. Tai and Kai, Blaze and Noelle, and Ember and Alaric searched together in groups of two. If anyone had happened upon them, they would have been frightened by their size or amazed at their beauty. A huge black wolf with glowing gold eyes walking through the wilderness with a shimmering silver white bear with glowing green eyes was quite a sight, let alone two sets. 'Yeah, it's a good thing we haven't seen anyone,' Ember thought to herself as she ran through the deep snow with little effort, enjoying the freedom of being in her Bear form, with Alaric in his Wolf form running at her side.

Tai jumped out in front of them in his immense Bear form and gave a growl, herding them back down the mountain. It was a race down the steep side of the mountain, and not surprisingly, the two wolves won. At the end of the race and back where they had started, the two wolves raised their noses towards the sky and let out long, melodious howls. It sounded like a symphony when the wolves within the park joined in. The girls, who had already shifted back to their human form, had tears in their eyes as they listened to the hauntingly beautiful sounds.

When the song ended, Blaze and Alaric shifted back and had huge grins on their faces. "We know where to go. We know where the Dragon that isn't a Dragon has been," Alaric said, grabbing Ember's hand. "How? Where?" asked Ember. Blaze said, "The Park wolves told us to look behind the Falls. The Lower Yellowstone River Falls, to be more exact. The wolves said they had seen a large white creature flying to the falls and disappearing. They said there is a hidden cave behind the falls." "We can transfer us right there. It was one of our favorite spots to sit and enjoy the beauty, but it drops over 300 feet. Do we start at the top or the bottom?" asked Noelle.

Tai and Kai exchanged a glance and, at the same time, said, "Bottom." Ember raised an eyebrow and asked, "Why?" Kai said, "Easier to climb up than to climb down." "Oh, yeah. This is going to suck," murmured Ember. They all grabbed hands and disappeared, reappearing below the

308-foot waterfall. They had appeared next to the river below the falls, so they had to walk about one hundred yards before they could start climbing. It was icy and snow-covered, and the falls were mostly frozen. "How are we going to get behind the falls? It's frozen," asked Noelle. Tai said, "There's a faint trail if you look closely to the right of the base. We'll start there."

The six of them began the treacherous walk to the right of the falls, slipping and sliding until Noelle stopped and said, "Nope! Enough. Come here." Ember joined hands with Noelle, and they began to glow softly. After a few moments, there was a melted path to the base of the falls. "You're going to have to put it back the way it was when we leave," Kai told the girls, who nodded but continued walking on the now dirt path.

When they reached the spot where the trail began, Noelle gasped. "The trail goes behind the falls!" she exclaimed. Tai went first, followed by the teens and Kai. They walked up the trail and followed it behind the falls into a world of ice. It looked as if the trail had melted into the ice. Following it further in, it opened up into a large cave that looked to go into the mountain 200 feet.

"Do you smell that?" cried Ember excitedly. Everyone nodded, and Noelle waved her hand, and the entire cave lit up with a soft glowing light. "Oh, my Goddess," breathed Noelle. On the walls of the cave were drawings and paintings. They showed humans transitioning into Dragons and back again. "These are old, very old," said Tai, reaching out and tracing a drawing of a small boy changing into a small Dragon. "This is a family," breathed Kai. As they looked around, they discovered that the drawings were indeed of a family of Dragon Shifters. Something unheard of in Marqueria.

"Look, the drawings change over here. The family is gone, and the boy is alone," said Alaric quietly, his voice somber. "Do you think this is our Dragon that isn't a Dragon?" asked Ember, looking around at the group. "I think so. Look here. The boy changes into a white dragon," said Noelle. "There doesn't appear to be anyone living in this cave now. In fact, I don't think anyone has been here for a couple of years," said Kai, slowly walking around and occasionally sniffing the air. Tai agreed, saying, "I believe you're correct. At least we now know we're dealing with a shapeshifting Dragon, something I never thought I'd see."

"I wonder what happened to separate him from his family? Why was he left alone?" murmured Ember as she ran a finger over one of the last pictures drawn. It was of the boy in this cave, drawing on the walls. Alone. "He must be so lonely," she whispered. Noelle walked to her sister and wrapped an arm around her shoulder, pulling her in close. "I can only imagine how lonely it must be for him. Even with mom and dad away, we have each other," Noelle said softly, leaning over and kissing her sister's head. Ember nodded and laid her head on Noelle's shoulder.

"Let's head back to the Lodge. I don't think we need to look around here any longer. We can search around Butte and our house. Look for all the hidden places where he can disappear and blend in," said Noelle, turning towards the entrance of the cave. "Let's put the melted path back to normal, and then we can transfer while we're still in the cave," said Ember. "Yeah, I feel exposed out there for some reason," said Noelle. The girls joined hands, closed their eyes for a few seconds, and glowed briefly. Then, Ember walked to the entrance of the cave, peeked out, and said, "It looks as if we were never here. Let's go back to the Lodge." Tai and Kai exchanged a glance, and Kai said, "Take us back to your room. Then Tai and I can do some sleuthing around and see why those two were so interested in us."

Chapter Fifty-Eight

The six of them reappeared in Noelle's room, and Tai and Kai immediately left. The four teens decided to hang out in the bedroom, play The Isle on their laptops, and drink hot chocolate. "Why do you think that couple was so interested in us? How did they get so close to us at Mammoth without our hearing them?" asked Ember, taking a sip of her hot chocolate. "I don't know, but they were extremely rude, and I didn't like the way they invaded my personal space," replied Noelle. "I wonder what happened to the boy's parents," murmured Ember, looking up from her laptop with a frown. "That's something we will find out when we find him," Noelle replied.

As Noelle finished talking, there was a knock at their door. They all looked at each other. Then Blaze got up, went to the door, and asked, "Who is it?" "It's Tai and Kai, Blaze. Open the door, please," Tai's voice from the other side of the door sounded strange. The teens moved quickly. Blaze and Alaric had their weapons in hand, and the girls stood at the ready. Ember moved to the door and unlocked it, then moved back as she opened it. Tai and Ka came through the door one at a time, but right behind them were the couple, Brad and Annabelle, both holding handguns pointed at Tai and Kai. The teens moved to the other side of the room, putting the bed between them, Ember and Noelle holding hands. Tai met their eyes and gave a wink.

Keeping her weapon aimed at the two Bear brothers, Annabelle closed the door and locked it. "Now, isn't this cozy?" she asked in a voice very different from the one she used at Mammoth. This voice was low and firm, with a growly bass. "You two, put your weapons down on the bed now," she said to Blaze and Alaric. They looked to Tai and Kai, who both nodded. "What is going on?" asked Ember while glaring at the two holding the guns. "You're not afraid, are you? Interesting," replied Brad. "Put the gun down, and I'll show you how unafraid I am," Ember growled. "Oh, brave. Stupid but brave. You'll make a nice addition to our collection," Annabelle laughingly crowed. "What collection?" asked Noelle.

"Our Were collection. We know you're Shifters and that you're looking for Dragon shifters. Hilda started our little project years ago after she married that rich husband of hers. Your family was never on the radar until she found out your mom mated with a Shifter, and you two were made. We've been watching you for months," Annabelle said with a cold smile, then she laughed and continued, "Oh, and forget about finding another Dragon Shifter. We got the only two in existence in our facility in Wyoming."

Unbeknownst to Annabelle and Brad, Noelle and Ember had been communicating via their mind-link. With lightning-quick speed, Annabelle and Brad were disarmed and encased in a soundproof binding dome. Inside the dome, the two of them were banging their fists on the walls, trying to find a way out. Tai, Kai, Blaze, Alaric, and the girls stood and watched them yell obvious profanities at them, causing the six to laugh.

With floating hair and glowing skin, the girls removed the clips from the handguns and made sure they were completely unloaded before they froze and shattered them into thousands of tiny pieces. The girls stood in front of Brad and Annabelle, saying nothing, just staring with their fiery green and gold eyes. For the first time, Brad and Annabelle became still, and a hint of fear showed on their faces. Ember turned her head and asked Tai and Kai, "What should we do with them? We don't need them anymore. Noelle and I looked into their minds, and we know where their horrible facility is located."

Tai and Kai had completely emotionless expressions, and they, too, were staring at the two in the dome. Tai shrugged and said, "I think we should kill them, but it's not my call." All eyes turned to the girls as they continued to glow. Ember and Noelle looked at each other for a few moments, and then they both smiled. It was a rather chilling smile but fitting under the circumstances. "We think they need to be transferred somewhere far, far away with only the items they possess now. Oh, minus the cell phones and any other electronics they carry," murmured Noelle in a low voice, still staring at the couple coldly.

"Where have you been that is far away, and no one will find them for a while?" asked Kai. The girls smiled, and it sent a chill down Kai's back. "The Bering Land Bridge Preserve in Northwest Alaska," the girls said together, turning their glowing eyes to look at Brad and Annabelle again. Tai burst out laughing and said, "That's a fitting punishment, but you do realize they will die out there? Right? You're okay with sending them to their deaths?"

He watched the girls closely as they turned to him, anger causing gold sparks to shoot out of their eyes. "They have been kidnapping Shifters. They have been performing experiments on these Shifters. This is as the Goddess commands, and we are just fine with it," Noelle said. "We've seen inside their minds. They have no redeeming qualities, none. All they think about is money. How much could they get for us, what would they buy with it, and if they could get into Marqueria and get more shifters? They know about Marqueria and cannot be allowed to live," Ember growled. Noelle turned towards the dome again, glared at Brad, and growled, "And I've seen inside his mind. I've seen what he wants to do to Ember and me."

Tai and Kai became eerily still. Blaze and Alaric stepped closer to the dome, low growls emanating from their throats. Their eyes glowed golden, and the energy coming off them was lethal. Brad and Annabelle shrank back, sheer terror showing on their faces. Tai and Kai move to stand next to Blaze and Alaric. Annabelle fell to her knees, covering her head with her arms and sobbing. Brad moved as far away from the four Weres as he could, bumping into the wall behind him. Tai growled low in his throat, "You better send them now before this room looks like a bloodbath. We are having a hard time containing our animal sides."

Ember and Noelle stood facing each other, palms touching. Their hair floated softly around their heads, and their skin gave off a silvery white glow. They began to chant.

This time of darkness, these malevolent souls
To a cold, barren land, we banish those.
By the light of the Moon and the strength of will
We invoke the elements to fulfill.
With Earth, Air, Fire, and Water so bold.
No harm shall they bring, no more pain they'll sow
In the cold, barren land, where they must go.
To the cold, barren land, where they shall dwell
Locked away in icy chains, their power quelled.

Silvery white ropes wound around Brad and Annabelle's wrists and ankles, lifting them into a standing position, arms and legs spread. Noelle and Ember faced the dome and pushed their hands toward the couple in the dome. With a whoosh sound, Brad and Annabelle and the dome were gone. "They will never be found," whispered Noelle. "Where did you send them?" asked Blaze, coming to Noelle and pulling her into his arms. She laid her head on his chest and said, "Somewhere hidden." "How do you know they won't be found?" asked Tai, watching as Alaric gathered Ember into his arms and sat on the couch, holding her close, his face buried in her mass of cinnamon curls. Ember spoke up now, saying very softly, "Because we left the dome on them and the magic ropes and put them behind the waterfall in the hidden cave. We placed a spell upon the opening that will prevent anyone from seeing it as a cave." Tai and Kai both nodded in approval.

Blaze led Noelle to the bed and tucked her under the covers, then climbed in next to her and wrapped his arms around her. Alaric and Ember were on the couch, he on his back, and she was lying half on him and sound asleep already.

Alaric looked up at Tai and Kai and asked, "Will you stay in this room with us tonight?" They both nodded, Kai saying, "I will go get our bedding. I'll be right back." He quickly left the room and returned within a few minutes, as his room was right across the hall. Tossing a couple of pillows and blankets to Tai, he left again and came back with more. Then he closed and double-locked the door, wedging a chair up under the door knob. He made his bed right near the door, and Tai made his bed under the window. It took a long time for either of them to fall asleep.

Chapter Fifty-Nine

The next morning, Tai, Kai, Blaze, and Alaric were carting trays of breakfast to the room they had shared during the night. While the guys went down to the dining room, the girls cleaned up the room, folded the blankets, and packed all their backpacks. By the time the four Weres were back, Ember and Noelle were ready to go, but smelling the food on the trays triggered their appetite, so they decided to eat before getting on the snow coach.

There was a subdued atmosphere in the room, and nobody wanted to break the silence. Tai had suggested to the other three males that maybe they should let Ember and Noelle take the lead on how much they wanted to talk about the night before. They all agreed it was probably best that way. When the girls had polished off two cups of coffee each and most of the pastries, Ember stood up and said, "So. Is it going to continue to be this awkward silence, or are we going to discuss what happened last night?" Alaric smiled and said, "We were waiting on your lead. What would you like to talk about?" Ember returned his smile and said, "Going to the facility in Wyoming and rescuing the Weres they have been kidnapping and holding." Noelle stood up and said, "Yep.

Looks like we're taking another road trip. Do we have all the weapons we need, or should we transfer back to the house and grab some more?"

Tai shook his head, and Kai said, "We have enough. There's a hidden compartment in the Sequoia, which we filled with weapons of all kinds. Your dad is a planner, isn't he?" Noelle grinned and said, "He is. All the vehicles have hidden compartments. I just forgot about them." "What's the plan?" asked Blaze, picking up his and Noelle's backpacks. Ember and Noelle exchanged a small smile and said, "We need to drive back to Livingston and get on the Interstate. From there, we will go through Billings and turn down towards Sheridan, Wyoming. It's going to be a long drive, and we will have to stay in Sheridan for the night." Ember said, "Which is a good thing because they have a breakfast cafe that is so good." Noelle laughed and said, "It's always about the food, isn't it, sis?" Ember gave her sister a wink and then went to take her backpack from Alaric.

Following Tai, they left the room with Kai behind them. When they got to the snow coach loading area, there was a commotion. Tai stopped one of the workers who was walking past and asked, "What's going on? Is there something wrong with the coach?" The employee shook his head and said, "No, it will leave on time. We just have a couple of missing guests. They haven't been seen since last night at dinner." "Oh, no. Who is missing?" asked Ember, her expression worried. "The couple who rode the snow coach with you, Brad and Annabelle. They didn't check out and haven't checked in for the coach. We're checking their room now," the employee said before hurrying up the stairs.

"Shall we get on and settled while they continue their search?" Tai asked the group. They all nodded and walked over to the Coach. There was an employee standing next to it with a clipboard. "Are you the Tai Mathan party?" the employee asked. Tai nodded and said, "Yes, we are. Are we allowed to get on, or do we need to wait for the rest?" The employee said, "You all can load up. We aren't waiting for anyone else. We have a schedule to keep. As soon as you are in your seats, the driver will begin your trip back to Mammoth." "Excellent," said Tai and motioned for the other five to get in the snow coach. Even though they were the only passengers, they still sat in the back, taking up the last two rows.

When they were all seated, the driver put the coach in gear and left the Lodge. Ember said to Tai and Kai, "I didn't even think about your last name. Is it something you chose when you came to the Mortal realm?" Kai nodded and said, "We needed documents, and they needed last names, so we picked one with personal meaning. Mathan means 'Bear' in Scottish." Ember nodded and said, "I think that's what my dad did, too. Our last name is Alexander. It means protector."

"We don't use last names like that in Marqueria," said Blaze. "Yeah, we just have our given names and our Clans," said Alaric. "How do you say it then? Your names and Clans?" asked Ember. Alaric put his arm around her shoulder and pulled her close to his side, then said, "Prince Alaric of the Wolf Clan. You would be...huh, you're of two, that's right. Princess Ember of the Elf and Bear Clan. No, wait. It's going to be Princess Ember of the Elf, Bear, and

Wolf Clans." This got the attention of Tai, Kai, and Blaze. They all looked at each other with looks of surprise. "What?" demanded Ember.

Tai had turned around and was looking at the four teens sitting behind him, as was Kai. Kai said, "Never in the history of Marqueria has there been one ruler of the Clans. When your mom steps down, it will fall to you two as the female Elves chosen by the Goddess. But you are also in line to be the leaders of the Bear, and with your mating to Blaze and Alaric, the Wolf clan becomes yours as well." "But, would Ulrika become the Wolf ruler and Noelle become the Elf and Bear? I'm the younger daughter," said Ember. Tai shook his head and said, "The Wolf and Bear Clans are ruled by a committee. That is to say, if there are siblings, then the siblings rule together. The Elven line has always been the son, no matter how many children are born. But Elves so rarely give birth; there was never an issue until Hilda was born. But you, Noelle, Blaze, and Alaric will be leaders of all three Clans when it is your time to take over."

The four teens were silent for a while, and then Ember said, "We have a long time before that happens and a lot to accomplish before we even turn sixteen and seventeen next month." Noelle nodded, yawned, and said, "Speaking of which, we need to contact our parents and let them know what happened here." "Let's wait until we are in our own vehicle. Mammoth is just a couple hours away," murmured Tai, glancing around at the driver and tour guide, both of whom were talking quietly between themselves. "That's okay. I need a quick nap anyway," yawned Ember. She then cuddled up to Alaric, laying her head on his shoulder and closing her eyes. She was asleep within seconds. Surprised, Tai looked over at Noelle, who was asleep as well, head resting on Blaze's shoulder. "I think yesterday and last night wiped them out. It's as if they need to recharge," whispered Kai. Nodding, Tai turned around and faced the front. Kai did as well, and soon, all four teens were asleep.

Chapter Sixty

Kenna, far above the trees of Marqueria on her Dragon, Nyx, was eyeing the space between the trees intensely. She was hunting Hilda and the Darkness again. She and Jamie had taken to the skies every day for the past couple of weeks, trying to prevent another tragedy at the remaining magical playgrounds of the outlying villages. They had stationed guards from each Clan at the remaining sites, and so far, there had been no more attacks. So, while Luna and Ulric searched the ground, Jamie and Kenna searched from the sky.

Nyx was flying towards the Grove and where the Tree once stood. It had disappeared on the day Noelle and Ember had gone through the Tree with Blaze, Alaric, Tai, and Kai. It hurt to think about not being able to physically hold her daughters. The ache of missing them was too much to bear at times, and she wouldn't be able to do her duties without Jamie to keep her sane. She hadn't heard from them in a few days and was feeling itchy with anxiety.

Nyx gave a chuff and, using their mind link, said, "Little one, it does no good to worry. Your younglings are well protected. Not only by the four Weres but by their own powerful magical abilities. You will see your daughters again soon, little Elf." Kenna sighed and said, "I hear what you're saying, Nyx, but it doesn't help that I'm missing them. The Tree is missing, and I don't have access to our girls to ensure they are doing well. It creates a physical ache, this longing to hold them." Nyx gave a chuff and chirp and purred, "I know, little one. All will work out as it is meant to, and I promise you will be reunited with your daughters."

Jamie and Sika were flying in front of Kenna and Nyx, although slightly lower. Jamie used his mind-link to tell Kenna of the movement below them within the Grove. Nyx and Sika made a sudden turn and dive, heading to the Grove. Despite the speed of their descent, they landed lightly. Jumping off and gliding quickly to the ground, Kenna joined Jamie, and together, they entered the Grove on high alert.

Standing next to where the Tree used to reside was the Darkness, or rather Hilda, with the Darkness trapped within her. Hilda turned towards Jamie and Kenna, but she looked different from the last time Kenna saw her. Now, she had long jet-black hair, black lips, and eyes, and her long nails were black as well. There were black veins visible on her bare arms and exposed neck and face. There was a black fog swirling around her feet and legs, with tendrils undulating and wrapping around her body. Hilda, with The Darkness in complete control, stood still and watched as Jamie and Kenna walked into the Grove. "What have you done with the Tree?" the Darkness asked in a layered, echoey low voice. His voice made Kenna shudder with revulsion on the inside. Kenna didn't show what she was feeling; she knew she needed to remain neutral and not allow her emotions to be detected by the Darkness. 'Show no weakness,' she thought to herself.

Kenna chuckled softly, raised an eyebrow, and said, "We have done nothing with the Tree. Maybe the Goddess has removed it." The Darkness gave a chilling laugh and said, "I see you've lost none of your spunk. I wonder if you will be so when I've taken your daughters over? Hmmm. I do look forward to tasting their magic." Taking a step forward, Jamie growled, "You will never get the chance to find out." The Darkness turned its gaze to Jamie and said, "The Bear speaks. Amazing that an animal has such abilities as speech. Do you know that Hilda has been collecting shifters in the Mortal world since she found herself that rich husband? He never questioned all the trips she took alone, never asked where she went or who she was meeting. Pathetic human. Ahhh, I see you didn't know about the shifters. Did you even realize there were shifters in the Mortal world? No? Well, Hilda knew, and she hunted them down with the help of her husband's money. You see, she feels as I do when it comes to animals because make no mistake; that is all shifters are. Animals. Yes, she has a facility in the wilds of Wyoming, which holds many different species of shifters. Did you know she has the only two Dragon shifters in existence? Her little zoo holds Bears and Wolves, too. Do you know what they do to the shifters there? Anything and everything they want to."

While it was talking, The Darkness had been watching Jamie and Kenna closely, trying to detect any signs of emotions. The only thing it found was surprise at the knowledge of the other shifters and the facility. Kenna and Jamie had mind-linked with their Dragons while the Darkness had been speaking. All of a sudden, everything happened at once. They both dropped to the ground. At almost the same time, Sika and Nyx flew behind them, and each shot a torrent of scorching flames at the Darkness. But at the exact moment that the Dragons blew their flames, the Darkness shot a dark ray, which hit Jamie square in the chest as he was starting to drop. Jamie fell to the ground, still. The inferno engulfed the Darkness in an intense, fiery brilliance. As the Dragons swooped back up into the sky, Kenna quickly jumped up. Jamie remained still on the ground, and Kenna began to glow brightly in silver and white. Engulfed in flames, the Darkness screamed in agony and rage. Kenna's power was ready when and if it decided to attack, but with one last enraged scream, the Darkness disappeared, along with the Dragons' fire.

Kenna ran to Jamie and put her hands on his chest, sending silver-white light into his body. As she was healing Jamie, the scorched, blackened areas where the fire had torched the earth were slowing healing. The snow-covered trees, grass, and flowers return to their original state. Jamie began groaning, and Kenna stopped glowing, moving her hands to his face. "Jamie, are you okay? Please be okay! You can't leave me. Don't you dare leave me alone! Wake up!" Kenna cried, tears streaming down her face. Jamie opened his golden eyes, meeting Kenna's tear-filled dark green ones. "I'm okay, wife. I would never leave you," he croaked, his voice rough and hoarse.

Jamie sat up and pulled his shirt up to look at his chest and stomach. There was a dark purple and blue bruise forming on his chest, right in the middle. "Ouch. That really hurts," Jamie groaned. Sika said, "It's a good thing you had your special riding gear on; otherwise, you'd be dead. Your riding gear is spelled to protect you against spells from the Darkness." Sika and Nyx had landed softly behind Jamie and Kenna, chirping and chuffing. Nyx chuffed and said, "The Darkness is not destroyed, only badly injured. It will take time for it to heal itself; how much we do not know. As long as the Darkness is trapped within Hilda's body, it is vulnerable and easier to fight." Giving a loud chuff, Sika said in his low baritone, "Yes, but this will also make it more dangerous. It will become more hidden and harder to track, knowing It is so vulnerable."

Kneeling next to Jamie, Kenna asked him, "Are you sure you're okay? Is anything broken?" "I think my ribs were broken and my lungs punctured, but you healed all of it. Now it just hurts a little," Jamie replied, kissing her gently on the mouth. Kenna nodded and then looked at the Dragons quietly before asking them, "Did you know there were Dragon shifters living in the Mortal world?" Jamie, too, had been watching the Dragons closely and said, "Yes, this is a question I'm very interested in hearing the answer to." Nyx gave a chortle and said, "Calm, little ones. We hide nothing from our Bonded Riders. No, we did not know of the Dragon Shifters. However, there is a myth pertaining to Dragon Shifters and the Spirit Dragon. We believed it to be just that, a myth." Kenna and Jamie both nodded their heads, and then Jamie asked, "What can we do about the facility in Wyoming? We need to get back to the Mortal Realm and rescue the Shifters being held there."

"That is currently being taken care of by those whose destiny it is," said a melodious voice from the area where the Tree had been. Startled, Jamie and Kenna turned towards the voice and discovered the Dryad of the Tree standing where the Tree usually stood. She glided gracefully over to Jamie and Kenna, reverently nodding her head to the two Dragons, who, in turn, bowed their heads to her. When she reached the couple, she said, "Your daughters and the four Were males are on their way now to the facility in Wyoming. They will be rescuing the shifters there and bringing the ones who are still living here through the Tree when it is time. As for the Dragon Shifters, there is more to that story than I am able to tell you at this time."

Kenna stared at the Dryad for a few moments and then asked, "Will you return the Tree so that we might join them and help?" The Dryad slowly shook her head, her large swirling eyes showing her regret; she said, "I'm sorry, Princess Kenna. That is something I cannot do. The Tree must remain hidden until the Darkness has been dealt with. While I don't get many visions, the ones that I do receive always come to pass. For the safety of the Mortal realm and the protection of Marqueria, this is non-negotiable." "What did you see?" asked Kenna, a frown etched between her eyebrows.

The Dryad moved closer to Kenna and placed a long, graceful hand on her cheek. Kenna felt a warmth seeping into her skin, and then images filled her head, images so frightening and devastating that tears began to roll down her cheeks. "No! Please, no," Kenna whispered. The Dryad removed her hand from Kenna's left cheek and placed her other hand on Kenna's right cheek. Kenna let out a gasp and closed her eyes. His golden eyes glowing, Jamie growled softly, "Please stop now." The Dryad reached out her hand

and placed it on Jamie's cheek, showing him what Kenna was seeing. "That is why you must remain here and allow your daughters and their companions to complete their task," the Dryad said softly, removing her hands from the couple's cheeks.

"What did you see the first time she put her hand on you?" Jamie asked Kenna. Kenna looked at Jamie with wide, devastated, tear-filled eyes. "I saw the end of our worlds. The death of everything and everyone we love," whispered Kenna. She moved into Jamie's arms and buried her nose in his chest, breathing deeply of his scent, calming herself. The Dryad said, "The first vision was what would happen if the Tree remained in Marqueria and the Darkness found Its way through. The second vision showed the way things are now, with the Tree hidden and your daughters on the other side of it. Princess Kenna, you and Prince Jamie must remain here and contain the Darkness as best you can until your daughters have completed their quest in the Mortal world. It is the way it has to be."

"I must return to the Mortal realm. I am needed there. Have faith in the strength of your daughters and the love they have for you. They will succeed and return to you. But fair warning, the Darkness won't be down for long. As strong as Dragon Fire is, it will not kill the Darkness or destroy Hilda's body completely. It is but a stopgap until the true weapon is delivered," the Dryad said in her sweet, melodious voice. The Dryad of the Tree drifted gracefully to the spot where the Tree originally stood; then, she faded away.

Turning to Nyx, Kenna said, "Would you please share with us the myth of the Spirit Dragon?" Nyx gave a chuff and said, "Yes, little one. Through our mind-link, I too saw what the Dryad's visions contained." In his low baritone voice, Sika said, "The Spirit Dragon myth has been passed down through generations upon generations. We Dragons are very long-lived, so this myth is ancient. According to the myth, the white Spirit Dragon is powerful and wise and embodies purity and all that is good. It is said to reside in a hidden realm and is believed to possess incredible magical abilities. It is also revered as a guardian and protector. The Spirit Dragon has the ability to bring peace and prosperity wherever it is needed and is a symbol of hope and salvation."

Nyx took over the telling of the myth, saying, "It is said that the white spirit dragon only appears during times of great turmoil and chaos. Its arrival is seen as a sign that balance and harmony will be restored. It is also believed that only those who are pure of heart and possess a strong connection to nature can communicate with the white spirit dragon. The myth of the white spirit dragon serves as a reminder of the power of goodness and the importance of maintaining balance in the world. It is a symbol of hope and inspiration, reminding us that even in the darkest of times, there is always a chance for redemption and renewal." Nyx purred deep in her throat and nuzzled Kenna gently.

"Your daughters are the ones who will find the Spirit Dragon and bring them to Marqueria. That is the full vision of the Dryad, that which she didn't show you," Nyx said softly. "Come. We must return to the Castle and let the others know what has transpired here in the Grove. Climb on, little ones, and let's take to the air and fly away our sorrows," Nyx chirped. Kenna and Jamie transferred up into their seats on their Dragons, then Nyx and Sika jumped up into the air and flapped their massive wings, and they were soon high above the tree tops, flying towards the Elven Castle.

Chapter Sixty-One

Ember finished fastening her seatbelt in the 3rd row of the SUV, then leaned down and opened the sack from the grocery store. She took out a bottle of water, which she handed to Alaric, who was sitting next to her, and then grabbed one for herself. "Anyone want a water? Or a snack?" she asked loudly. "No thanks, we got our own up here," called Tai from the front seat. Noelle said, "We have our own, too, but thanks for asking, sis."Ember pulled out a bag of Oreos and waggled her eyebrows at Alaric, who laughed and took the Oreos from her.

The six had arrived in Mammoth, climbed into the SUV, driven to Livingston to fill up on gas and grab food, then got onto Interstate 90 and headed for Billings, where they were currently parked at another gas station. It was dark, and the roads were snow-covered and icy, so they hadn't made good time. "How far to Sheridan? Do you think we should stay in Billings tonight?" asked Blaze. Noelle shook her head and said, "No, we need to push through to Sheridan. Then, we can crash for a few hours and get an early start. We have to head west out of Sheridan on Highway 331 for several miles. It's impossible to miss, as there are several buildings. It's a small private community, and we will need to approach it at night. There are cameras and high fences around the entire facility. I'm open to suggestions on how we enter unnoticed."

Tai maneuvered the SUV onto the Interstate and headed toward Sheridan, Wyoming. "Have you been able to contact your parents yet?" he asked the girls. "We'll try again now that we've had some rest," replied Ember. Both girls leaned their heads back on the seats and closed their eyes. In seconds, they began to glow faintly. After about five minutes, the girls opened their eyes and sat up. They both looked shaken.

Blaze pulled Noelle closer and asked, "What happened?" Noelle took a deep breath and said quietly, "We were able to get in touch with our parents. They've had an interesting few weeks." Ember leaned forward and said, "The down and dirty is this: They hunted the Darkness down, and the Dragons used Dragon Fire on It. It was engulfed in flames, screaming in agony, and then suddenly disappeared, but not before it shot a black barb at Dad, and then Mom had to heal him. He's fine now, just badly bruised." Noelle picked up where Ember had left off, saying, "The Dryad showed both of them the visions she had about us and the Spirit Dragon, which our parents shared with us." "What about you and the Spirit Dragon?" asked Kai.

Ember chirped up from the rear seat, saying, "Apparently, our little group here is supposed to free the Shifters, bring the ones that want to come with us to our house in Montana and find the Spirit Dragon. So, no pressure at all." There were a few moments of silence as everyone digested that piece of news. The girls told them about the myth of the Spirit Dragon and how it pertained to them.

"Wow. It just never stops, does it? How much more is going to be piled on us? Sometimes I just want to run away," grumbled Noelle, popping open a bag of chocolate chip cookies and shoving one in her mouth angrily, then chewing aggressively. From her seat behind Noelle, Ember laid a hand on her sister's shoulder and asked, "Sis, do I need to remind you exactly who you are?" Noelle growled, "I know who I am." Ember whispered mischievously, "I think you've forgotten. The granddaughter of Santa Claus would never want to run away." Noelle choked on the mouthful of cookies and started coughing. When she was able, she murmured, "Ember, I love you." Then she laughed along with the rest of the occupants of the SUV.

Chapter Sixty-Two

In the Grove behind the red house in the country, the boy with the snow-white hair was sitting on the bench next to the Tree, hoping the Dryad would visit with him tonight. He had been rather bored over the past few days because the group of six shifters who lived in the red house hadn't been home. So, he was waiting for the Dryad, hoping she would come keep him company. The boy sat for quite some time when, finally, the Dryad appeared.

"I have been waiting for so long tonight. The family in the red house is gone, so I had no one to watch over," the boy said as he stood up and hugged the Dryad. She wrapped him in her arms and held him tightly. Kissing the top of his head, she said, "I'm sorry, little one. I was needed elsewhere tonight. Let us sit on the bench and chat." She guided him back to the bench and sat down next to him. "Are you sleeping and eating enough, little Dragon?" she asked him softly, brushing his snow-white hair off his forehead. He smiled at the Dryad and nodded. "Yes, I am. What I don't catch and hunt for, I get from the stores or the cafes. I have been getting hot chocolate from the little coffee place down the road. I sleep in my hidden cave up there." He pointed behind the Grove to where his cave was.

"Little Dragon, do you understand why we need to wait for the return of the people in the red house? Why can't we go through the Tree yet?" she asked softly. The boy gave a sigh and said, "Yes, I do. I have a part to play in destroying the Darkness, don't I? When it's time for me to go through the Tree, will the ones living in the red house come with me?" The Dryad smiled kindly at the boy and nodded. "Yes, you will be going through the Tree with all of them when the time is right," she said.

The boy gave a wide yawn and tried to hide it behind his hand. The Dryad laughed softly and said, "I think it's time for you to go get some sleep, little one." The boy nodded and stood up, giving the Dryad a hug and then saying, "Goodnight! I will see you tomorrow," before he shifted into his Dragon form and took to the skies. Even though he was tired, he decided to fly around a little before going to sleep. Flying always made him feel happy and content. Flying made him forget that he was alone in this world.

Chapter Sixty-Three

The next afternoon, the six travelers left the hotel in Sheridan and climbed back into the SUV. They were headed west, driving towards the facility they had been told about. It was said to be just sixteen miles out of the city near a place called Wolf Creek. Ember smiled to herself, thinking, 'Wolf Creek. An appropriate place to hide Shifters.' "Why are you smiling?" Alaric asked, putting his arm around her shoulder. Ember told him, and they both chuckled.

"So, what's the plan? Are we going to storm the facility or sneak in stealthily?" asked Noelle. Tai and Kai, sitting in the front while Tai was driving, briefly glanced at each other. Then, Kai gave a one-shoulder shrug and turned to face the four teens. He said, "We were thinking we'd storm the facility while invisible." The four teens just stared at him, confused. Then, Ember said, "You can turn invisible? How? Can you turn us, too?"

The Bear brothers chuckled, and Tai replied, "No, we don't know how, but you and your sister do." Noelle said, "No, we don't. What gave you the idea we knew how to become invisible?" Kai replied, "Because you do. The knowledge is within you; you just have to reach in and grab it." Ember scoffed and said, "Oh, is that all? And just how do you suggest we do that?" Tai laughed and said, "The same way you connected with your Bear. Go deep within." Ember groaned and said, "Noelle, let's try this now before we get there."

Noelle reached over the back of the seat and grabbed both her sister's hands. Ember said in a deep voice, mocking Tai, "Go deep within." Noelle and Ember giggled and then closed their eyes. They sat in silence for several minutes, holding hands and glowing faintly. Then, as Alaric and Blaze were watching, they disappeared. "What the Hell?!" cried Alaric. Tai chuckled and said, "I knew they could do it." "You can't see us?" came Noelle's voice from her seat next to Blaze. "Nope," said Blaze, then laughed. "Can you turn us invisible?" asked Alaric. After a few moments, the SUV was driving down the two-lane road and appeared to have nobody in it. Noelle and Ember laughed loudly, and then everyone appeared to be visible again.

Tai called back to the girls, "It's a good thing we didn't pass anyone while you were pulling that little stunt. Now, we will need to check the facility for cameras and infrared. We won't be invisible if they have infrared cameras." "We could just do a spell to mask our body heat," said Ember. Kai replied, "Yes, that could work. Good idea."

"According to this map, we are just a mile from the property line. There is a treed area up there on the right. I'll park the SUV within it, and hopefully, nobody will discover it. Then we will go in on foot when the sun goes down. That should be about twenty minutes," said Tai. "Sounds good," murmured Kai, on alert and looking around.

Thirty minutes later, the six of them were walking in the dark towards the ten-foot chain link fence, completely undetectable. They stopped when they reached the fence, and Ember said, "It's weird how I can't really see you, but I know exactly where each of you is." "It's our magic you're sensing," said Kai. Tai interrupted them and said, "Have you noticed there is no movement at all within the grounds? It's completely still."

Noelle whispered, "I can sense life within the walls of that large building on the left, towards the back. The blue one." "Yes, I can, too. I don't think there is anyone else around; they all seem to be concentrated in that blue building," murmured Ember. Tai said, "Then it's the blue building we need to go check out." "Can we just transfer over there? It will get us over the fence and outside the doors," murmured Blaze, his voice coming from behind Noelle. "Good idea. Grab hands," whispered Ember. "I can't see your hands, so how do I grab your hands?" asked Alaric in exasperation. Ember giggled and said, "Everyone, put your hands out in front of you and walk toward the sound of my voice. I'll have my hand out."

Finally grasping hands, they transferred over to the doors of the blue building. "What is that stench?!" whispered Ember, gagging, and then the sound of vomiting could be heard off to the side. Noelle was gagging, too, and then whispered, "Use your magic, Ember. It can make the smell less disgusting." Ember breathed a sigh of relief and said, "Thanks, sis. That was truly disgusting." Alaric gagged, then whispered, "Extend that courtesy to us, please." After a moment, there were murmurs of "Thank you" from the others.

"I'll go first," said Tai as he turned the knob to the door on the right. He pushed the door open, and the six stealthily snuck in. What they found left them all speechless. Within the large blue warehouse building stood row after row of cages. Most were just big enough to fit a man, and some were large enough for massive bears and wolves. Taking up half the warehouse were two huge, deep garnet red Dragons with gold horns and spikes. The Dragons were splayed out on their stomachs, four legs chained in manacles and pulled taught. Their wings were spread and pinned down with large iron spikes hammered through the thick edges. Sparkling lilac-purple fluid pooled under them, running in rivulets down the concrete to join the river of dark red blood flowing from the figures in the cages.

"Oh, my Goddess! What have they done to these poor souls?" whispered Tai. The six were all visible now, the shock of their discovery making Ember and Noelle forget to feed the magic for the invisibility spell. As they walked closer to the cages and down one of the rows, they found that some of the cages held animals and some held humans. "I think these are all shifters," murmured Kai. "Are they all dead?" asked Noelle, her voice shaking. "No. I can sense life here. We need to find the ones who are still alive as soon as possible," Ember said as she walked closer to the Dragons.

Noelle joined Ember, and the two of them walked to the nearest red Dragon, laying their hands on its head. It was a magnificent creature, deep garnet red with gold horns and spikes. Its wings were also a deep shade of red but with ancient gold designs etched within the wings. As the girls began to glow, the iron stakes holding the wings down and the iron shackles binding its legs disintegrated. The glow from the girls began to creep over the Dragon, soon covering it completely. Suddenly, where there once lay a Dragon, now a black-haired woman lay. She was pale and emaciated, covered in sparkling lilac blood. She didn't stir but for her breathing, which was slow and even.

The girls moved on to the next Dragon and performed the same magic on it. It shifted into a man. A pale, too-thin man with black hair. He, too, was breathing slowly and even but didn't move otherwise. Tai called out from down one of the rows, "I found one alive!" he yelled. The girls went to him and found him kneeling next to a small brown bear cub. The cub was lying on its side, breathing fast and shallow. It gave a pitiful groan when Tai picked it up gently and cuddled it to his chest. "Can you heal her?" Tai whispered. The girls nodded and laid their hands on the tiny body.

After a few moments, the bear cub shifted into a small, brown-haired girl. She appeared to be about two years old and was covered in blood and filth. She raised huge, bright golden eyes up to Tai, who was holding her in the cradle of his arms. The little girl said nothing, just stared at Tai, then she laid her head on his chest and closed her eyes. "Are there more?" asked Ember, turning around to look at all the cages. "Here!" called Alaric towards the end of the row she was standing in.

The girls made their way to the next one, which was a black bear cub. They healed it, and it shifted into a small black-haired female child. She, too, had shining golden eyes, and her skin was ebony. Alaric held her in his arms, cradling her to his chest. His eyes were devastated when he looked up and met Ember's gaze. "Who would do this and why?" he growled. Kai, who had joined them, asked, "Girls, will you please make the rounds and heal all those who remain alive?" The girls nodded and made their way down the rows of cages. Sadly, they found just two more shifters who were still alive. They were tiny white Wolf pups locked together in the same cage.

When they were finished healing the two pups, and they had shifted into identical small white-haired girls with golden eyes, around four years of age, Ember and Noelle led them to the doors where the others had gathered. Tai said, "Ember, Noelle, Alaric, and Blaze. We want you to transfer the children and the two dragon shifters to our hotel suite in Sheridan. Kai and I need to stay behind and look for the purpose of this facility. We need to find their notes, and we also need to burn this warehouse to the ground, with all the dead inside. They can't be found. If the mortal world discovered the existence of shifters, it would be a hunt like the Witch hunts of old."

Chapter Sixty-Four

The four teens nodded in understanding and took the four children to where the two Dragon shifters lay, still unconscious. After arranging the hands of the two Dragon shifters so the female's hand rested within the male's and each teen holding a child, Ember and Noelle ensured everyone was touching and transferred. They appeared in the middle of their suite, still touching the Dragon shifters and holding the children. The children hadn't made a sound since they had found them and still remained silent, but their eyes were huge in their thin faces as they looked around the hotel suite's sitting room.

"I'm going to transfer the two Dragon shifters to the bed in my room; then we need to get these kids cleaned up, dressed, and fed," murmured Noelle softly. She put the child she was holding down and bent to touch the couple lying on the floor and disappeared with them. A few moments later, she returned to the sitting room. "They're cleaned up and tucked into bed. Hopefully, they'll wake up soon so we can get some answers about that facility and where all the shifters came from," Noelle said when she returned. Ember asked, "How did you clean them up so quickly?" Noelle chuckled and said, "Magic. I used a cleaning spell. I figured if it will work on dishes, then it should work on people." She turned to the four children, all of whom were sitting on the floor with Alaric and Blaze.

Noelle gracefully waved a hand over the children's heads, and they instantly became clean; even their clothing, what little they had on, was now clean. The children started and looked at each other, their expressions amazed. Ember said, "Now we need to think about some food. From the looks of these four, they haven't had enough food for quite some time." "Are you hungry, little ones?" Blaze asked the four girls sitting on the floor in front of him and Alaric. The two older white-haired girls looked at each other, then at the two younger girls huddled between them. They then turned back to face the brothers and slowly nodded their heads.

"What do you feed two-year-olds?" Ember asked, biting her lip. Alaric laughed and said, "The same thing you feed teenagers. Well, mostly the same." Ember was on her phone, scrolling and tapping. "What are you doing?" Alaric asked. "I'm putting in an order for food to be delivered," Ember replied. "Order a ton, please. I'm starving too, and I bet Tai and Kai will be as well," said Noelle from the doorway to the room where the Dragon shifters lay unconscious.

The four teens sat on the couches with the four children cuddled up to them. Ember and Alaric sat on one couch with the two youngest, while Noelle and Blaze sat across from them on the other couch with the white-haired twins. The twins had each eaten a hamburger and some French fries and then promptly fell asleep and snuggled up to the teens.

Ember was stroking the black hair on the head of the little Bear shifter lying across her lap and cuddled in her arm. Softly stroking the ebony skin of her cheek, Ember whispered, "What happened there? How did they find so many shifters in the Mortal world?" Noelle, with one of the sleeping white-haired twins in her lap, quietly replied, "I don't know. I don't know the answers, but I do know only evil could do what they did. So many dead, and half of them children. It makes me so angry; I want to hunt them down." The other three teens nodded in agreement, their faces briefly showing their rage. "Are these two Spirit Wolves?" Noelle asked Blaze, who was holding the other white-haired child. Blaze and Alaric stared at each other for a few moments, and then they both nodded.

"Weird how a Spirit Dragon, two Spirit Bears, and now two Spirit Wolves show up within weeks of each other. All of which are supposed to be myths. What is going on?" whispered Ember as she stroked the soft hair of the child in her arms.

Just then, the door to the suite quietly opened, and Tai and Kai walked in. They looked exhausted, and their faces showed their sorrow over the night's events. After the door was closed, the two walked further into the room and absorbed the scene in front of them. "There are burgers and fries on the counter in the kitchen area for you if you're hungry," Ember whispered. The brothers smiled sadly at her and went to the kitchen area. They made short work of the meal and returned to the sitting area, sitting on the floor with their backs against one of the couches.

Tai rubbed a hand over his face and then up through his blond hair. His eyes closed, and he whispered, "It was Hilda. She started hunting down shifters after she married Maxim's dad. She built the facility to do experiments on them. They kept meticulous notes. All the horrors they did were documented. Before Hilda disappeared, she killed all the workers and abandoned the facility, leaving the shifters in their cages to die. We found the dead workers piled in another building containing all the evidence of the atrocities they committed."

Kai murmured softly, "We started a hot fire and burnt every building to the ground. When we were driving back, we passed a couple of fire trucks and emergency vehicles. They will find nothing but ashes. There will be no evidence of Shifters." A tear slowly rolled down his cheek, and he buried his face in his elbow, which was resting on his bent knee. Tai reached over and grasped Kai's shoulder, "Brother, they will be avenged. Hilda will answer for what she has done."

"How will we get everyone back to our house in Montana?" Noelle asked, leaning down and placing a soft kiss on the sleeping girl she held. Looking up, she met Blaze's shining golden eyes and gave him a soft smile as she watched him smooth the snow-white hair of the little one he was holding. Ember, who was staring down at the beautiful child in her lap, said softly, "We will transfer them. Even if we need to make a few trips, we will get them back to our home."

From the doorway of the bedroom where the Dragon shifters had been placed, a low growl came, "Where the Hell are we?"

Chapter Sixty-Five

The six turned towards the door where the male Dragon shifter stood in clean but ragged clothing. His jet-black hair hung past his shoulders in waves, his skin was pale, and he was too thin, but he gave off a lethal air. "I asked where the Hell have you brought us?" he growled, eyeing them angrily. From her position on the sofa, Ember eyed the Dragon shifter, her glowing green eyes with golden sparks narrowed. She said very softly, "If you wake these poor babies up, I will personally put you back to sleep." This seemed to surprise the Dragon shifter, as the anger melted from his face, only to be replaced with speculation as he eyed all six of them, saying nothing.

Noelle stared at the Dragon shifter for a few moments and then asked, "Where did you come from? We weren't aware of the existence of Dragon shifters." He started and looked at Noelle in surprise, then he raised his nose and sniffed the air. His body relaxed, and he let out a soft sigh. "You are shifters, but for the two females. They are that and something more. What are you?" he replied softly, looking between Ember and Noelle. Ember grinned at him and said, "We are Bear and Elf." He raised an eyebrow and said, "Elves don't live in the Mortal realm. I haven't seen an Elf in many, many centuries."

As he was speaking, the six had moved their eyes to look behind him. This caught his attention, and he turned to see the female Dragon shifter standing there. "My love, you should be resting," he said, putting his arm around her and pulling her into his side. She barely reached his chest, and it wasn't that she was petite; it was that he was huge. He stood at 6'7", and despite being too thin, there was power radiating from him, which increased in the presence of his mate. She was 5'10" and lovely, if very thin and undernourished. Their love for each other shone in their eyes...their red eyes. The irises of their eyes were a deep dark red, like their Dragons. Ember thought to herself, 'I hadn't noticed his red eyes before. They looked dark brown until she had joined him. Weird.'

Tai and Kai stood up and moved towards the pair. This caused the man to gently push his mate behind him. Tai and Kai stopped, and both raised their hands and palms towards the couple. Tai said, "We mean you no harm. We are the ones who freed you and healed you. We brought you here to our hotel suite, where you could recover." Kai added, "If you are hungry, we have food. Why don't you both come sit and eat, and then you can explain what happened to you?" The couple looked at each other, and the female nodded. The male gave a sigh of frustration, causing Ember to smirk and chuckle.

"Remind you of another couple?" Ember asked her sister, Noelle. Noelle grinned and nodded, then said, "Mom and Dad." The couple went to sit at the small dining table while Tai and Kai prepared their meal from the groceries Ember had ordered earlier. Ember said quietly, "Let's go put the little ones in our room, in the beds." "Good idea," murmured Alaric. The four teens stood up carefully, trying not to jostle the children, and then walked into one of the bedrooms.

"How many survived?" whispered the female Dragon shifter, her face showing her grief. Her mate took her hand and softly said, "Just us and the four younglings in there." She raised tear-filled eyes in shock. "That's it?" she cried softly as the tears streamed down her face. Interrupting them, Tai set two plates with roasted chicken breasts, broccoli, mashed potatoes, and rolls on the table in front of the couple, then handed them each a fork and knife. Kai handed each of them a couple of napkins, then went to one of the sofas and sat down, elbow on his knees, head in his hands. Tai joined his brother on the sofa just as the four teens walked out of the room where the little ones were sleeping.

The four teens sat on one of the sofas, the girls in the middle. They looked exhausted, and they all had a haunted look in their eyes. As the Dragon shifters were eating, the six on the sofas were speaking quietly among themselves. "Are you two okay?" asked Ember, looking across at Tai and Kai with concern. Kai gave a sigh and nodded. Tai shrugged and said, "We will be. How about you four? How are you processing what you experienced tonight?" Alaric put his arm around Ember and pulled her in close to his side. She snuggled into him, breathing in his scent deeply, letting it calm her. She then said, "If I let myself think about it too long, I'm afraid I'll never stop crying. How do I process this, you asked? With anger. White hot rage. Because otherwise, the sorrow will paralyze me."

Noelle, who was cuddled into Blaze, lifted her head off his chest and looked over at her sister. They stared into each other's eyes for a few moments, and then each nodded and laid their heads down again. Tai and Kai had been watching them, and both gave a quiet chuckle. Tai asked, "What are you planning, my Princesses?" There was a small gasp from the small table where the Dragon shifters were finishing their meal. The six seated on the sofas all looked over to see what caused it and found the two Dragon shifters staring at Noelle and Ember.

Ember, never one to shy away from anything, asked rather harshly, "What?! Something catch your attention?" The two Dragon shifters stood up and made their way to the empty sofa at the end of the U-shaped furniture placement. After they had taken their seat, the female leaned into the male, and the male asked, "You are Royalty? From where do you come?" Noelle exchanged a glance with Ember and then said, "We will tell you about us in exchange for more information regarding you and the other shifters." The girls stared at the two Dragon shifters, waiting. This caused a small smile from the two Dragon shifters, and they both nodded. The female said in a low, soft voice, "Let's start with the basics, shall we? My name is Adeen, and this is my mate, Rory. As you already know, we are Dragon shifters." Her voice contained a slight raspiness; whether this was due to her captivity or was natural remained to be seen.

Tai leaned forward and asked, "Where did you come from? In our world, there are no Dragon shifters, and as far as I knew, there were none in the Mortal realm either." He eyed them quietly, waiting for their answers. Rory, the male

Dragon shifter, said, "We will answer your questions, but first, we would appreciate the names of those with whom we are speaking." Ember gave a soft laugh and winked at Tai when he looked at her. He gave her a rueful grin and sat back. He nodded to Rory and began the introductions.

"The four teenagers on the sofa there are Blaze and Alaric, Princes of the Wolf Clans. The females are Noelle and Ember, Princesses of the Elf and Bear Clans. I am Tai, this is my brother Kai, and we are Princes of the Bear Clan," Tai informed the Dragon shifters, Rory and Adeen. There was silence in the room as the two Dragon shifters stared at the two girls on the sofa. Their expressions were ones of surprise and hope. "You are both Elven and Bear? How did that happen?" asked Rory, staring at Ember and Noelle. Ember raised an eyebrow and said, "Do we really need to explain the birds and the bees to you?" Adeen, the female Dragon shifter, laughed softly and said, "There is no need for that, spirited one. We are just surprised a union between different clans was allowed. It isn't something we have never seen. We mean no disrespect, Princess."

Noelle spoke up and said, "Our mother is the Elven Princess and is the mate to the Bear Prince, our father." "Thank you. Now, from where do you hail?" asked Rory. The four teens looked to Tai and Kai, not knowing if they should tell them about Marqueria. Kai shrugged and said, "We are from Marqueria." This caused the couple to look very startled and unsettled. They became eerily still, staring at the six Marquerians. "You are from the same realm as the monster who captured us and held us captive for years," rasped Adeen softly. Rory's red eyes began to glow, causing the six to instinctively react in kind.

Ember and Noelle began to glow softly, and a protection dome suddenly popped into existence over them, separating them from the two Dragon shifters. This caused Rory and Adeen to jump up and move away from the dome. They gazed at the six contained within the dome in utter amazement. "You can manipulate the magic in the Mortal realm? You can tap into the power of the Goddess?" gasped Adeen softly. Ember and Noelle, eyes glowing green with golden sparks, skin softly shimmering, and hair floating up off their shoulders, both nodded at the two Dragon shifters.

"I apologize for my reaction. It was instinctual. We will not harm you. You do not need a protection circle. I was very surprised to learn you are from the same land as the monster who killed so many of our kind," Rory said, leading Adeen back to the sofa to sit. Ember and Noelle looked at each other for a few seconds, and then the circle fell. "It seems we need to tell our story first," said Ember, and then continued, "But first, I need some hot chocolate. Would anyone else like some?" Everyone present nodded, so Ember waved her hand gracefully from left to right over the coffee table set in the center of the three sofas.

A tray with eight cups of hot chocolate topped with whipped cream, a plate of cookies and crackers, and a plate of tiny triangle sandwiches appeared on the coffee table. "I'm starving," whispered Ember as she picked up a cup and snagged four sandwiches, handing the cup to Alaric along with two sandwiches. She then grabbed her cup, sat back, and took a sip. She eyed Rory and Adeen and said, "It's not poisonous." They both smiled at her and helped themselves. When everyone had their cups and snacks, Tai began to speak.

Chapter Sixty-Six

Tai told Rory and Adeen the tale of why they were in the Mortal realm. He explained about Hilda, how the Darkness was trapped inside her, and her connection to Ember and Noelle. They asked questions, and the six answered as best they could. By the time the tale was told, it was midnight. When Tai finished speaking, there were a few minutes of silence as the six from Marqueria allowed the two Dragon shifters to digest what they had been told.

Ember asked softly, "Would you mind telling us your story, or would you rather wait until morning?" Rory and Adeen stared at each other for a few seconds, obviously communicating via a mind-link. They both nodded, and Adeen began their story.

"We come from another realm, one long since destroyed by the Darkness. Yes, it was in our world, too, but we were unable to fight it in the way you have. It took over many of our shifters, and there was a war amongst our own kind. Where there had once been only love and harmony, our world became fractured with hate and greed. The clans fought not only with each other but also within the clans, and there was division. The Darkness took over every corner of our world, and we barely escaped with our lives and those few we could save and bring with us," Adeen said as she took sips of her second cup of cocoa. "The shifters in the warehouse were the last of our world. The ones in this hotel suite are all that are left, as far as we know," Rory said softly, his eyes sorrowful.

Adeen continued, "We had a son after we came to the Mortal world. He is lost to us now. He was in our cave when we were taken." Ember gave a loud gasp, and everyone looked at her questioningly. She excitedly leaned forward and exclaimed, "We found your cave in Yellowstone!" The two Dragons gazed at her in complete surprise. Adeen asked, "How?! It was hidden behind the falls." Ember explained their search and why they were searching for it. "Is your son a white Spirit Dragon?" Noelle asked them. They nodded, and with tears in her eyes, Adeen asked, "You have seen our son? You know where he is?"

The six nodded, and Noelle said, "He has been hanging around our house in the mountains and the nearby town of Butte. We have caught his scent many times and seen him but once near our Grove." "You are welcome to stay at our home while we help you search for him. We can transfer all of us in the morning," said Ember, covering a yawn with her hand. Rory and Adeen nodded, their eyes shining with happiness and holding each other's hands tightly.

Ember stood up, along with the other three teens. "We need to get some sleep. We will sleep in with the younglings. Goodnight, everyone." The rest said their goodnights, and the teen quietly entered the room with the sleeping children. "Where will they sleep? On the floor?" asked Adeen. Tai and

Kai chuckled softly and shook their heads. "Knowing the girls, they have probably magicked a huge bed in place of the two which were in there," said Tai with a grin.

The two Dragon shifters stood up and said their goodnights before they, too, went to their assigned room. Tai and Kai looked at each other ruefully, and Kai said, "Well, it looks like we got the sofas."

Chapter Sixty-Seven

The next morning, the four shifter children had perked up a bit after a good night's sleep and a nourishing breakfast. They were sitting on the floor behind one of the sofas, playing with toys the girls had magicked for them and wearing new clothing as well. Their giggles brought smiles to the faces of all of them and temporarily made them forget about the horrors of yesterday.

When breakfast was finished and everyone was dressed and ready to go, Ember asked, "Are you sure we can transfer all of us and the SUV?" Rory smiled at her and said, "Yes, we can. With our magic bolstering yours, it will be possible. While we can't access the Goddess's magic as much as you two, we are able to use some." Tai said, "When we are all loaded into the SUV, you four can transfer us to the driveway at your house."

Ember and Noelle joined hands, and both looked a little nervous. Adeen walked over and took one of each of their hands in hers. "I feel the power within you both. It's like nothing I've felt in this Mortal realm. Your power is even more than I felt from anyone in our own realm. We can do this," she said in her low, raspy voice." The girls stared into Adeen's eyes when Ember suddenly exclaimed, "Your eyes are gold today!" Adeen and Rory laughed, and Rory explained, "Our eyes are usually gold, but when we are in pain, weak, or in fight mode, they glow red like our Dragons." "That's so cool," whispered Ember, making everyone laugh.

Twenty minutes later, they were all squished into the SUV. It was made to seat only eight, so the children sat in the rear seat with Blaze and Alaric. Ember and Noelle sat in the middle with Rory and Adeen. Tai and Kai were in the front seats. "Okay, join hands. Noelle, you and Rory also need to touch the sides of the vehicle while we are holding hands. Close your eyes and picture where you want us to go. Keep the picture in your mind," Adeen said very softly. The girls' skin began to shimmer softly, and after a few moments, the SUV disappeared.

The SUV reappeared in the garage, which was attached to the red house in the country. Everyone within the SUV had transferred as well. "Yes! We did it!" exclaimed Ember, much to the amusement of the other. Noelle said, "Come, let's go into the house, and we will show you around. Our home is yours for as long as you have need of it." The four doors of the SUV opened, and everyone piled out. The small children were handed out to the four adults, and then they all followed Ember and Noelle into the house.

"You have a lovely home. The love your family has for one another has soaked into its walls. That in itself is a powerful barrier against evil, but with the protection circles you've cast, this home is the safest place in this realm. Thank you for sharing it with us," said Adeen as she set one of the white-haired twins down in the living room.

"Something has just occurred to me. We don't know their names. The children. Do you, perhaps?" asked Noelle, looking between Rory and Adeen. They both shook their heads, Rory saying, "They were infants when they were brought into the facility. I don't think they have names." Ember sat on a sofa holding the black-haired Bear child, who had her arms and legs wrapped around her. The toddler had her head resting on Ember's shoulder, and Ember was stroking the soft, long black hair flowing down her back. "Maybe we should give them names, then," Ember murmured softly. Noelle was holding the other Bear child, the one with long, brown curly hair, and she said, "Maybe we should ask them what they want their names to be." At this, everyone nodded in agreement.

"Sweetheart, what do you want your name to be?" Ember murmured softly to the girl in her arms. The toddler leaned back and put her tiny hands on Ember's cheeks, looked into her eyes, and smiled. She then said softly, "My name is Honey." Ember asked, "Honey? Why Honey?" The adorable toddler grinned and said, "Because I love honey." Everyone chuckled, and Ember said, "Then your name is Honey." The girl threw her arms around Ember's neck and hugged her. "We want names," two soft voices said in unison. Turning towards the voices, they found the twins standing in the doorway, holding hands.

Alaric held his hands out to the girls and said, "Come here, little pups. Tell us what you want to be named." They ran to him and jumped up into his lap. With an arm around each girl, he bent his head down and asked, "What do you want to be named, little wolves?" "We want to be Snow and Ivory," they said together in their soft little girl voices. "Why those names?" asked Ember, smiling at the two girls. "Because we have white hair, and Snow and Ivory mean white, don't they?" the girls said in unison. Everyone nodded. Blaze spoke up and said, "Those are perfect names for white Spirit Wolves."

Tai was holding the brown-haired little Bear shifter on his lap, and he bent his head down and asked, "What do you want your name to be, little cub?" She looked up at him and shrugged her shoulders. Then, in a very soft voice said, "I don't know. You name me." Tai looked up and met his brother's eyes. Both brothers had a stunned look on their faces. "What's wrong?" Ember asked the brothers. They just shook their heads and remained silent.

Alaric spoke up and said, "Naming someone is powerful. When you name a child, you take on the responsibility of them, completely. They are yours to raise." "So what you're saying is when you name her, she will become your child?" Ember asked Tai and Kai. They both nodded, and after staring at each other for a few moments, Tai said, "Takara. Her name is Takarra." Kai nodded and smiled at the newly named Takarra. The toddler Bear shifter smiled up at Tai and then at Kai and said, "Thank you. I am Takarra, and I am your daughter now." She promptly laid her head down on Tai's chest, popped her thumb in her mouth, and watched the others.

"Okay, we have named the children. We have the Bear shifters, Honey and Takarra, and we have the Wolf shifters, Snow and Ivory. Welcome to our home, girls, for as long as you have need of it. Come with us; we will show you where you will be sleeping. I'm afraid you will be sharing with us, but our room is huge, so there is plenty of room," said Ember, and as she stood up, Noelle, Blaze, and Alaric followed her, each carrying a youngling.

"That is a huge responsibility you've just taken on. What about the other three?" asked Adeen. Kai nodded, then shrugged and said, "Yes, but if not us, then who? As for the other three, they will stay with us. When the door to Marqueria is open, then we will take all four of them through the Tree with us. You are more than welcome to join us after we find your son, that is." The Dragon shifters both nodded, and Adeen asked, "When can we start looking?" Kai stood up and said, "Well, we can go out back and hike to the Grove now if you'd like."

Chapter Sixty-Eight

While the teens were upstairs with the little ones, Tai and Kai took Adeen and Rory up to the Grove. When the two Dragon shifters entered the Grove, they both took deep breaths and sighed. "This feels amazing. I haven't felt magic like this since we left our realm. It's invigorating and soothing at the same time," breathed Adeen as she slowly walked around the large Grove, breathing the magic deep into herself. Rory took her hand, and together, they stood under the Tree and began to glow with a faint red shimmer.

As the two Dragon shifters bathed in the magic of the Grove, Tai and Kai kept watch and noticed movement from near the Tree. Turning quickly, they saw the Dryad of the Tree gliding slowly towards the two Dragon shifters, her vibrant hair flowing in the breeze. She stopped a few yards from the couple and waited. When Adeen and Rory were acclimated to the Grove, they opened their glowing red eyes and smiled in gratitude at Tai and Kai. "Thank you for sharing your home and the magic of your Grove with us," Adeen said softly. Tai and Kai both bowed their heads briefly in acknowledgment, their eyes moving to the Dryad.

Rory and Adeen turned quickly and gasped when they saw the Dryad. They both knelt in front of her and said, "Esteemed one. We are honored by your presence." "Please, do stand. I am the one honored to be in your presence. I have been waiting for your arrival for many years, my brave Dragons," replied the Dryad in her soft, melodious voice. The couple stood up and exchanged confused looks. Rory asked, "Why have you been waiting for us? How do you even know about us?" The Dryad gave them both a loving smile and said, "I've known about you for millennia. You were one of my first visions. You and your son."

The two Dragon shifters stared at the Dryad in stunned silence, and then Adeen asked in a voice filled with hope, "You know our son?" The Dryad again smiled softly and said, "Oh yes, I know your little sapling. He has been my ward for the past few years when he made his way to my Grove and sat under my Tree." Rory asked hoarsely, "Where is he? Is he okay?" Just then, a shadow crossed over them from above, and they all looked up at the sparkling white Dragon flying overhead. Adeen dropped to her knees and covered her face with her hands, her mate resting his hand on her head, murmuring, "Love, it's okay. Our boy is alive."

Tai and Kai looked behind them, sensing that the rest of the household had joined them. The four teens and the four young ones moved to stand next to Tai and Kai, and they all stood quietly, watching. The white Dragon landed softly at the end of the Grove and quickly changed into a boy with snow-white hair. He walked slowly to stand next to the Dryad. Then, taking her hand and looking up at her with huge golden eyes, he asked, "Is now the time? Do I get to join the ones in the Red House now? Is this going to be my family now?"

Adeen and Rory were both standing now, staring at the beautiful boy in front of them. The Dryad smiled down at the boy and said, "This is your family now, and these are your parents. They have been found." The boy turned to the couple in front of him and asked, "Do I get to live with you, and will we be a family?" It was more than Adeen could bear, and she rushed forward and enclosed him in her arms, sobbing in joy and anguish. The Dryad took a few steps back and allowed the family to be reunited.

Rory knelt down in front of Adeen and the white-haired boy. He wrapped them in his arms and held them tightly. He, too, was unable to hold back the tears. Adeen leaned back and held the boy's face in her hands, saying, "We didn't want to leave you. We were taken and held against our wills. We promise never to allow us to be separated again, my son." The child solemnly nodded his head and then asked, "What is my name?" "Your name is Teague," replied Adeen. The boy smiled brightly at his parents and said, "Teague. My name is Teague." He turned to the Dryad and said with excitement, "I have a name! My name is Teague!"

Teague ran to the Dryad and threw his arms around her waist, hugging her tightly. Looking up at her with his large, shining gold eyes, he said, "Thank you for being my friend. Will you stay and join my family? It's a big one now." The Dryad wrapped her arms around Teague and placed a kiss on his head, then said, "I will always be a part of your family,

Teague, and we can visit whenever I am able. You have filled my heart with joy these past few years, and I would miss you terribly if we couldn't have our visits."

Taking her hand in his, Teague tugged her towards his parents and the others from the Red House. Then, standing between the Dryad and his parents, he faced the ten shifters and said, "Hello, I'm Teague. I have been watching you and wanted to join your family, but the Dryad said I had to wait until the time was right. Now that my parents have returned, I would like to ask if we can join your family and live in the Red House with you." Wiping the tears from their faces, Ember and Noelle walked over to Teague.

Ember said, "We would be honored to have you and yours join our family. Noelle and I always wanted a big family." Noelle nodded her head and added, "Until we can all return to Marqueria together, our house is yours too." Teague gave the sisters a wide grin and said, "The Red House in the Country. My home is the Red House in the Country! I have a home." This was more than the girls could bear, and they rushed forward and wrapped Teague in one of their family hugs, holding him tightly and kissing his head.

After a few moments, the Dryad spoke up, saying, "Until it is safe for you to travel to Marqueria, the thirteen of you will remain in the mortal world for the time being. Use this time wisely." She looked towards Tai and Kai and said, "You brothers will teach these young ones how to fight and protect themselves, but don't forget the most important thing. They are children and have never known love. Fill their lives with love." Eyes shimmering with a sheen of tears, Tai and Kai, who were holding the two Bear girls, both nodded in agreement.

The Dryad turned to Blaze and Alaric and said softly, "You brothers will teach the Spirit Wolves how to be Wolves. Though they are still very young, they play a role in defeating the Darkness." Blaze and Alaric, who were both holding the hands of the two Wolf girls, nodded in understanding. The Dryad then turned towards Teague's parents and said, "Your son is the Spirit Dragon of the myths, and his role in defeating the darkness is a heavy one. While you are learning to be a family again, you will also need to teach him everything you know about his inner magic and how to use it. He has just tapped the surface of his magic, and he will need your guidance through the rest." Eyes showing their concern, Adeen and Rory both nodded.

While the Dryad had been giving her instructions to the rest, Teague returned to his parents, and Ember and Noelle moved to the side to watch and listen. The Dryad turned to the sisters and said in her soft, melodious voice, "Oh, my little saplings." She glided to them and wrapped her arms around both, pulling them in for a long hug. After a few moments, she stepped back a pace and took their hands in hers. "You two have much on your shoulders, and I'm so very sorry you aren't allowed to be carefree teenagers like your friends in town. The Universe is asking a lot of you both, and you have met the challenges with strength and will. I know you have had times of doubt and have wanted to quit, but you didn't. You did what needed to be done without losing your joy for life and your love of others. You are the Spirit

Bears, and that added responsibility you won't have to carry alone. You will have the Spirit Wolves and the Spirit Dragon to help you defeat the Darkness. Together, you will learn to use your special abilities as the Spirit animals of your kind. I will always be here when you need me. Our mind link will always be connected, and I will come when you call me." She leaned in and gave them another hug and then turned towards Teague and his parents.

"Teague, I would like to share a mind link with you. It will enable you to contact me whenever you have a need," she said as she glided over to stand in front of him. Teague smiled up at her and asked, "For real? Like a phone?" This caused those around him to chuckle softly, and the Dryad smiled. "Yes, like a phone in our heads. We will be connected, just as I am connected to Ember and Noelle, and soon, we will be connected to Snow and Ivory," she said. Kneeling down, she pressed her forehead to Teague's, and a soft glow began emanating from the place their skin touched. After several seconds, she stood up straight and ruffled Teague's snow-white hair, saying, "I will come when you have need of me."

The Dryad gracefully approached Blaze and Alaric, who were holding the hands of the two Spirit Wolf girls. She knelt down, facing the sisters, and said, "Hello, my little darlings. Would you like to be able to call me whenever you need me?" The sisters looked at each other for a few moments, obviously communicating through their mind links. They then turned towards the Dryad and nodded. The Dryad bestowed the mind link on both girls and then stood up.

Surprisingly, she moved to Tai and Kai, who were holding the two sleeping Bear toddlers. "You both have lost so much to this war and the Darkness, more than most. The younglings you hold in your arms are yours. They are your daughters now and are to be raised as such. You both carry the capacity of immense love, and these two cubs need the love and protection you can provide. Let them heal your wounds and bring you joy, as you will heal theirs," the Dryad murmured softly. She bent down and placed a kiss on each of the girls' foreheads and said, "They too will have a mind link with me, so if ever they have the need, they can reach out to me. Teach them, love them, and cherish them. This is my gift to you, brothers, Princes of the Bear Clan." She glided over to the Tree and disappeared into It.

There was total quiet in the Grove as everyone absorbed what had just transpired. Noelle had her arm around Ember's shoulders, and Ember had hers around Noelle's waist, both leaning into one another. Ember looked up and noticed the two Dragon shifters observing them. She raised an eyebrow and asked, "Yes?" This brought a smile to Adeen's face, who then laughed and asked, "You are fiery, aren't you?" Ember gave her a grin and asked, "Are you going to tell us what's on your mind?"

Adeen took a deep breath and let it out slowly, then asked, "You and your sister are Spirit Bears?" The sisters nodded and waited. "You are Spirit Bears, have a direct line to the Goddess and the Dryad of the Tree, carry immense magic within you, and are of the Royal houses of the Elves and Bears. How old are you?" The girls gave nonchalant shrugs, and Noelle said, "We are 15 and 16, but our birthdays are in a couple of weeks, so we will be 16 and 17." Ember grinned and said, "In fact, on the 13th of January, Noelle and I will both be 16. On one day of the year, we are the same age."

Adeen looked surprised and glanced at her mate, Rory. He, too, looked rather surprised. "What?" asked Ember. "Teague's birthday is January 13th," Rory stated. Adeen nodded and said, "The number 13 is a powerful number. It stands for power and purity, prosperity and life. It is the number most associated with the Goddess and her divine feminine energy." Rory said, "There are 13 of us in this group. I don't think this is a coincidence. The Goddess is at work here." Ember just stared at the Dragon shifters for several seconds, saying nothing, and then said, "Okaaayy.... Well, I'm starving. Who wants to go back to the house and get some grub?" This caused Tai and Kai to laugh, and Tai said, "We will make pizza. Come on, everyone!"

The group of 13 adults, teenagers, and children started back down the path towards the Red House in the Country. There was cheerful chatter amongst the group regarding sleeping arrangements, shopping for food and clothing, training schedules, and such. The Dryad had appeared next to the Tree, and she watched as the group happily planned their day. A tear slowly ran down her cheek before she faded back into her Tree.

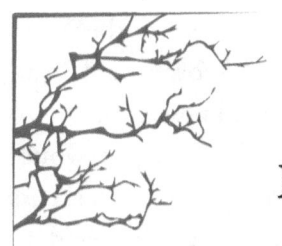

Epilogue

In a deep, dark cave, in the farthest reaches of Marqueria, the Darkness lay. Hilda's body was slowly mending, but the Darkness had to bind her mind to keep her from going mad from the pain. He himself did not feel pain, hunger, want, or need. He just was. He had an innate drive to spread. To destroy. It wasn't a need or a want; it just was. As he lay in the cave and waited for Hilda's body to heal, he planned his next move. With the Tree gone from Marqueria, he was trapped here. He needed to turn it into his advantage. Maybe it was time to leave Hilda's damaged body and take over a younger and fresher vessel.

At that thought, the Darkness stared over to where the half-human lay on the cold, damp floor of the cave. Maxim. Yes, that was his name. Hmmmm. Strong, with powers yet untapped. Not as powerful as Kenna, but the Darkness had come to the conclusion he was not going to be able to take her over. With her daughters safe in the Mortal world, he would have to find a new way to infiltrate the Elven Castle. What better way than to take over the body and mind of the son of Hilda? He could arrange to be found by the searchers, and no one would be the wiser. Yessss. This just might work.

'In the body of Maxim, I will have access to the Elven Castle and the leaders of the Bears and Wolves, and I can destroy them from the inside,' The Darkness thought to himself. When he was finished with Marqueria, he would then move on to the Mortal Realm and spread his darkness there. "Yes, that will be the new plan," he whispered in Hilda's hoarse burnt voice, "I will have all of Marqueria soon."

Don't miss out!

Visit the website below and you can sign up to receive emails whenever Shana Ren publishes a new book. There's no charge and no obligation.

https://books2read.com/r/B-A-XRPCB-QBQTC

BOOKS 2 READ

Connecting independent readers to independent writers.

Did you love *Comes the Darkness*? Then you should read *Through the Tree*[1] by Shana Ren!

[2]

Living in the Mountains of Montana, miles from the nearest small town, the family of four has always lived a quiet life. Kenna was raised in the foster care system and aged out at 18. She had lived a violent childhood before entering the system, so her peaceful home and family are everything to her. While kind and giving, the two daughters are fearless, outspoken, and incredibly courageous, always ready for a new adventure. Join in on the adventures when the two teenage daughters, who, when they were toddlers, discovered

1. https://books2read.com/u/bMnWpV

2. https://books2read.com/u/bMnWpV

an ancient Birch Tree, which was a doorway to the Land of Marqueria, where magic is real and Unicorns exist. Now, as teenagers, they must lead their mother through the Tree so she can become who she was born to be. From Montana to Marqueria, the family is tested by danger and adversity. Still, they are bound by love, loyalty, and a determination to protect all they hold dear from the encroaching Darkness.

Read more at https://www.shanaren.com.

Also by Shana Ren

The Land of Marqueria
Through the Tree
Comes the Darkness

Standalone
Comes The Darkness

Watch for more at https://www.shanaren.com.

About the Author

Shana is a retired RN, who when not writing, can be found romping through the mountains of Montana with her family, cooking new and exciting(?) meals, playing with her grandson and her crazy Mastiff, and caring for her two chronically ill teenage daughters. She's a wife, a mother to four daughters, a mother-in-law to a wonderful son and she is YaYa to her darling grandson.

Read more at https://www.shanaren.com.